Apocalypse Nyx

cally heartless, Nyx is the bounty ...... to call when the stakes are high, the payouts are iffy, and the morality is optional."
—Nicky Drayden, author of *T*

"*Apocalypse Nyx* is exactly t —it's dark, violent, and has, at its ho is hard as steel and has whiskey , x is a bad-ass, and so is her author, Kameron Hurley. If you're anything like me, you already know this is the book you need to be reading right this minute."
—Michael Patrick Hicks, author of *Broken Shells* and *Mass Hysteria*

"This is a dystopia that revels in it in a big, joyous way, with cracking one-liners and tight squeezes to escape . . . If you like your heroines as kickass as Dutch from the TV series *Killjoys* you'll love Nyxnissa."
—*Starburst*

"The five novellas that make up *Apocalypse Nyx* are packed with more glare, grit, and snarl than a junkyard full of mutated jackals, landing their punches with all the tooth-loosening, hardhat-launching, lunchbox-swinging frankness of a noontime construction worker brawl. Hurley's world of mercenaries, magicians, blood, and bug guts is dusty enough that you can feel it grinding between your molars and insistent enough that it'll yank you by the collar and not let go, a no-frills hang-the-hell-on death-rattle-and-roll Keith Moon drum solo of staccato narrative bursts."
—Brooke Bolander, author of *The Only Harmless Great Thing*

"With Nyx, Hurley masterfully writes about a strong woman who is also a very broken human being—something women are rarely allowed to be."
—Stina Leicht, author of *And Blue Skies from Pain* and *Cold Iron*

"Nyx is back and just as good as ever. In this new collection of five novellas, Kameron Hurley serves up courses of crunchy action and intrigue layered with tender character moments that bring real depth to this intense, unique world."
—JY Yang, author of *The Black Tides of Heaven* and *The Red Threads of Fortune*

"Great for all you hard-drinking, hard punching, embittered readers who like a lot of grit in their post-apocalyptic hard-SF Biopunk."
—Bradley Horner, author of *Darkside Earther*

"*Apocalypse Nyx* is grim, unapologetic science fiction at its best."
—*New York Journal of Books*

"If you're new to Nyx, this may be a good place to start, taking place before the current series of which she's the star. If you're already a fan, this adds some wonderfully bloody, emotionally sharp texture to an already intriguing world and characters—get on it."
—*Sci-Fi and Fantasy Reviews*

Praise for *The Geek Feminist Revolution*

"A call to arms for those who care about the future of science fiction and fantasy."
—John Scalzi, author of *Redshirts*

Also by Kameron Hurley

Bel Dame Apocrypha
God's War (2011)
Infidel (2011)
Rapture (2012)

Worldbreaker Saga
The Mirror Empire (2014)
Empire Ascendant (2015)
The Broken Heavens (forthcoming)

Novels
The Stars Are Legion (2017)
The Light Brigade (forthcoming)

Nonfiction
The Geek Feminist Revolution: Essays (2016)

APOCALYPSE NYX
KAMERON HURLEY

APOCALYPSE
NYX

KAMERON
HURLEY

TACHYON
SAN FRANCISCO

Interior and cover design by Elizabeth Story
Echo cover art copyright © 2016 by Wadim Kashin

Tachyon Publications LLC
1459 18th Street #139
San Francisco, CA 94107
415.285.5615
www.tachyonpublications.com
tachyon@tachyonpublications.com

Series Editor: Jacob Weisman
Project Editor: Jill Roberts

Print ISBN: 978-1-61696-294-4
Digital ISBN: 978-1-61696-295-1

Printed in the United States by Worzalla

First Edition: 2018
9 8 7 6 5 4 3 2 1

THE BODY PROJECT

"When you feel the suffering of every living thing
in your own heart, that is consciousness."
—*Bhagavad Gita*

THE MAN'S RUGGED VISAGE—hanging from the upper window
of the tenement building—was captivating. The rest of him
was less so, as it was a mangled wreck of shattered limbs and
shredded torso strewn all over the street at Nyx's feet.

Nyx toed at the burst flesh of his admittedly once-fine
form, now split and oozing a sour blend of offal that brought
to mind the pungent stink of rotten bodies at the front. That
memory, paired with the profile of the man's head, sparked a
sudden familiarity. She had a powerful feeling that she knew
him.

Nyx squatted next to the body. Turned over the sunbaked
left wrist with some effort. The stiffness told her the body had
been there most of the night.

A familiar purple tattoo in the shape of an unblinking
eye stared back at her. A wave of remorse rolled through her,
more intense than she expected. She rubbed at the loose skin
absently. Gazed back up at the swinging head.

His name was Jahar, and he was already supposed to be dead. She knew, because it was her mistake that killed him.

"Is he a deserter?" Her contracted magician, Rhys, stood just behind her, speaking low in his thickly accented Nasheenian.

"A man under forty in the city?" Nyx said, rising. "Sure is."

"We're here for a parole violator, not a deserter," Rhys said, paging through the slick green papers of his little book of bounty contracts. "Should I update Taite on the delay?"

Taite was Nyx's com tech, responsible for monitoring and hacking into chatter conveyed through other hunters' communications. She had picked up a lot of free tips on other hunters' bounties by having him monitor their communication streams.

"Not yet," she said. Taite was securely nestled away in the dilapidated upper level of the storefront she'd been renting for the last eight weeks. He was probably eating take-out curry and confessing his worries to some Ras Tiegan idol. She wasn't sure how deep this was going to get yet, and didn't want to involve any more people than she had to until she understood why a good man who died a thousand miles from here lay mutilated on the streets of Bahora.

She glanced at Rhys, and wondered if she was going to have to bag him and dump him after this run. He had only been in her service for three weeks, and she was already reconsidering her choice of magician. Nobody liked dealing with Chenjan refugees, and it would be worse if she started looking into the death of a military man. Rhys had better manners and a better head for numbers and paperwork than she did; she got her letters backward, and hadn't attended the state school for more than a couple years. His education, best she understood it, had been a bit more lavish than hers. Every good bounty hunter had a magician on their team. But she suspected she was the only hunter foolish enough to have a Chenjan one.

"Maybe it's best we leave deserters to the bel dames," Rhys said.

"You aren't scared of a few bel dames, are you?" Nyx said. "This sort of kill isn't their style. And this soldier didn't deserve it." Though killing Jahar and other deserters like him was pretty much the entire job description of bel dames these days, they generally cleaned up what they put down.

Nyx knew. She used to be a bel dame, before she'd pissed them off enough to get blacklisted.

Rhys sighed. "I didn't say they did it. I said we best leave it for them to handle." The hood of his burnous was pulled up, hands tucked neatly into its broad pockets. A single cicada clung to his sleeve; one of a coterie of useful insects he kept at hand to send messages, sniff out traps, open locked doors, and perform other tasks that Nyx couldn't manage herself with a gun, fist, or a sword. It was broad daylight in the bustling border city of Bahora, and men with the darker cast of a Chenjan, like him, were likely to be treated even less hospitably than a deserter like Jahar. If not for Rhys's grating Chenjan accent, he might have been mistaken for a Tirhani on pilgrimage—they looked about the same, on first glance. All he needed was a pilgrim's pass prominently displayed on his chest. But he nattered on too much to hide his accent. People figured out what he was very quickly.

"You know him?" Rhys asked.

"I served with him," Nyx said. "Taught him to be a sapper." And a good many other things. She found herself looking at Rhys's slender hands. Wondered if he would be as skilled at putting together an IED with a bug cistern, secretion spool, and household carrion beetle colony as Jahar had been. Probably not.

"Doesn't appear to have done him much good," Rhys said.

"I expect blowing things up wasn't involved in whatever this was."

At street level, Nyx couldn't tell how Jahar's head was suspended in the window six stories above them. A noose, maybe, or some trained bug swarm. From the look of what remained of the body, the head and limbs had been torn or chewed from the body, not cut or hacked. Not a butcher's job, then. Nor a bounty hunter's. Looked more like some kind of bug attack orchestrated by a magician—one with a lot more skill than Rhys.

"Seems the body spent the night with dogs," Rhys said.

"It was bugs," Nyx said.

"I've studied every kind of bug injury," he said. "This isn't one. Not even those roving packs of beech creepers leave marks like this. These are teeth."

"You aren't exactly the world's most skilled magician."

"And you're a butcher, not an investigator," he said coolly. "Yah Tayyib told me all about what you're good at, and it's not details. Could you sign a more skilled magician? Certainly. But not one with a better eye for detail than me."

"Are all Chenjans so humble?"

"Honesty is a virtue, even in this blighted country. Or

have your mullahs further twisted the words of the Kitab to make liars into martyrs?"

Nyx chanced a look at the suns, hoping for some respite, but it was still hours from afternoon prayer. The only peace she got from his preaching was when he was at prayer.

"You add a seventh prayer today?" she asked. "Or is this little rant just for me?" She hadn't knelt on a prayer rug since she got back from the front, burning God behind her along with her men. Fuck the war. Fuck Rhys and his self-righteous talk.

"Those *are* the marks of a dog's teeth," he said, less aloof this time, "and he has something in his other hand that you missed."

She frowned. "I was getting to that."

In truth, she'd missed it. She had been looking for defensive wounds and chemical residue.

They were alone on the street; the suns were too high and hot for reasonable people to be outdoors. But even in cooler weather, Nyx suspected the body would not draw a crowd. Bahora acted as a conduit for goods from the interior to the border cities that lined the raging warfront between Nasheen and Chenja. Merchants did well here, as did butchers and organ dealers. Plague Sisters also trained here to serve casualties from the front. Many underwent their metamorphosis here, shedding their lower limbs for something altogether more unsavory, but useful for assisting in the rapid reanimation of the half-dead and dying. The more bodies the Plague Sisters saved, the longer the war raged. The market for fresh limbs and organs was strong, and it led to both legal and illegal trading in blood and bugs.

Nyx herself had sold off most of her organs for cash at one time or another.

Nyx massaged open the body's other fist. It clutched a dead locust, the guts smeared across Jahar's palm.

"Can you get anything off that?" she asked Rhys.

He crouched beside her. "Did all your men desert, or just this one?"

"The rest are dead," she said. No need to mention Jahar should have been, too. Rhys was staring at her with his big dark eyes, but she avoided meeting his gaze. Better to think of him as a means to an end, like everyone else.

Rhys gently took the crushed locust into his palm. For a long, dark moment she wondered what kind of a Nasheenian she was, to offer an employment contract to a man whose people she had spent so many years slaughtering. She had signed him away from Yah Tayyib, his mentor and sponsor, in a fit of spite. Tayyib had crossed her once too often, and an old friend bet Nyx the Chenjan with a magician's waiver of amnesty wouldn't sign with her fledgling bounty hunting team.

Nyx liked a good wager.

Rhys murmured something over the locust's body. Nyx smelled saffron and vanilla. The locust trembled, then stilled.

"Whatever it recorded is salvageable," he said. "Are you sure you don't want to leave this for the bel dames? This could get very bad."

Someone called to them from the amber-tiled doorway of the building. Nyx saw bullet wounds above the door, and fresh shattered tile littering the stoop. But the door itself was intact, a green slab made of bug secretions, shot through with shards of stone. Someone opened that door. Nobody forced it. She wondered if Jahar had opened it, or the woman. Or someone else.

"You the bel dame?" the woman in the doorway called in a Mhorian accent. Her dusty brown hair was pulled up into a riot of dreadlocks. She wore a colorful scarf around her neck, and neat short trousers and a long-sleeved tunic and lace-up vest; clean, merchant-class garb that looked out of place on this side of town.

"Sure am," Nyx said, rising.

Rhys said, low, "You can't just tell people you're a government assassin."

"It's not important what you are," Nyx muttered. "It's what people *think* you are." Then louder, to the Mhorian, "Who are you?"

"Henye bhin Heshel. Come quickly."

"If she finds you out, she could kill us," Rhys said.

Nyx patted his arm. He flinched. "I'll protect you."

"From order keepers? From bel dames?"

"I'm scarier than both."

"Only because you're somehow less hygienic."

"He's one of my men," she said. "My responsibility. I wouldn't expect a man who'd never served to understand that." She'd fucked it up once—she wasn't going to do it again.

Nyx pulled away and went to the door. Henye ducked inside, beckoning.

"Wait, Nyx. Don't go in there," Rhys called.

Nyx stepped into the building. From the outside, she assumed it was just a bank of low-rent apartments. But she had not guessed its residents. Walls of trembling mucus lined the corridors. The mucus crawled with white and brown larvae. She saw glassy blue butterflies trapped within the viscous goo, and shiny green jewel beetles. The circular doors along the corridor were covered in fine webbing, sprayed with old magical hexes for various types of restorative amalgamations. Above the lintel of one doorway she saw a mummified human arm.

"It's a bug farm," Rhys said, stepping up beside her. "I could sense them from the street."

"Could have mentioned it."

"Didn't know you were just going to barge in," he said.

"Do you have a bag for this corpse?" Henye asked. She stood just behind a low reception desk, arms crossed. She had a face like a hatchet; Nyx suspected the bel dame ruse wouldn't work for long. The woman would nose her out soon enough.

"How'd he die?" Nyx asked.

"What does it matter? He's a deserter, isn't he?"

"Paperwork," Nyx said. "Humor me."

"I don't know," Henye said. "I came to the shop this morning after breaking fast and there he was, all over the street."

"And the head?"

"Haven't gone up yet. Called you straight off."

"You rebuild people here?"

Henye's eyes widened.

"Rebuilding?" Rhys asked. "What is that?"

"I've seen a rebuild shop before," Nyx said.

"I run a clean operation," Henye said. "I have all my permits. We even have a registered Plague Sister." She reached under the desk.

Nyx placed a hand on the butt of her pistol. She wore a coiled whip on the other hip, a scattergun behind her, and a sword across her back. Those were just the visible weapons. The razor blades in her sandals and poisoned needles in her hair were for seriously deteriorating situations. She doubted this would end up one of those. But you never knew.

"Getting my permits!" Henye said, jerking her hands out from beneath the desk and placing them flat in front of her.

"I don't care about your permits." Nyx nodded at the severed arm over the door further down the hall. "I know that mark means you rebuild here, and not just broken limbs, right? This man come here to be rebuilt?"

"I wouldn't know."

"Who would?"

"Meiret was working last night. She closed up."

"Who is she?"

"My daughter. She works the night hour. If you need help to mop up—"

"I'm not here for a bribe," Nyx said. "Just information. Open the rebuild room."

"I will not. I have my permits."

"Then I'll force the door." Nyx pulled her scattergun from her back, and raised the heavy butt of the gun to the door's weaker hinges.

"Don't! I'll open it." Henye leapt forward, faster than Nyx thought a plump little woman like that could move, and pressed her palm to the door's faceplate. The door opened. A bitter almond scent wafted into the corridor. Nyx had a powerful memory of another dark room that stank like this, and her own burnt, blackened skin being peeled from her body by serious-looking magicians. She'd been riding a morphine and black beetle juice high, then, when they rebuilt her body and brought her back from the edge of death.

Nyx pushed through. Reached for the light.

Something skittered in the darkness.

Nyx had just enough time to swing her gun forward. Four giant fox spiders, legs as long as her arms, broke away from a crumpled figure on the floor and mobbed her.

She kicked the first in the face and blasted the scattergun at another. The massive spider ruptured, spattering eyes and guts and limbs across the room.

"I have them!" Rhys said behind her. He moved into the room next to her, hand raised. Four cicadas had crawled out of his sleeve, and made an annoying buzzing sound.

The two remaining spiders stopped, motionless, two paces from them, their massive jaws working at nothing.

"Can you control them?" Nyx asked.

"They aren't under the hold of another magician," he said. "They're just wild intruders. I can turn them away."

"Do that." Nyx didn't like giant bugs any more than the next person, but fox spiders were useful scavengers.

Rhys flicked his wrist. The spiders obediently trundled back toward the rear of the room, crawling over the dark shape they'd been huddled around when Nyx pushed in.

Nyx palmed the light. Above, the glow worms in the ceiling lights squirmed, emitting a dull orange glow over the rebuild room.

The spiders squeezed out through a broken section of the far wall, its edges rimmed with scorch marks. Nyx followed the stain of smoke up along the shelf-lined wall. Broken jars littered the floor; spongy hearts and lungs, tongues and eyes, fingers and ears lay among the glass, as did another body—the crumpled form the spiders had been feeding on was a woman dressed in the white muslin habit of a Plague Sister. Her lower limbs were just visible—a tangled collection of six appendages that looked more spider than human.

"This woman yours?" Nyx called back to Henye.

Henye crept inside. She put a hand to her mouth in horror, and said something that sounded like an oath or prayer in Mhorian. "That's Siraji, the Plague Sister assigned to our operation," she said.

"She assigned to work here last night?"

"No, I . . . She was still here when I left, but said she'd only be another hour."

"Then it looks like we need to talk to Meiret," Nyx said. "Because whatever happened here happened on her watch."

"Glorious God, this is terrible," Henye said. "I must call the order keepers now. This is far worse than a deserter."

"Wait a minute on the order keepers," Nyx said. It was bad enough that real bel dames were on the way. Once order keepers locked down the scene, she wasn't going to be able to get back in. "Rhys, check out her permits. Make sure she's really allowed to do rebuilds here."

Having a Plague Sister on staff lent legitimacy to Henye's story, though. Plague Sisters were a guild of magicians that specialized in rebuilding the mangled bodies of soldiers. The sisters were only assigned to reputable rebuilders. If anyone here had been giving deserters new faces, even the most lax Plague Sister wouldn't stand for it. Anybody a Plague Sister patched up went back to the front until they'd served their time—two years for women, and twenty to twenty-five for men.

Of course, this one was dead now, which might indicate something at the operation had changed the night before.

"I'm going upstairs to get his head," Nyx said. "I need any codes or patterns to get access up there?"

Henye shook her head. "The top two floors are still under construction. We've not locked them. Glorious God, this is terrible. Terrible."

Nyx made her way up six floors, passing two floors of convalescing quarters and two more floors locked off with additional security. She made a note to have Rhys sniff those out with a hornet swarm later. It also wouldn't hurt to get Taite to do a search for the building records for the site. What people said they were to somebody they thought was a bel dame was sometimes a lot different than what they told a building inspector.

The fifth floor was indeed under construction; buckets of broken tile and plaster lined the hall, and all the windows were uncovered—no screens or organic filters to keep out the cancerous light of the suns. She saw scattered patterns in the debris on the floor of the landing here—the scuffed impressions of sandaled feet. A neat spatter of blood made a fine arc against the far wall. She pulled out her scattergun, just in case, and ascended to the final floor.

She stepped into a wide open space, gutted to its raw bones of stout amber pillars. The windows were all broad, which was why it was so easy to see the head suspended in the one to her right.

Jahar's head floated in midair, three paces from the

window. The sight of it just . . . hanging there caught her off guard. She'd expected more blood. Maybe more bodies. But it simply hung there like some kind of lost, semi-sentient insect that had lost pheromone instructions from its magician.

She approached the head slowly, circled. No blood on the floor, or the walls—not even spatters like downstairs. Aside from being severed, the head was otherwise undamaged. Nyx did note some bruising around the eyes, which was a telltale indicator of sorasa use—military-grade narcotics often prescribed to war-addled veterans. She'd been on them for a year after getting back from the front, and quit because living life on sorasa was like being wrapped in gray gauze and left to observe the world from the depths of some great pit.

Nyx lowered her gun and went to the window. He'd been killed on the street, then, not up here. Somebody had gone to a lot of trouble to bring his head up. Why? A warning? A party decoration?

She heard a scraping sound. Pivoted.

"Stand down!" A woman's voice, from across the room. Ventilation? Ventilation in old buildings like this was nonexistent, or extremely tight.

Nyx stepped behind a nearby pillar for cover, brought up her gun.

"You first!" Nyx said.

A lithe woman slid out from behind a pillar at the far side of the room. She pivoted her hips, gun out and pointed down, presenting the smallest target possible.

Nyx gritted her teeth. Foolish catshit, not to clear the room. She hadn't thought there was anyone small enough to hide behind the pillars. Stupid mistake. It was a wonder she'd kept her head on a full five years after leaving the front.

"I could shoot you again, if you want," the woman said.

Nyx recognized the voice. "Anneke?" she said.

Anneke tilted her head to the side. Nyx caught her profile. Anneke, all right—she was a popular hired gun for other bounty hunters and mercenary groups working the border cities. She was also one of the few people who'd shot Nyx and lived to tell about it.

"Who you with?" Nyx asked. "Come to put a bullet in me again?

"Nobody gives a shit about you now you're not a bel dame," Anneke said. "I'm on my own. You know Jahar?"

"I did. You?"

Anneke took a few tentative steps forward, cautious as a cat. Her jaw worked; she spit chewed sen on the floor. Her teeth were bloody with the stuff.

"Was in prison with her," Anneke said.

"One of you must have been a guard, then," Nyx said. There were no coed prisons in Nasheen.

"She and I shared a cell," Anneke said.

"Jahar was a man," Nyx said.

"You sure about that?"

"Fucked him," Nyx said. "So yeah, pretty sure."

"Well . . . she changed a lot, if parts matter. But Jahar was always 'she' to me."

"Reassignment is expensive."

"What do you want here?"

"Figuring out who killed him. Was that you?"

Anneke snorted. "Too easy."

"You going to put down your gun?"

"When you put down yours. I know your rep."

Nyx eased herself out of cover, pivoting her left hip forward, like she was about to start a fight. "Listen, if you'll ease up I'll—"

She heard footsteps on the stairs, then Rhys's voice, "Nyx—"

Anneke fired.

Nyx got off two rounds in response. She slid back into cover, cursing. Unlike Anneke, she was far too broad for the pillar to provide good coverage.

Rhys dropped to the floor, hands out.

"Rhys?" Nyx said.

"Is that a fucking Chenjan?" Anneke yelled.

"You're one to talk," Nyx said. "I heard half your family owns a tea house on the other side of the border."

"Totally different."

"He's with me, Anneke. Stand down for fuck's sake."

"How do I know you're not here for Jahar's head?"

"Because you'd be dead already." Nyx bluffed. She was too far away from Anneke to use the scattergun, and with anything else, from any distance greater than twenty paces, she was a piss-poor shot.

"Can I get up?" Rhys said.

"I'm putting away my gun," Nyx said. "Let's have my magician look at Jahar's head. We're on the same team, Anneke."

"I'm on my own team," Anneke said.

"You're on Jahar's team," Nyx said. "So am I."

Anneke lowered her gun. Stowed it at her back. Strode forward. Nyx let out a breath and holstered her pistol. She spread both palms, an old bel dame habit to show she was unarmed.

They met at the center of the room and clasped wrists. Anneke was a head-and-shoulders shorter than Nyx, slim in the hips. From behind, colleagues often mistook her for a child. The heavy, double-barreled acid rifle at her back was plenty lethal, though. She wore a belt of acid-tipped bullets and two cylindrical grenades in banded leather cases. Her arms were marked in prison tattoos.

"If you've decided to be friends," Rhys said, "can I get up now?"

"You know what happened here?" Nyx asked Anneke.

Anneke walked over to the head. "No. Got here too late."

"Rhys?" Nyx said. "Can you figure out how this head is . . . floating?"

He pushed himself up from the floor in one smooth movement, quick and spry as one would expect from a dancer. For all his complaining, he'd adjusted quickly to her line of work. She had seen him dance, and he was a far better dancer than he was a magician.

Rhys passed a hand above and below Jahar's motionless head.

"Bugs?" Nyx said.

"Magnetics," Rhys said.

"What?" Anneke said. "You a magician or organic scientist?"

"I can sense strong fields, pheromones, gases," Rhys said. "I need to in order to control the bugs."

Nyx grabbed Jahar's head and gently pulled it forward. As she did, the full weight of it fell into her palms. She let out a breath. Stared into Jahar's dead eyes. So strange, with the dead—when it was all over, they looked like dolls, for a time. Then . . . meat.

"How's she suspended?" Anneke asked, poking at the space where the head had been with the point of her gun.

Rhys flinched. "Do please watch where you point that. There's a magnet above and below. Must also have something in his head, which is why it levitates."

Nyx rolled the head over, saw nothing but festering flesh. "We'll have to crack it open, back at the storefront," Nyx said.

"Crap idea," Anneke said. "Let me look after it."

"I have more resources," Nyx said, "unless whoever your current employer is knows about your little side project. And I doubt that."

"Got no reason to trust you."

"No reason to trust you, either," Nyx said. "But you've got information I don't. I have resources you don't. Truce, Anneke. For this run."

Anneke pursed her mouth. Then, "Fine. This run."

Rhys stepped into the space where the head had been. Stared at the ceiling. "They brought his head up to put it here. Right here."

"Warning or something?" Anneke said.

"Ritual?" Rhys muttered.

Nyx pulled off her burnous and wrapped Jahar's head in it. "Let's take him home and find out," Nyx said.

"What about the body?" Rhys said.

"That too. Call Taite and have him drive the bakkie over so we can load up the body."

"There's a problem," Rhys said.

"Shit doesn't need more problems."

"I came up because the bel dames are here," Rhys said. "The real ones."

Nyx swore. "You could have mentioned that earlier."

"When you were shooting at me?"

"Are there order keepers, too?"

"Not yet, but Henye did call them."

"Stay here and call Taite. I'll distract the bel dames."

She handed over Jahar's head to Anneke. "Can you get out through this window, meet Taite on the street? If the bel dames get this head, we've got nothing."

"Sure. But how you gonna distract the bel dames?"

"Serve them tea and halva?" Nyx said. "Fuck if I know."

"Shit," Anneke said. "Signed with another genius boss, didn't I?"

"It's all right," Nyx said. "I'm good at pissing off bel dames."

"That doesn't make me feel better."

Two bel dames stood in the foyer talking to Henye. Nyx knew them both, which wasn't uncommon. Bel dames were a tight, elite group. Even if she hadn't met somebody, she'd know them by reputation. The skinny one with the deformed hand she refused to fix was Almira Sameh. Almira was Nyx's age, mid-twenties—middle-aged, for Nasheen. She had a plump face and lean figure. Her bright red burnous looked too big for her, but Nyx expected it afforded her a lot of cover for the no doubt substantial arsenal she carried with her.

The other, Dahab, was older. She was a broad, hefty woman who could bench her own weight—a hundred and twenty kilos, if Nyx remembered right. She'd lost an arm at the front, so her right arm was a lighter color than the left—she'd had it rebuilt in some place like this one.

Nobody would mistake them for anything but bel dames. It was something about how bel dames took up a room, like they knew they were the most dangerous thing in it.

"Nyxnissa so Dasheem. . . . I thought you were eaten in prison," Almira said.

"In more ways than one," Dahab said, chuckling.

"Sorry to disappoint," Nyx said.

Dahab said, "Now, why in the world would a little bottom-feeding mercenary like you present herself to this fine businesswoman as a bel dame?"

"Is that what I said?"

"You did!" Henye said. Her face was livid. Mhorians could get alarmingly red.

"Bit of confusion on everyone's part," Nyx said.

"You tamper with anything up there?" Almira asked. She eased back the right side of her burnous, and rested a hand on the butt of one of her ivory-hilted pistols.

"I didn't touch anything you wouldn't," Nyx said.

Almira waved her clawed left hand. Nyx heard it had been crushed in some machine at a factory, back before Almira had been accepted into bel dame training. The refusal to fix it always amused Nyx. She wished she and Almira got on better. Nyx would have loved to take her to bed and seduce out the story behind that hand. But bel dames fucking bel dames always ended badly. Nyx preferred not to head down that road.

"I find myself un-reassured," Almira said.

Nyx heard Rhys come down the steps behind her, and

resisted the urge to turn. Both bel dames watched him like hungry ravens.

"You're fucking kidding me," Dahab said. "He with you?"

"Sure is," Nyx said. "You look at the Plague Sister's body yet? Seems somebody blasted their way in."

"Meant to look that way," Almira said. "Henye here says there's a head upstairs. We still going to find it there?"

"See for yourself," Nyx said.

Dahab drew her gun. "Almira could see from the street it wasn't there, Nyx."

Nyx held up her hands, spread her palms. Forced an extravagant grin. "Go ahead and search us."

"We'll do more than that," Almira said. "The order keepers will be here in a quarter hour. Why don't you two cool off in the rebuild room with the Plague Sister and me while Dahab checks things upstairs?"

Nyx hated getting into situations she couldn't shoot her way out of. Killing bel dames was illegal, though it took a lot to kill them. She knew.

"You don't have the authority to hold me," Nyx said.

"How about your partner?" Dahab said. "Looks like a fucking Chenjan terrorist to me."

"You're the one holding the gun," Nyx said.

Almira motioned them both toward the rebuild room. Nyx glanced back at Rhys. She didn't know him well enough to read him, and he kept his face pretty stoic. His gaze stayed on the floor. Nyx took stock of the room again. They could make a break for the blown-in wall at the back of the room, but she didn't know where it led. The ceiling was low, unblemished. At the center of the room was a great stone tub with pulsing semi-organic hoses coming out of it, all attached to various broad glass jugs of viscous fluid teeming with different types of bugs. Nyx had spent more time than she cared to remember in a tub very much like it.

She tried to catch Rhys's eye again, but he wouldn't look at her.

The bel dames had just put a magician into a room filled with the tools of his trade. Nyx might not have an edge here, but he did. Did he have the guts to make a move?

Dahab walked past them and up the stairs. They had maybe ten minutes before Dahab got up there and figured out the head was gone, and fifteen—fourteen, now—before order keepers swarmed the place. By then whatever tenuous lead Nyx had on figuring out who killed Jahar would get eaten up with bleeding all over paperwork and shitting in holding cells.

"Why were you really here?" Almira asked. She blocked the doorway.

Nyx put her hands down, but kept her fingers splayed to show she wasn't carrying anything. Nyx herself had shot more than one person in holding for making fists.

"Just passing by," Nyx said. "Saw the body, had a look in case there was a bounty on it. You?"

Almira shook her head.

"What," Nyx said, "you think I can't hack a com? Who assigned you two to this one? It was a civilian call-in, not an assigned note."

"Bel dame council rep assigns all the call-ins," Almira said. "That hasn't changed."

"Who is that now?"

"Nyx, I have a caravan of relatives coming in for a wedding tonight. Don't pull me into this. It's a simple grab and go and you're messing it up."

"You were always softer than Dahab."

"And you were always a fucking psycho."

"That puts it mildly," Rhys said.

Nyx glared at him.

"I'd get a new employer, gravy eater," Almira said to Rhys. "You know all her partners end up dead?"

Rhys finally looked at Nyx. "I didn't."

"Dead in all sorts of interesting ways," Almira said. "Eaten by organic filters, stuffed full of carrion beetles. Heads chopped clean off . . ." She smirked at Nyx. "I saw the deserter's file, Nyx. He served under you. Why am I not surprised he ended up dead here?"

"Was he one of mine?" Nyx said. "Hard to keep track."

"You'll be in a holding cell at least a week."

Nyx laughed. She reached up casually, as if to scratch at the back of her neck. Instead, she grabbed the end of one of her poisoned needles, and braced herself to get shot, hopefully some place non-vital.

Rhys stepped back. From the corner of her eye, she saw him raise his hand. Almira's attention twisted to him.

The four jars full of watery insects exploded. Glass shredded Nyx's right side. She moved left, flinging the poisoned needle as she surged away.

Almira brought up her hands, deflecting the needle and much of the glass. But just as she recovered, Nyx was on top of her. Nyx pounded her in the face once, twice, three times. Yanked the gun from her hand.

"Rhys!"

"Right behind you!"

Nyx bolted out the door, flying past Henye, who sat on the floor by the reception desk, hands covering her head.

"You just assaulted a bel dame!" Rhys said.

"Can't take all the credit," she said. "Nice distraction."

Nyx slid out into the hot street. Jahar's body was gone.

"Where's the bakkie?" Rhys asked.

"You called Taite?"

"Yes!"

She took his hand. Pulled him forward, toward the narrow alley across the way. There was more cover between the buildings.

Nyx heard shots. Ducked. Looked back. Dahab stood in the open window six stories up, taking aim.

A bakkie rounded the street to Nyx's left, spitting dead beetles from its back end as it belched toward them.

Anneke leaned out the passenger window of the bakkie, big gun at her shoulder, popping off rounds. "In, in!" she said.

Nyx used the bakkie as cover and pulled open the door on the far side. She pushed Rhys in ahead of her. Got her leg inside and yelled at Taite. The bakkie jerked forward so fast she had to hold on to the door to keep from flying out.

She swung herself into the back and slammed the door.

Seeing Rhys gawking at Dahab, Nyx pushed Rhys's head toward his knees. "Keep your head down!"

Anneke sent off six more shots, then slid all the way back into the vehicle as it peeled down the next street.

Skinny, pocked-marked Taite hunched over the wheel, visibly shaking. His hands were smeared in old blood. He was in his mid-teens, and experienced with a lot of mercenary crews, even if he didn't look the part in a firefight.

"Body in the trunk?" Nyx asked.

"You're bloody welcome!" Taite said.

Nyx chanced a look behind them. Her storefront address wasn't listed anywhere, but she didn't want to chance going back there.

"Drive us to the safe house," she said.

"Which one?" Taite said.

"The one with the most whiskey."

Anneke slumped in her seat, clutching her arm.

"You hurt?" Nyx asked.

Anneke shook her head. "Just pulled it. Don't want to make a habit of this."

"Then let's go find Henye's daughter before the bel dames do," Nyx said.

The soaring Hazrat Ahmadin mosque at the edge of Bahora had been located at the center of the city a century before. That was before a Chenjan burst demolished three-quarters of the town, burying it in a stinking mire of contaminated sludge that hardened into a cakey powder, poisoning the air and the soil. Subsequent generations of magicians had made the area half-habitable again, but aside from poor squatters in the old trader's mall, the place remained a sandy ruin. The Hazrat Ahmadin had been rebuilt on the other side of town, leaving the wreck of its ancestor where it had fallen the day of the incursion.

For Nyx's purposes, the mosque was a perfect refuge—as one of the four minarets was still standing, and gave impressive views of the terrain in all directions. The hike up the winding stairs of the minaret with a body wrapped in muslin and a burnous-bound head was less ideal. Nyx hadn't heard so much fucking complaining since she asked her sapper squad to blow up the Chenjan city of Bahreha—kids, cats, and all. It reminded her she was dealing with mercenaries and refugees, not professionals. It soured her mood.

Taite pulled out the whiskey, halva, and an assortment of dried fruit from their cache in the upper room of the minaret. Jahar's body stank, so they left it on the landing just below and shut the door.

"What happened back there?" Taite asked.

Nyx said, "Got Rhys down on all seven bones outside of prayer."

Rhys stood over her with a container of aloe-soaked cicada wings to plaster over the shredded skin of her right side. "You want me to patch you up, or throw this at you?"

"Notice you came out unscathed," Nyx said.

"You said it was a good distraction," Rhys said.

"She has a problem with thanks," Taite said.

"I've noticed."

"Enough, both of you," Nyx said. She snatched the container of cicada wings from Rhys. She could do it herself. She nodded at Taite. "You know Anneke?"

Taite gave Anneke a curt nod. "Yeah. I'll put some tea on for her."

"Too early for tea," Nyx said.

"I don't drink liquor before sunset," Anneke said.

Nyx looked from Taite to Anneke. "You both worked together on another mercenary crew, as I . . . recall. Anything I should know?"

Anneke shrugged. "I don't have a problem with Taite."

"Good," Nyx said. "You'll want to go to prayer with Rhys, then. I drink through prayer and Taite worships idols so—"

"Not with a Chenjan," Anneke said.

"Saints, Nyx. They're *saints*," Taite said, setting Nyx's whiskey glass in front of her.

"Whatever."

"I don't need watching," Anneke said. "Especially not by a Chenjan."

"I'll decide that."

"I don't work for you."

"We're both working for Jahar. I'm still not clear on your motives. So let's talk about that."

Taite broke the carapaces of a handful of fire beetles and started a fire in the mud-brick oven. Nyx had slathered the thing together herself, back when she first came to town and was squatting here.

Anneke slumped in a rickety chair.

"Jahar tell you why he got reassigned?" Nyx asked. "Making a full body switch like that isn't cheap."

"Are you sure it's related?" Taite asked.

"It's expensive, Taite," Nyx said. "I got burned up at the front, and I was indentured to the magicians for a year to pay for it. Only a First Family could afford a reassignment, or the government, not some breeder baby scuttled off to the front. If somebody reassigned him—especially if it happened a couple of times—it was because he did them a very expensive favor, or they thought he'd be a very expensive tool."

"First Family security's hard to hack, Nyx," Taite said, "and I don't have a proper com console here. If this goes that deep—"

"Why was Jahar in prison?" Nyx asked.

Anneke stiffened. "Leave that in prison."

"Catshit," Nyx said. "Don't pretend it's some honor-bound social club."

"Tell me all about being a bel dame, then," Anneke said.

"That's different," Nyx said.

"She . . ." Anneke crossed her arms. "She stole some things."

"From government or First Families? If it was government, he wouldn't be in a general prison."

"First Family," Anneke said. "They used it against her once she got out, too. She couldn't shake them. Always owed them."

Taite cursed in Ras Tiegan, something about shit and cabbages.

Nyx pointed at Jahar's burnous-wrapped head. "Taite, I need you to get on that. There's something in his head. Somebody took it off and set it up between two magnets."

"Magnets?" Taite said. He pulled the head into his lap. Unwrapped it. Nyx saw his eyelids flutter, and put out a hand to steady him in case he fainted.

Taite shook his head, breathed deeply. "Sorry."

"Anneke, can you cut the head open?" Nyx asked. "Taite, have a look at it."

Anneke snorted. "This is what you get when you have two draft dodgers on your team instead of women."

"I'm a Ras Tiegan citizen," Taite said, indignant. "I'm not subject to the Nasheenian draft."

"We can't all be butchers," Nyx said.

Anneke grabbed Jahar's head and went to the low table on the other side of the room. She pulled a heavy knife from her belt. Nyx went over to help her, and together they sliced and pulled back Jahar's scalp of dark, shaggy hair, then cracked open his skull.

Rhys stood a pace distant, peeking over Nyx's shoulder. The blood had all coagulated by now; she knew Rhys didn't much care for blood either, an even greater handicap for a magician.

Upon cracking open the skull, nothing looked immediately out of place to Nyx's eye, but then, she only cut off heads. She didn't often open them.

"The base of the brain," Rhys said, pointing.

Anneke cracked off more bits of the skull. It was tougher than Nyx had expected. At the base of the brain was a fig-sized green fistula. Nyx cut it open. Inside was a small copper-colored ball, covered in clear mucus.

"Taite?" Nyx said, holding it up between thumb and forefinger. "You know what this is?"

"Oh, shit," Taite said. He took it from her. Pinched a pair of specs on his nose, and tapped them twice to zoom in. "Sure do," he said. "That's a polarized, semi-organic key. Must have given him horrible headaches."

"Key to what?" Anneke said.

"A magnetic lock," Taite said.

"Shit," Nyx said.

"What?" Anneke said. "What's that mean?"

"There was a safe in that rebuild shop," Nyx said. "That's why somebody attacked him in the street and walked his head up six floors." She looked at Anneke. "Jahar ever tell you about having a safe? In prison, maybe?"

"You still suspect me?"

"He tell you about the key in his head? Tell you you'd get a cut of whatever's in the safe?"

"She told me to meet her there this morning."

"He looked a lot different after prison. How'd you find him?"

"*She* found *me*."

"How?"

"Jahar got a lot of people new skins," Anneke said, "after she got hers. New bodies, new faces. She liked switching bodies. Liked being anybody she wanted. But it doesn't work for everyone. Lots of people don't take to the switch. Always feel out of sorts."

"You know more than you're saying, Anneke."

"Only saying what you need to know. Not more."

"Jahar must have been some friend to you."

"She was . . . an old boss."

"You this loyal to all your bosses?"

Anneke grimaced. "Only the *good* ones."

"Where was the safe?"

"Told you. Don't know. Got up there right before you."

Nyx gave a huff of displeasure and moved away from her. "Taite, what do you need to get me the address for a girl named Meiret bhin Heshel?"

"Regular public terminal," he said. "But the bel dames are probably already headed in that direction."

"If she's in on this, she isn't going to be at home," Rhys said.

Nyx glanced over at him. Sometimes she forgot that for all his grimacing he knew what it was to be a fugitive, if not a criminal. He was, after all, a Chenjan in Nasheen.

Taite said, "If I can get a secure com console I can tap into her withdrawal records and monitor the surveillance drones. If she's running, she'll need money."

"People who run take cash."

"Only if they planned ahead," Rhys said. "If she got into trouble she wasn't expecting, she'll make mistakes."

"Then let's hope she's an amateur," Nyx said. She squeezed the copper ball in her hand, and wondered what sort of collateral somebody kept hidden with a key buried in their skull. She had some guesses, none of them uplifting. For all her own mistakes and vices and black market bartering, she'd never betrayed Nasheen to the enemy. She'd never needed a drop box like Jahar's. Jahar had been a good kid. Good kids didn't sell bioweapons to Chenjans, did they?

She was going to find out, whether she liked the outcome or not. She set Taite on hunting down Meiret. Rhys started work on the locust they'd retrieved from Jahar's palm. But after half an hour, Rhys hadn't made any progress.

"You said you could fix it," Nyx said.

"I'm sorry," Rhys said. "Conditions aren't ideal and I need—"

"You said you could fucking fix it!"

Rhys's expression hardened. He turned away from her.

Nyx went outside on the balcony of the minaret to get some air and decompress. Too many voices.

She spread out her burnous and leaned back against the hot stones to take a nap. She pulled her hood close and dozed.

She wasn't sure how long. What woke her was the sound of Rhys's voice. He was speaking in the same reverent tone most people used to recite the Kitab, but she didn't recognize the words from the holy book.

She cracked an eyelid. When she didn't see him, she leaned forward, just far enough to see him sitting around the curve of the tower.

"What is that?" she said sharply.

Rhys started. "I apologize—"

"No," she said, standing, walking toward him. "It's fine. But what is it?"

He cleared his throat. "Poetry."

"Not Chenjan?"

"No, it's Nasheenian. I'm . . ." He made a face. ". . . working on my accent."

Nyx plopped down beside him. "Read me some."

"All right," he said. "But I don't expect you'll like it."

She grunted, and watched him turn the pages with his delicate fingers. He had lovely hands. She'd noticed that first thing.

He recited, "'My mother was a bird of fire. She bore me swaddled over the ruined cities of my sisters. We rained a sea of flame upon our brothers, and brought them aloft again. Transformed. Our mothers burned the cities. We keep the ruins.'"

"Nice," Nyx said.

"That was horrible," he said.

"You read a lot of poetry in Chenja?"

He smirked, one of his you're-a-stupid-Nasheenian smirks that set her teeth on edge. "Chenjans can read, yes."

"Didn't mean it like that."

"I thought this was a business arrangement and we weren't going to ask questions of one another."

"What, it's a personal question?"

"Isn't it?"

"Not like I asked you what you're running from."

He sighed. "Nyx—"

"I don't care if you're a deserter," she said, "or some poor rich kid run off to piss on his parents. I asked you about the fucking poetry."

Rhys closed the book. "This is clearly not going anywhere." He stood.

"Rhys?" She grabbed at the edge of his burnous.

"What?"

"No questions," she said. "You remember that, when you hear things about me from bel dames, or Anneke, or anyone. I burned my past. I'm starting over. Everybody on my team gets to start over."

"I understand that," he said. "It's why I signed with you. I think it's *you* who needs to remember you're supposed to be a different person now."

"I was rebuilt," Nyx said. "I can start over."

"I don't think it's me you're trying to convince," he said.

She pulled her hand away.

Meiret bhin Heshel waited under the broad awning of a wait station for the local train shuttle. Luck was with Nyx on this one—transportation hubs and waiting areas always had some kind of surveillance, and Taite had found Meiret easily after hacking into the delicate code that bound her government residency files.

Meiret probably wasn't a day over twenty. She was soft and plump like her mother, but Nyx knew well enough that looks could be deceiving, especially when it came to Mhorians. Fat meant rich. Fat meant status, power. They weren't from Ras Tieg, where the rich sought to starve themselves to corporeal perfection to make up for their worldly wealth. More telling was Meiret's expression, which was pinched in fear and worry. She kept looking at the great face of the water clock in the public square. She carried a shaved ice cone in one hand, slathered in blue syrup, and a large carpet bag in the other.

Nyx strode across the square alone. It was mid-afternoon prayer, and the streets were mostly empty. Unfortunately, it meant Rhys and Anneke were both unavailable for half an hour, since both did the full ablution beforehand, and Nyx wasn't going to risk Meiret stepping on that shuttle amid the crush of after-prayer bodies flooding the streets.

Meiret spotted her when she was still forty paces from the platform, and froze. Nyx wasn't good at making non-threatening faces. She tried looking away.

Meiret dropped the shaved ice and bolted.

Nyx ran after her.

Meiret might have been younger, but Nyx boxed in her spare time, which meant putting in a fair amount of running every day. Hung over, sure, but running. She slammed into Meiret. The girl went reeling.

Nyx pinned her to the street. Meiret wailed.

Another sound cut through the thump of their bodies—

the mournful melody of the burst sirens. Nyx dug her knee into Meiret's sternum, pinning her to the ground.

Meiret squealed. "Please! The sirens."

Nyx leaned over her. Gritted her teeth. "Then the Chenjans will blow us both to hell."

The burst sirens wailed.

"Please," Meiret said. "We need to get inside."

"I need answers." Nyx pressed harder. "About Jahar."

Meiret gasped. A blue blast of color burned overhead—Chenjan aerial bursts. Nyx listened to the whump-whump of the anti-burst guns. Nyx heard those sirens a lot in the border towns, less on the interior. But Meiret looked terrified.

"It was Harun!" Meiret said.

"Who?"

"Harun of Family Sharaset. Please let me get inside."

"Who the fuck is Harun?"

"Jahar worked for her. She came for documents he had in his safe. I hid. I watched her kill him!"

"Where can I find her?"

Meiret choked on a laugh. "You can't hurt her. She's First Family. Jahar took the fall for her work."

"And how did you know this?"

"Jahar and I were involved."

Nyx recoiled. "You?"

"He was very charming. I knew he was a deserter. I didn't care. Your war is a blemish."

"Encouraged by fat little countries like yours," Nyx said. "Don't shit me. You were doing black market rebuilds and you killed him to keep it quiet."

"We didn't. He worked for Harun. Please. I loved him."

Nyx yanked her up, stared into her wet eyes. Fear, love, terror? It often looked the same, to her. "You have proof?"

"No, I . . . yes. Harun has it. Please." She clutched her big carpet bag to her chest. "We have a list of reassignments at our center, if you want to see them, everyone Jahar referred to us. I know it's illegal. That's why I need to leave. But I just did what Harun asked. She's a First Family. You can't say no to a First Family in Nasheen."

"I've said no plenty," Nyx said.

"Then you're a fool."

"Don't leave town. We have you locked in."

"Who are you?"

"Not somebody you want to piss off," Nyx said. She stood, releasing Meiret. A bright red burst popped in the sky behind her. The sirens howled. "If you lied, you're fucked."

"I'm done anyway," Meiret said.

Nyx grabbed her by the collar and pulled her up. "Get inside."

Meiret ran across the street to the burst shelter, marked with double green triangles.

Nyx walked back to the shuttle station. She kicked away the largest of the bugs that had swarmed the overturned shaved ice cone, and picked it up. Sat on the cold stone bench. She gazed at the sky. Blue, amber, and green bursts spilled across the air, blown apart by the anti-burst guns. She took a mouthful of the slushy ice. Hooked her free arm over the back of the bench.

"Fuck of a thing," she muttered. A poor interrogation, but under the circumstances, she'd take it. Prayer would be over soon, and this air raid wouldn't last much longer.

She finished the shaved ice and strode across the square, making her way to the mosque where Anneke and Rhys would pour back out into the world, into the deep afternoon light; peaceful and pious, perfect.

Someone had to be imperfect, or there was nothing to strive for in that big worshipful love letter to God.

Nyx didn't mind being the broken piece.

Harun's family house stood on a craggy hilltop at the center of Bahora in a part of town so nice that Nyx suspected their bakkie already had a wasp swarm attached to it as surveillance, on suspicion they were casing a house.

"This is their local residence," Taite said from the passenger side of the bakkie. "They have a big family place in Mushtallah, of course, but this one is pretty much what you'd expect. Security's impossible."

Nyx didn't believe in impossible. "Anneke, Rhys, you get out here like we discussed. Good?"

Anneke muttered something about catshit.

"Tell me when Harun's in residence, and Taite will pop the alarm."

"You really think the bel dames aren't right behind us?" Rhys asked.

"Bel dames would shoot themselves before stalking a First Family," Nyx said. "They run the fucking country, no matter what the Queen says."

"Perhaps there's a lesson in that?" Rhys suggested.

"Like, let's not mess with First Families?" Taite said.

Nyx leaned back and opened the rear bakkie door from her place at the wheel. "Out," she said.

Rhys sighed and exited. Anneke slid after him. She came up to the driver's side window: "If we're just bait—"

Nyx pulled on her smoked driving goggles. The contaminated grit from the road burned her eyes. "Let's see how it rolls, all right? You get in the shit, well, you're skinny enough to hide in a ventilation grate, right?"

"One job, Nyx."

"One job."

Nyx accelerated away from the curb, blowing dust and dead beetles behind her.

Taite sat up front with her, playing with the misty blue projections coming from the radio. Images of First Family high council members droned on about rationing and Ras Tiegan refugees and recommendations on increased border security. Taite tuned the dial to a more upbeat station— northern dance music set to foggy green images of women hanging out the windows of their bakkies in a drifting street race.

"Can you trigger that house alarm from here?" she asked.

"You didn't hire me for my looks."

"Got any boyfriends you need to say goodbye to?"

"That would be telling."

They drove around the corner and parked. Taite reached under the seat and pulled out a bulky transponder. The under casing sloshed with blue bioluminescent worms strung together with silvery tapeworms, each as long as a string of intestines. Taite flipped open the top, revealing a little shelf of tiny bug and scent jars.

Com techs tended to have some minor ability with controlling bugs tailored for engineering and communication uses. Unlike magicians, they couldn't create new strains of bugs, or control those not created expressly for communication and engineering purposes, but they could sense and control lower-level transmissions meant for directing the tiny mites that carried most audio and image data.

Taite popped open the transponder's reservoir and reached for one of the jars.

Nyx caught a flash of movement from the corner of her eye. She glanced at the rearview mirror. Saw two women quickly approaching. They wore long trousers and short coats. Their faces were smooth and lovely, heads wrapped in red scarves. They bore pistols on their hips; both carried large truncheons with angry red glowing ends—the charge from those sticks could put down a two-hundred-kilo person with ease. They were the weapons of personal security officers for the Firsts, not order keepers.

"Taite, drive." Nyx popped open the bakkie's door and climbed out. She pulled her scattergun.

"What?"

"Break, go! Drive!"

Nyx slammed the door as Taite dropped his transponder and slid over into the driver's seat.

Nyx showed her teeth at the women, gun pointed at the ground, still hopeful she could talk her way out. "Can I help—" she began.

The woman on her left shoved her truncheon forward, just as the bakkie peeled away from the curb.

Nyx dodged the thrust. Shot the second woman in the

gut, then flipped her scattergun around and bashed the first woman in the face with it. Both women went down neatly. Nyx quickly stowed the gun and pulled her burnous more closely around her, to hide her prickling cache of weapons.

She took the corner wide—there was a vast spread of garden here, with tall trees and hedges that blocked her view of traffic—and had just enough time to see six more security women rushing out the front gate of Harun's estate.

How many security people did one First Family member need? Nyx tried to casually cross the street, but they spotted her. No random security check, this. They knew who she was, if not why she was there. Had Meiret tipped them off?

Nyx looked for an alley, but this part of town was too nice for dirty, close quarters. The sidewalks were broad and the buildings spaced too far apart for adequate cover.

In truth, she wasn't worried so much about her odds as she was about the number of bodies she'd leave on the street. Bodies meant questions from order keepers about why the bel dame council had stripped her of her title instead of killing her. She'd like to know the answer to that, too.

She saw a slick, smoked-glass bakkie rolling toward her, and timed her move.

When the bakkie passed her, Nyx turned. Scattergun out.

The first two security techs were twenty paces away, so she had a fighting chance of hitting something. She fired three times and rolled behind the bakkie. Yanked out a pistol. Keeping her head low, she dashed for the other side, using the pistol to put down cover fire.

She darted around another corner, now visibly armed and undoubtedly dangerous. A hornet swarm moved past her.

She saw six locusts take flight from a nearby residence. Most locusts were surveillance drones.

Nyx pressed herself against the big security fence of the residence behind her and waited for the pack of women.

Four took the corner wide. She shot two.

Two more came around from the other side of the residence—they'd been smart enough to break up and try to flank her. She shot one in the face with her pistol; the other pistol rounds went wide.

Their sticks were out. The fact that they weren't shooting her was . . . troubling. This wasn't the way she wanted to get inside Harun's place.

The three she hadn't hit moved in with their sticks. She blocked with the scattergun. Struck another in the face with her pistol. A swarm of locusts passed directly overhead.

Nyx broke someone's arm. The woman shrieked and backed off. Then the others pulled away, as if on a single command. Nyx kept her back to the fence.

"Shit," she said, and looked up.

The locust swarm massed by a second time; this time they sprayed her with a fine yellow mist of sticky, tannin-tasting liquid.

Nyx gagged and stumbled forward.

The liquid burned her eyes, throat, and nostrils. A heady black wave of nausea filled her. She vomited.

The security techs moved in again. Nyx emptied her scattergun clip. Drooled yellow bile.

Hands gripped her. Nyx bit their fingers bloody.

"Spray her the fuck again!" somebody yelled.

They zapped her with their truncheons.

Nyx clawed forward a full pace before losing all feeling in her fingers. The numbness suffused her body, fingertips to arms. Her head felt full of gauze.

Voices murmured around her, like ghosts from another country, "That was like trying to put down a fucking freight train."

"You know what we do here, darling?"

Nyx tried to focus. She was bound at the feet and wrists with sticky organic bands. Her mouth felt dry and swollen and tasted of acorns. Slowly, she made out the form of a set of bare brown feet a few paces from her. The skin was smooth and unblemished. That alone told her it was a First Family woman, not a security tech. The floor was warm tile, and oddly pleasant. Nyx wanted to take a nap on it. She followed the feet up to the ankles, then up the long white muslin tunic the woman wore.

The woman was broad, regal, with a spill of black hair that artfully escaped the back of her white head scarf. Her face was unlined, and so beautiful it made Nyx wince. She didn't trust pretty people. It meant they had enough money to spend a lot of time inside, behind the sun filters, plotting and politicking.

"You must be Harun," Nyx said.

"And you're the fool who took something that belongs to me," Harun said.

"Don't think so . . ." Nyx said. Her tongue felt heavy. She slurred, drooling.

Harun paced. Clasped her delicate fingers behind her back. Nyx tried to figure out where they were. It was an open room, supported by arches. She craned her neck and looked up into open sky, protected by a shimmering organic filter. Anything trying to get in or out that way would get eaten by the filter. She saw security techs near the archways—counted eight. Hadn't she shot them? Yes, those were familiar faces. She'd blown those faces apart. Only a bel dame could come back from a grievous wound like that, and no bel dame came back so *fast*.

The heavy fog in Nyx's head began to lift. She struggled.

Harun shook her head. "I wouldn't try," she said. "My people are far more difficult to kill than even you. You can slow them, certainly. But they'll come back. They self-repair. No need for Plague Sisters or magicians or tubs full of bug goo."

"What are they?" Nyx said.

Harun leaned over her. "They are the end result of a great deal of hard work, work that needs to stay in Nasheen. Where are Jahar's files?"

"He another tool, like these?"

"Every one of you colonials is a tool," Harun said. "You provide a service."

"And Jahar?"

"Provided a service."

"But he overstretched, didn't he?"

"She was a better woman than either of us."

"And you let him be whatever he wanted."

"Jahar was always Jahar, no matter the skin or the pronoun. But he overstepped. Jahar started giving boys new faces. Not just the ones we approved for new identities or reassignments for my security detail, but friends of his. Deserters. Terrorists, even. That had to stop."

"And all record of your involvement purged."

Harun sighed. "Where's the information from the safe, Nyx?"

"I tell you and you kill me."

"I kill you regardless."

"Then I'll die knowing I pissed you off."

Harun made a noncommittal noise. Nodded to her security staff. "Get her up. Bring her to the tank."

Four women hauled Nyx to her feet and half-dragged her through the courtyard. Nyx let them carry her full weight—it slowed them down and she needed the time to fully recover her muddled head. Nyx couldn't recall ever being inside a First Family's house, even if it was just a second or third residence. Most First Families lived in Nasheen's capital, Mushtallah, in the hills overlooking the city, ringed in layers and layers of security. In Mushtallah, she wouldn't have even been able to get into the First Family district without spending several days hacking through or blowing up two tiers of organic filters and eight security points. Harun was operating outside Mushtallah; Nyx suspected Bahora's tolerance for dicey illegal human experiments was higher than the capital's. She'd sold enough of herself to butchers in border towns like Punjai to know you could get away with just about anything.

As long as it wasn't with the body of one of Nyx's people.

They brought her down a sinuous hallway lined in tiled mosaics—passages from the Kitab, lovingly detailed and painted over in silver and gold gilt.

"My people tell me you're a hard woman to break," Harun said, "so I'm skipping to the end."

Harun unlocked a door at the far end of the house and opened the portal wide. A massive stone cistern dominated the room, ringed in jars of insects suspended in fluid, much like the ones at the rebuild tank in Henye's shop, only on a much grander scale.

"Planning a party?" Nyx asked.

Harun flashed a smile. Nyx was dazzled by how white her teeth were. "Of a sort," she said. She beckoned for the security techs to bring Nyx to the edge of the cistern.

For a moment, Nyx thought Harun meant to rebuild her into some kind of brain-addled monster. She looked over the rim of the cistern and found that most of it was actually underground—it must have been a good ten paces in depth.

And there, chained to a large ring suspended over the basin, was Rhys.

He looked up at her with his big dark eyes, and for a moment Nyx thought he looked terribly like Jahar. On seeing her, there was hope in that gaze. The same hopeful look Jahar gave her when she took him to bed. The look that said, "You've found me. You'll protect me. You'll never leave me."

It scared the shit out of her, because she was not here to save him.

Saving people like Rhys and Jahar was never part of the plan. It's why she no longer believed in the war. It's why she left the service. She knew just how highly her government valued the bodies it flung at the border. She feared becoming as callous as they were. But she already had, hadn't she? A long time ago.

Nyx glanced behind Harun. Just more security techs. She

needed to keep stalling. She scanned the edges of the room, looking for Anneke. If Anneke wasn't in the pit, they didn't have her. Nyx would have dumped the whole team in here to pry information out of a bel dame. You never knew, on a really close team, who the bel dame was fucking. Sometimes it mattered. Sometimes it didn't. Nyx had planned on getting in here by throwing Rhys outside the door, but not this way.

"Give me what was in the safe," Harun said.

"We didn't find a safe," Nyx said. "Whatever his head opened, you already emptied it."

"Me?" Harun laughed. "When we blew that tenement open, Jahar and the Plague Sister were already dead, and Meiret was missing. I know exactly one person in this horrible little town who could achieve that."

"Well, I'm the wrong horrible person."

Harun gripped a large lever beside the tank. Pulled.

Water flooded into the cistern.

"You left Jahar to die," Harun said. "Who did you expect him to turn to when we brought him back—you? You abandon your own people to save your feral little skin. Tell this one how many partners you had before putting together this little team? You're a fuck-up, Nyx. Your service record is a series of fuck-ups."

"Maybe so," Nyx said. Rhys was watching her as water filled the basin. She started cutting away her own common sense; she severed the silvery string of compassion she kept slick for negotiating personal interactions. She went numb. Looked at her situation as if from a great height.

This was the plan.

Sacrificing Rhys was part of the plan.

He was just a fucking Chenjan.

Nyx clenched her jaw. Her whole body went tight, as if expecting a blow. She wanted to look away, but couldn't. It was true about Jahar—she left him to die, back at the front. Him and the rest of her squad, when she fled past them after triggering an acid burst. They'd been melted down into nothing. She thought them all dead where she'd abandoned them, until she saw Jahar's head staring down at her from the rebuild center's window.

Harun had put Jahar back together again, tattoo and all. She had saved him. Nyx had not.

"You make a habit of collecting dead people and tossing them into rebuild chambers?" Nyx said. She watched the water stir around Rhys's ankles. He looked from Nyx to Harun and back.

"Dead people have more to live for," Harun said. "I gave Jahar another chance. The magicians left him for dead. So did you, he said."

The water rushed to Rhys's knees.

"I don't have what's in the safe," Nyx said. "I suspect Meiret played us both."

"Meiret is a timid Mhorian. Jahar had her well under control."

"May have been the other way around," Nyx said.

Nyx had killed a lot of people. She'd let even more die through neglect. Rhys was just one more. I'm the same person, aren't I? she thought. She had burned herself up, only to come out the other side exactly the same.

Taite's signal would get out, Nyx knew. It would be soon enough to save *her*.

But it would not be soon enough for Rhys.

Nyx hardened her jaw. Her hands and feet were still tied. They'd stripped her of her most obvious weapons. She could just wait this out.

She saw Rhys register that. But there was no shock. Just resignation. He knew her for what she was.

Butcher. Monster.

The same old monster.

Harun grabbed a gun from the nearest security tech and shoved it in Nyx's face.

"How many do I have to go through?" she said. "How about your sister, instead?" Harun turned, called to her women, "When he's dead, find Kine so Dasheem and bring—"

No, Nyx thought, watching the water bubble up to Rhys's waist as his burnous swirled around him. No, not yet.

Her squad screaming. Jahar's accusing eyes.

Nyx thrust out her bound hands and gripped Harun's right arm at the elbow. Hard. Nyx yanked them both over into the cistern.

She heard gunfire as they hit the water.

Icy cold engulfed her. Nyx thumped Harun in the sternum with her bound fists. She snapped up in the water and head-butted Harun. Harun crumpled. Nyx freed Harun's gun and turned it on Rhys.

Rhys cringed.

Nyx took aim.

Above them, she heard the sound of Harun's women yelling. The water in the tank bubbled up past Rhys's neck. He gurgled at her.

Nyx took the shot.

Three of them.

Rhys's restraints popped under the bullets. He yelled something. She saw blood.

She'd shot through one of his hands.

Nyx grabbed the front of his tunic and pushed him behind her. They splashed to the rim of the tank.

Harun's women lined the opening above them, guns leveled.

"Now what?" Rhys said, cradling his injured hand. "Was this seriously your plan? You're going to shoot your way out?"

Nyx wondered if saving him had really been a great idea.

Nyx had maybe four more shots, six if Harun had loaded the gun with an extended clip, which wasn't likely. There were eight women lining the tank. Math wasn't usually her thing, but this looked especially bad.

"Get me loose," she said, spitting water. Fuck, she hated water. "There's a razor blade in my sandal."

"Give me the gun, Nyx," he said.

"Why? You want to pray over it? Get my hands free!"

Rhys dove into the water. Yanked off her sandal. Just as he reemerged, one of Harun's women plunged into the cistern.

Nyx shot her, and dove for cover, taking Rhys with her.

Dumb way to die, Nyx thought, but at least she got to drown Harun in the process.

And the last thing she saw wasn't going to be that awful look on Rhys's face.

Under the cold water, Rhys broke away from her. She surfaced under Harun's body, using it as cover as she broke for air.

As she did, she heard the sound of more shots—not from outside the tank, but inside it.

She peeked out from under the body. Rhys hung on to the side of the cistern, the dead security tech's organic pistol in his hand. As Nyx watched, he cleanly popped off seven shots, every one of them hitting a security tech in the right shoulder.

"Next will be the head," Rhys said. "Move back."

They retreated.

Nyx swam to the edge of the cistern, spitting water.

"Where the fuck did you learn to shoot like that?" she said.

"Camp."

"Camp what? Camp target practice for self-righteous dancers?"

"Something like that."

The injured security techs had fled to the far end of the room, but already looked like they were rallying. Rhys cut her bonds.

"You got something against killing?" Nyx asked.

"I won't kill for you, or anyone. I told you that the day we met."

"These ones aren't going to stay down long."

"If they get up," he said, louder, "I'll hit them again." Rhys got to his feet. He pressed his bleeding left hand to his side.

"Let me see your hand," she said. She pulled herself out of the cistern.

"It's fine."

"Let me—"

"You'll only make it worse."

"You treat your family like this?"

"Did you shoot yours?"

"Come on," she said, and wrapped her arm around him. He clung to her with his good hand. He leaned hard on her.

She realized, with a stabbing pain of horror-stricken desire, that she wanted to spend the night with her hands on more of him. Not the fucking *Chenjan*, she thought.

"Surprised you jumped in after me," he said.

"Seemed like a good idea at the time."

"Regret it yet?"

"Yes."

Nyx heard the heavy sound of someone battering at the front door. "Time to go," she said, loud. Not for the security women or the order keepers, but for Anneke.

"Who's out there?" Rhys asked.

"Order keepers," Nyx said. "Taite triggered the house alarm for this residence remotely. Whole district's order keepers are about to descend us."

A ceramic ventilation grate on the far wall shattered inward. Anneke poked her head out. "Hurry the fuck up," she said. "It was tight in there."

"What happened?" Nyx asked. "No assist?"

"You said I don't move until the alarm," Anneke said. "I waited for the order keepers. I count forty outside. Need to move."

Nyx pulled herself away from Rhys and motioned him forward.

"I don't understand," he said. "Anneke was in on this? I thought we were bait? I thought you threw us both out front just to get caught?"

Nyx grimaced. "No. *You* were the bait, Rhys."

"We were going to trip the alarm," Anneke said, "and have the order keepers pick you up, then slip in during the confusion while they processed you."

"That's . . . a horrible plan," Rhys said. He met Nyx's look a long moment, and she knew that no matter how drunk she got him, he wasn't going to sleep with her.

"You're as bad as they say."

"If that was true, I'd have let you die." She heard footsteps in the hall. "Go."

"You first," he said. "I don't want you at my back."

"Fair enough," Nyx said, and crawled after Anneke.

"I'm sorry, mistress," the ticket vendor said, "your identification papers are invalid."

Meiret took the papers back, clutching them to her chest. Nyx watched her from a bench in the train station, yawning. Evening prayer had come and gone, and the station was busy with people on the move after end-of-week prayers. It had been a long day. She still had water stuck in her left ear. She could hear it sloshing around. She yawned again, then stood.

She came up behind Meiret and put her arm around her. Meiret froze.

"Hello, honey pot," Nyx said, guiding her away from the ticket counter. "You and I need to have a little chat."

"It isn't what you think," Meiret said.

Nyx kept her voice low. "I have a sniper up in the second level there," she said, nodding to where Anneke was posted on the far side of the station. "And a magician over there." She smiled at where Rhys waited near the train platform. "And to make this even cozier, I've got a com tech recording this entire conversation for posterity." She tapped her ear.

"I don't have the information."

"Then I'm afraid you're not ever leaving this country," Nyx said.

Meiret gritted her teeth. "This is very serious organic science," she said. "I need this. My people need this."

"What, to make some kind of super regenerating soldier?" Meiret shook her head. "That's unstable. It's the sex reassignment. Mhoria is a divided nation, Nyx. An agent with the ability to pass across the divide between the male and female spheres of our society—"

"Wait, what? You want to use it to spy on your own people?"

"I don't expect you to understand Mhorian society. It's necessary for the sexes to be separated, as God ordained."

"So you're a government agent for the women's side? You spy on your own men?"

Meiret laughed. "You hunt down the men who flee from your war as if they're feral dogs. You have no right to make judgments about Mhorian society."

"I need what was in the safe, Meiret. You're not leaving here with it."

"I need . . ." Meiret's eyes filled. "I need it. Please. You don't understand how this will change things, for so many people."

Nyx reached forward and gently took the carpet bag from Meiret's hands. "Sewn into the liner?" Nyx said.

Meiret began to weep. "Please, if we don't bring something back they'll kill us. My mother and I. And if I stay, your government will kill me."

"Did this act work on Jahar?"

Meiret's crumpled face softened. She took her hands away

from her face, and gave Nyx a hard look. "Damn you, and your foolish country," she said.

"Let me guess—Mhoria didn't want you experimenting on Mhorians, so they sent you here and you wormed your way into Harun's cold little heart."

"Jahar led me to Harun," Meiret said. "My mother reassigned Jahar before the war, so he could be male and serve at the front for life with his brothers."

"And when Harun rebuilt him, he started delivering more boys to you who wanted to be reassigned. Nice little organic science lab you had going here. Too bad it was all illegal."

"They were all willing."

"And you took advantage of that," Nyx said. "Sorry, but changing people's identities so they can avoid the draft is illegal, whether or not I agree with it."

"It's a crime to throw bodies into the maw of a war that will never end."

"One your government happily supports by selling us bomb components," Nyx said. "You and Tirhan and Ras Tieg and the rest are just as culpable. You know the war keeps Nasheen and Chenja busy, so you can consolidate your own power."

"Politics is difficult," Meiret said.

"So is prison," Nyx said.

Almira stepped away from the crowd and took Meiret by the elbow with her clawed hand.

Meiret's eyes widened. "Who. . . ?"

"Guess who handles foreign espionage in Nasheen?" Nyx asked.

"Bel dames," Almira said.

Two more bel dames peeled away from the crowd, and took hold of Meiret.

"This won't stand!" Meiret cried. "The Mhorian ambassador will be notified. This won't stand!"

They hauled her away.

Almira smiled at Nyx. "Thank you, Nyx."

"Just don't be some cat bitch about it."

"Such language."

Nyx handed her the carpet bag. "I hope you're running this for the government and not for some big bidder."

"Don't insult me. I'm true to my vows, Nyx. This information won't leave Nasheen. The Queen herself put Dahab and me on this note."

"I knew it wasn't a fucking random assignment."

"They never are," Almira said. "Go peacefully with God, Nyx."

"I'll go drunkenly, how's that?"

"Whatever pleases you."

"You put in a good word with my bel dame sisters," Nyx said.

"We're not your sisters anymore, Nyx," Almira said.

Nyx watched Almira walk out of the train station where Dahab and three more red-clad bel dames met her. Nyx saw the delight in their faces. Lots of grinning, back slapping. They'd go out for drinks, later, fruity ones with little mango wedges. She wondered if Almira liked whiskey. Realized she was never going to find out.

Rhys came up behind her. "You really miss being one of those?"

"No," she lied. "Let's go get drunk."

"You get drunk," he said. "I'll drive you home."

"Home, or into a wall?"

"Let's not ruin the surprise," he said, and moved away from her.

She watched him go, admiring the outline of his form in the long tunic he wore. It was going to be a long night. Maybe a longer year.

They met at a cantina on the outskirts of Bahora, near the contaminated zone. It had a good view of the ruined mosque from the front bank of windows. Nyx was three whiskies in when Rhys finally gave in to the urging of two young, conservatively dressed magicians to dance.

Nyx had seen him dance before, back in the magicians' boxing gym where she recruited him. Watching him stirred something she preferred left dead, though. She decided she wasn't drunk enough to watch Rhys dance, so she switched chairs to face Anneke, her back to Rhys. Taitehad had sidled up to a young man on the other side of the bar, another Ras Tiegan, from the look of him. No matter how far into the interior they went, Taite always managed to find a sloe-eyed young man to talk to.

Anneke snickered into her own whiskey. "Can see why you keep Rhys on. What the fuck kind of name is that, though? That's fucking Heidian, not Chenjan."

"Planning on dissolving his contract, actually," Nyx said.

"Why, you want to fuck him?"

Nyx took a drink to disguise her discomfort. Was she that fucking obvious? "Do you?"

Anneke grimaced, like she'd eaten bad fish. "My fucking is my business."

"So's mine," Nyx said. "One rule on this team. We keep it business. I don't question your past. You don't question mine. We let shit lie. I expect you weren't born with the name Anneke any more than Rhys was born Rhys."

"Who says I'm staying?"

"What, you think you'll get a better offer?"

"Always better offers."

"How about this . . . I get you a bigger gun. Biggest you can carry."

Anneke raised her glass. "To bigger guns, then."

Nyx stood. "Going to get some air."

"Sure thing, boss."

Nyx walked up through the back of the cantina and out onto the roof. The air smelled like burnt raspberries. There had been another air raid after evening prayer. Now it was nearly midnight, and she already felt hung over.

She heard someone behind her, and turned.

Rhys strode over, mopping at his brow with his sleeve. She noted his other hand, bandaged neatly. "Plotting?" he asked.

"You know me well enough to know I don't think any of this shit through beforehand."

"So what do you think?" He leaned up against the edge of the roof beside her.

"About what?"

"About me on your team."

She shrugged. Tried to be nonchalant. "You signed a contract. You can walk any time. Didn't promise you this would be cheery. Wish you'd actually kill people with that aim. You're a better shooter than you are a magician."

"I signed with you for protection, Nyx. You almost let me die today."

"You don't look dead to me."

"The contract is a year," he said. "I can see it through, but only if you don't stab me in the back."

"Then why are you asking?"

He gazed across the city at the last gasp of the blue sun as it turned the horizon violet-topaz. "Just the way you've been looking at me."

"I don't look at you."

"You look like you're disappointed in how things went today."

"That's . . . not what that look means."

"What is it, then?" He leaned closer.

Nyx took a breath. Wasn't sure if she was going to reach for him, or another drink.

The drink, she knew, would be safer.

The muezzin sounded the call to midnight prayer, a sweet, lyrical call in the old prayer language that was both comforting and oddly mournful. The call brought her up short. She let out her breath and looked toward the old broken mosque.

"Let it be known that I bear witness: there is none worthy of worship but God, lord of all the worlds."

Nyx remembered sitting on the roof in the farm town she grew up in, Mushirah, listening to the faint sound of those words coming in from the mosque in the town center, so far away. She thought maybe someday she'd live there, become a muezzin herself. She liked to sing, though she wasn't much good at it. Simple path. Simple life. God carved it all out for you, everyone said. One's purpose in life was to worship and honor God. Five prayers a day, which God deigned to count as the prescribed fifty, if performed correctly. And the sixth prayer, Umayma's prayer, the prayer God required of those spared from whatever horror the first people of Umayma had fled from in the black void of the stars. Midnight prayer, to remind them all of who their bodies belonged to, birth to death. Reminded them of their unique purpose.

But it wasn't so simple.

There was the war. The Tirhanis. The Chenjans. The Ras Tiegans. The Mhorians. The world.

The war had remade her. Reshaped her purpose. Why couldn't she unmake it again?

"Better go," Nyx said, pulling away. "Ablution takes a while."

He paused a long moment, then, "I could wait."

An invitation. Open palm. Rebuild. She heard it and feared it.

"There's no water strong enough to get me to a state of purification," Nyx said.

"Then I need to go to prayer."

"And I need to pack up a body."

But they lingered there all the same, until the last note of the muezzin faded, and Bahora's sea of faithful moved across the city as one to bend their bodies in prayer.

Nyx tried to remember the words to the opening surah of midnight prayer, but realized she had forgotten it, somewhere between the front and the rebuild tank. They could rebuild all these bodies, here, every last one of them, but the lives, what came before—all ashes.

"I'm going, Nyx," Rhys said.

"Yeah."

When he left, she tossed her empty glass over the edge of the roof, into the contaminated sand on the other side, and yelled "Fuck!" at the sky.

She clasped her own empty hands in front of her. Held on tight. Every dawn was a chance to start over. Rebuild. Every day was another body.

THE HEART IS EATEN LAST

"Above all else, guard your heart, for everything you do flows from it."
—Proverbs 4:23

THE SABOTEURS FLED the bombed-out wreckage of the smoking chemical plant like roaches from a burning cane field. Black smoke clotted the air. The toxic bloom unfurled across the desert sky outside Alabbas like some black portent. It rolled over the fleeing insurgents, covering their escape into the warren of workers' houses and tumbledown ruins from the last time someone tried to build something worth a damn out here on the edge of the southern desert.

Nyxnissa so Dasheem—bounty hunter, mercenary, and former government agent—watched the explosion from the hot rooftop of an abandoned mosque half a kilometer away. She pulled on a respirator without taking her eyes from the specs that gave her a keen view of the action. Behind her, her magician, Rhys, was crouched against a nearby minaret, arms over his head, yelling about the end of the world.

Typical day, really.

"Put on your respirator," she said around hers.

"As if that makes a difference," he said. "That cloud will eat us down to bones in an hour. Why did you take this awful job? Why are we still here when we know what's really happening?"

Nyx adjusted her respirator and stuffed a pinch of sen into her mouth and sucked at it, considering the cloud. "Wind's the wrong way," she said. "It's heading out over the desert."

"Why didn't we stop them, Nyx?" Rhys said. "If nothing else we've done out here is worth anything, at least we could have stopped that."

Nyx watched the toxic cloud shift with the wind that now blew against her back, pushing the worst of the fallout in the other direction. Lucky break, that. Satisfied, she shoved the specs in her pack, pulled out the respirator, and spit bloody red sen on the sandy rooftop.

"No one's dead down there yet," she said. "We'll get to that next. Sometimes you got to let them burn and follow them back."

Rhys huffed out a breath. He was a handful of years younger than her, which put him in his early twenties. He had been on her bounty hunting team two years, though he insisted every six months that he was going to leave and find some new job, and this time he seemed to mean it. He was pretty enough, for a Chenjan, and she liked his eyes and his hands. But the complaining she couldn't stand, especially because it all came out in his terrible Chenjan accent. The accent reminded her she was supposed to be killing people like him on the other side of the border, not consorting with them. The accent took her back to the warfront.

She regretted taking this job, then. But the only time she

didn't regret taking a job was when she was drinking the money it earned her. Every other moment was stuffed with poisonous doubt. Served her right. She was a sucker for pretty boys and plain-faced girls, and the girl who had given her this job had been tough to refuse. What surprised Nyx was that even after saying yes, and finding out what she'd really been hired for, Nyx was still here anyway. Girls with silvery tongues had secrets, and Nyx couldn't help but try and fish them out. It was all too irresistible.

"Let's go start the cleanup," Nyx said.

"We're bringing the saboteurs in, then?" Rhys said. Hopeful. "I knew you would see sense!"

"We're finishing the job," Nyx said. She picked up her scattergun, and pointed it at his chest.

The day the girl with the job had walked into Nyx's gym in Punjai, Nyx was sitting at the front with the gym owner, Husayn, and nursing her usual morning hangover. Nyx dredged a hunk of stale bread into a cup of thick, dark buni so strong just the smell of it made her feel sober. Buni was the kind of thick, sludgy coffee that she had dreamed about often at the front.

Husayn sat opposite her, unwrapping her own hands after teaching an early morning class of eager young women how to throw punches. It had gone well enough until two of them got into a brawl over some slight, and one bit the ear off the other. The front of Husayn's breast binding was spattered in blood.

"What you teaching these girls?" Nyx said, nodding to the

bloody floor. The class had cleared out, and old Marise, the Ras Tiegan cut woman, was mopping the concrete floor.

"I don't have any control over what they bring into the gym," Husayn said. She sniffed at Nyx's buni. "Shouldn't eat right before a workout. Or are you just here to socialize?"

Nyx shrugged. "Bit of both."

"Avoiding that Chenjan at your office more like," Husayn said.

Nyx slurped her buni.

Husayn guffawed. "You never did take it well, not getting what you want."

"Got him on my team, didn't I?" Nyx said. "Can't imagine what else I'd want from a man like that."

A shadow fluttered in the open doorway, and Nyx squinted into the light; a shapely silhouette moved into the gym. Nyx sat up a little straighter.

The silhouette resolved itself into a thin-lipped woman in her early thirties. Her broad face was too smooth to be lower class, too marked to be First Family. Nyx guessed she was the daughter of some merchant family selling weapons or bugs; maybe landowners. Nyx had known farmers with plantations so large that they didn't bother working the land themselves, and it kept them out of the cancerous suns. Why bother when there was cheap refugee labor? Nyx flexed her own fingers, remembering the repetitive work involved in harvesting sugar cane and rye on her mother's farm. This woman didn't have the face or hands of someone who'd worked a day in her life.

The woman wore a long wrap of a dress, not trousers and certainly not a dhoti like Nyx's, and that was odd. That was a southern look, meant for impressing foreigners in cooler climates like the prudish, idol-worshipping Ras Tiegans. In Punjai nobody much cared about covering up in fear of cancers. This close to the contested border with Chenja, everyone figured a bullet or a burst would get them long before cancer from the blazing suns and toxic air. It was too hot, and life too short, to worry about it.

"You lost?" Nyx said, ripping off a hunk of bread with her teeth. She imagined doing the same to the woman's dress.

The woman narrowed her eyes at Nyx. She had gloriously shiny dark hair rolled up against her scalp—also a rural southern style. Nyx was leaning more and more toward thinking she was a land owner. There was a little scar on her upper lip; she'd clearly been born with a cleft palate, and been rich enough to get it fixed but not rich enough to remove the scar. She had a nose bold enough to be Chenjan, though her complexion was Nasheenian, and the thin lips and long face put Nyx in mind of some southern people like the Ras Tiegans or Drucians. In Nyx's line of work, it paid to pay attention to the cut of a woman's face. Could save you a whole lot of trouble.

"I'm looking for Nyxnissa so Dasheem," the woman said.

Nyx leaned forward while tucking her left hand behind her, closer to the scattergun stowed at her back. "That so?"

The woman held up her hands. She had long, slender fingers that Nyx imagined would feel delightful wrapped around her thighs. "I'm not armed," the woman said.

"Need a room?" Husayn said, snorting.

"I came to discuss a job," the woman said. "That's what you do, isn't it? *You're* Nyxnissa so Dasheem?" She was looking at Husayn.

Husayn laughed, and Nyx relaxed. An assassin would have moved already. And been better at making her.

"Get her some buni," Nyx said.

"I'm not a fucking bartender," Husayn said. "I'm going to have a rub down." She left them with her bloody hand wraps on the counter.

Nyx patted the stool next to her. "I don't bite unless you ask," Nyx said.

The woman looked visibly flustered at that, which Nyx found endearing. It had been some time since she had made a woman blush. Southern country kids, new to the city, were rarities this close to the border after a few hundred years of war. Only crazy kids and refugees came out here. Nyx supposed she herself was a bit of both.

"You have a name?" Nyx asked. She finished the bread and licked her fingers.

"Binyamin."

"That all? One name?"

"For now, yes."

"Huh," Nyx said. She held out her hand. Binyamin just stared at it. Nyx laughed. "You were brave enough to come out here, but too scared to play nice?"

Binyamin cleared her throat. "I have concerns about . . . disease. You spent a year in prison, didn't you?"

"Couple years ago," Nyx said. She wondered why that was relevant. "No more diseased in prison than anywhere else."

"I just thought that meant you'd look a little older, like your friend."

Nyx raised her brows. "I'm twenty-seven," Nyx said. "Husayn's thirty-two. Not a huge leap."

"I've known too many women like you and her," she said. "My mother says she can read faces like yours the way hedge witches read palms. But I'm not as good at that."

"I find it hard to believe you've ever met anyone like me," Nyx said, "on some southern plantation."

"How did . . ." She patted the rolls of her hair. "Ah, I suppose it's obvious."

"So what are you here for, southern girl? The killing will cost you, but there's plenty more that we could do for free."

"This is a serious matter."

Nyx stared into her cup and sighed. "Always is."

"There have been a series of explosions at weapons plants in the south. I'd like you to bring the saboteurs to justice."

"Nasheenian justice," Nyx said, "is a head in a bag. Why should I care about the south? Stuff blows up every day. Not my job to handle that shit. That's what bel dames and order keepers are for."

"It's . . . a domestic problem. Not a terrorist problem. If we thought it was Chenjans we would use more orthodox methods."

"These are your family's plants, then?"

She nodded. "It could be any number of people," she said, "but we have had some concerns with bel dames. That's our worst fear, that it may be a bel dame. You know that these former government assassins don't even answer to the government, once they are let loose."

"Then you should talk to the bel dame council. Only bel dames hunt down other bel dames. They exist as their own independent entity. They govern themselves."

"I went to them first," she said. "But they told me she was

just an apprentice, and never finished the training. That is close enough to a bel dame, to me, but not to them. They told me to speak to order keepers." She made a sound of distress, deep in her throat. "As if order keepers would make a difference."

"But I would?"

"You used to be a bel dame," she said. "Most die in service, but you served your time in prison and survived."

"So who is this bel dame apprentice?" Nyx said.

"My sister."

"Terrorism *and* family problems," Nyx said. "I'm not in the mood for either today." What Nyx wanted was a good fuck and a whisky tonight, not trouble with the bel dame council. She finished her buni. "I'm here to work out. You should go." She grabbed her gloves off the counter as she slid off her seat.

The woman flinched. "I can give you more than money," she said. "You'll have a favor from a very powerful family. We aren't First Family, but when it comes to wealth and influence, we may as well be. Isn't that something?"

"A favor? Like what?"

"Anything within . . . reason."

"Pardons for crimes?"

"Only the Queen can grant *that*. But we have other types of influence. Land grants, political pull with the high and low councils, contacts in land management—"

"What would I do with land?"

"There's a contested piece of property in Mushirah," Binyamin said. "Your mother owned it. She was Bakira so Dasheem, am I right? You see, we know something about you."

Nyx wrinkled her nose. "My mother granted that land to

my sister," she said. Spit it, really, because she knew where this was going, and she really didn't want to be interested. A soft country girl was one thing; a manipulative, wealthy, chemical weapons scoundrel who had done her homework was another. Now that Nyx was pushing thirty, she was trying to think with her head more often. So far that hadn't been working out very well.

"And your sister Kine has been stuck in a legal battle over it with the government for almost ten years. I can make that go away."

"What makes you think I give a shit about my sister, or that shitty plot of land?"

"Everyone cares about something."

"Not me," Nyx said.

Binyamin cut a sidelong look at her; big dark eyes, firm mouth, long, sad face. The sadness, the need, made Nyx hotter than she would admit. She wanted to bundle this woman up in her arms and save her—from what, she didn't know. Everyone needed to be saved from something.

Nyx slid her gloves across the table. "I'll take it if you spar with me," she said.

Binyamin looked at the gloves as if they were some dangerous insect. "I don't know how to box."

"Then I'll show you," Nyx said. She walked behind the counter and pulled out an extra set of gloves. "How serious are you?"

"Very serious."

"Then put on some gloves."

Binyamin looked at Nyx's wrapped hands. "Do I need that, the wrappings?"

"Not with how hard you're likely to hit," Nyx said. She pulled on her own gloves and danced out to the center of the gym, motioning Binyamin to follow her.

Binyamin went reluctantly after her, frowning at her gloves. "Shouldn't someone tie these?"

"Only if you intend to hit hard, like I said. You going to hit me, or what?"

Binyamin rubbed the worn leather of one of the gloves with her thumb. Shook her head. "I am not here to play games."

"Oh, I doubt that," Nyx said. She lunged forward to tap Binyamin's face with her left hand.

Binyamin flinched; her right shoulder came up, ever so slightly, and her fingers tightened on the gloves. She let Nyx tap her cheek, though, and it was the "letting" part that Nyx filed away for later.

Nyx rolled back on her heels and cocked her head at the little southern woman. She spared a glance for Binyamin's feet, and noted that she had slid into a right-handed woman's fighter's stance: right leg forward, left leg back.

She was not the soft southern woman she pretended to be, then.

"I'll think about taking the job," Nyx said. "You should go. I'll be in touch after I look into some things."

Binyamin hesitated a moment longer, then moved out of her stance and put the gloves back on the counter. She touched the jeweled beetle at her throat. It shifted to her finger. She placed it on the long table. "If you change your mind, you just tell her to find me," she said. The beetle scuttled to the edge of Nyx's empty buni cup and clung there, a shiny bauble.

Nyx's gaze followed Binyamin as she turned and sauntered

out, hips swaying beneath the long dress. When she came to the door, she became a black silhouette again, just another shadow, another woman with a dirty job that needed doing, and joined the bustling crowd on the street.

Nyx eyed the beetle. Gave it a little tap with her index finger. "Not falling for it," she said, but of course she was.

She always did.

The sign in the window of Nyx's cramped, battered storefront said, *Odd jobs and body reclamation,* which was a fair summation of what she did these days. She had been banned from one place already the year before when she found out a client's dead girlfriend wasn't dead after all. For the record, she preferred hunting down dead people or people she could legally make dead. The living were just too much trouble. She was best at killing, which is what made it so ironic that even the military had hastily discharged her after her two years at the front and never asked her to re-up. She'd always been a problem, far more hot-headed than any conscripted boy doing his thirty years of service and better at her job than even the most ruthless woman doing her own two years. Her reconstitution after she got blown up out there was part of her permanent file now, and it had been expensive. They didn't want to risk her doing some other dumb thing on their money. So instead she was here, trying to build a team of hard-bitten mercenaries that was now bickering like a bunch of fucking compound babies as she pushed inside.

Taite, her com tech, sat in the back at his console, arguing with Anneke, her hired gun. Anneke had a big shotgun hitched up over one shoulder; the gun was half as big as she was. Wiry, spry, and mouthy as hell, Anneke had her feet planted firmly in front of Taite, and though she did not unshoulder the gun, the flustered look on Taite's face told Nyx he fully expected her to at any moment.

Behind them, Rhys was hunched over his work table, probably dissecting some bug or some other thing that bug magicians did.

Nyx instinctively touched Binyamin's green beetle that she'd put in her tunic pocket. She considered breaking up the argument, but went to her office and rummaged around in the drawer for a bottle and a glass instead, only to find that the bottle only contained a few drops of liquor. She sucked on the bottle, long and slow, considering.

Taite peeked in. Raised his brows at her suckling. "I miss something salacious?"

Nyx wiped her mouth. "You wish."

Taite was in his late teens, spotty and scrawny, but good at hacking into transmissions and ensuring their internal com network wasn't hacked by some other com tech's buggy aerial concoctions. She didn't pretend to know all the particulars of what he did; it was good enough for her to know that she could communicate to her team on a job without somebody else listening in. She had added him to her team just after Rhys and Anneke, and he'd only been around six months, but she'd known him before then, when he worked for her former boss, Raine. She enjoyed taking Raine's employees away from him. Made her feel warm all over.

"Got a job for you," she said. "Need you to track down a woman named Binyamin. Her family owns chemical plants in the south, probably near Alabbas. See if she's got sisters, and tell me what happened to them."

"That all you got?" he said.

She pulled the beetle out of her pocket. "She gave me this to use to contact her. Can you tell me where it's tailored to report to?"

He took the beetle gently into his palms and peered at it. "I'll see what I can do. Rhys could probably figure it out."

"Work together then," she said. "Sooner the better."

"This a paying job?"

"Think of it like a job screening," she said.

He nodded. "There are some new jobs on the boards," he said. "Left it on your desk." He ducked out of the room.

Nyx sat hard in her chair and sighed, staring at the empty bottle. She had spent a couple hours at the gym, and the rest of the day loomed ahead of her, long and hot and dusty as her parched throat.

She cast about for the job letters Taite had pulled from the bounty boards, and found them under a pair of specs. She didn't much care for reading, and hadn't managed to wean Taite and Rhys off handing her reams of expensive paper that she was just going to feed to the bugs anyway. Rhys had a decent memory and recall, but Taite needed the paper. There were bounties out on two organ harvesters, a shifter who'd murdered and eaten her own mother, and two young indentured runaways, thirteen-year-old twins. She had asked Taite to stop pulling runaway kids, but there was a high price on these ones—double the usual. She turned the order over and found that the issuing authority wasn't the government, but the kids' own mother. That was new. Most mothers weren't shitty enough to formally indenture their own kids when they hauled them out of the compounds. If you were going to do that, better to leave them to be raised by the state. But she supposed some people got off on that—cheap labor, power delusions, that sort of thing.

She looked up from the paperwork and caught a glimpse of the call box in the foyer. She had to admit that reading about well-meaning but shitty family members just doing what they thought God wanted them to put her in mind of her sister.

But she'd need a few more drinks for that.

So she told the team she was going out to run reconnaissance. Which she did, a bit, in a cantina at the north end of Punjai where southerners and the occasional Drucian showed up to swill. She considered the drinks a business expense, especially the ones she bought for the grimy one-armed former chemical factory worker who had all sorts of things to say about working at a plant burned out six years before.

"There are two families that used to own the south," the woman said, knee pressing Nyx's. "The Yazeeds and the Muhktars. But last dozen years, there's these upstarts rolling in from northern Druce, half-breeds, *mixed*, you know, not real Nasheenians, even though they have Nasheenian names. And they started buying things up. Accidents started happening." She pointed the stump of her arm at Nyx, leaned in. "Got a lot of places shut down just cause of *accidents*. Bought them cheap, after. Some they bought just to close down. Fucking foreigners."

Nyx considered making out with her, but she wasn't really Nyx's type. When the woman's girlfriend showed up to retrieve her, Nyx was almost relieved, right up until she realized it left her alone in her own head again.

So she drank some more, drank so much she hoped she'd forget about her shitty mother and her shitty sister and her shitty military career and her shitty life.

When she stumbled back into the storefront, long after dark, she knocked her head on the door while trying to close it, and nearly tripped over her own feet. The only sound she heard was Rhys, back in his room, reciting midnight prayer. It was the call to prayer that had sent her home from the cantina. It hurt her head.

Nyx went right for the call box. Picked up the receiver. She knew her sister Kine would be awake because she, too, would be observing midnight prayer. She dialed Kine's pattern. When there was no answer, she dialed it again. And again.

At some point, Kine picked up.

"Who is this?" Kine asked; suspicious, guarded, as if expecting some sexual deviant or male deserter looking for refuge on the other end.

"I'm your fucking sister," Nyx said.

"Indeed," Kine said. "That hasn't changed."

Nyx leaned her head against the call box. Her stomach churned. She had no idea anymore why she'd wanted to call her sister. Maybe if she just waited here awhile, she'd remember.

"Nyxnissa, are you drunk?" Kine said. Nyx would say Kine sounded like their mother, but honestly Nyx couldn't much remember what their mother sounded like anymore. Their mother had taken up working at the birthing compounds for cash after getting kicked out of some government job. She'd died of yellow fever not long after Nyx's brothers died at the front.

"You think you look out for me," Nyx said. "But I look out for *you*."

Silence. Bloody silence. Nyx pounded the receiver on the wall and put it to her ear again. "You listen," Nyx said, "you never had to take care of me."

"Clearly," Kine said, coolly, "you give every appearance of taking such wonderful care of yourself."

"Listen—"

"I have dug you out of too many ditches, Nyxnissa. Carried you out of too many bars and brothels and butchers. Sleep this off and call me in the morning with what you have to say."

"Too late," Nyx said. "It'll be too late . . . Hey . . . you're on the coast. The south coast. Yeah, that's what I wanted to call about. See . . . you know about . . . southern families? Rich ones . . . the Yazeeds or . . . Makatar . . . Muktarata . . ."

"The Muhktars," Kine said stiffly. "What are you doing asking about them? What are you mixed up with?"

"Nyx?" Rhys's voice.

Nyx started. Dropped the receiver. She leaned her head against the wall. She must have lost some time, because the next thing she knew, Rhys was shaking her shoulder, repeating her name.

"Can you hear me?" Rhys said. He put the receiver back on the hook. "Nyx?"

She mumbled something and shuffled back toward her office. He followed her, but she paid him no mind.

"Gonna quit drinking at thirty," she said.

"Something tells me that's what you said at twenty-five."

She crawled underneath her desk, wrapped her arms around herself, and settled in to pass out.

"Nyx?"

She cracked open an eye and saw Rhys squatting before her.

"Too pretty for your own good," she said, and closed her eye again.

He sighed. "You haven't overdosed on liquor yet," he said. "God willing, your luck holds."

"God has nothing to do with it," Nyx said, and finally, blissfully, passed out.

"Report on the woman you asked about," Taite said, handing Nyx more slick green paper.

Nyx sat on the roof of their storefront under a tattered awning, wincing as the long wail of the midday muezzin rolled out over the desert. She wore smoked goggles and was swilling buni spiked with whisky. Anneke sat opposite her, feet on top of a bloody head in a sack, explaining why she needed more cash for bigger guns. Nyx had been setting up supply caches across the country the last couple of years, insurance for bad days. But stockpiling that many goods and weapons was expensive. Anneke had brought in a head from the boards the week before; easy sniper job on a prison escapee, she'd said, and it had paid off.

Nyx took the report and waved a hand at Anneke to still

the weapons talk. "Just give me the summary," Nyx said to Taite.

"I'm giving you a good summary, boss," Anneke said. "Just half the money from this one for the X32Z10 sand spitter and I'll—"

"Fine, yes," Nyx said. "Anneke, go buy something."

"Hell damn!" Anneke said, slapping her knobby knee. She threw the bloody sack over her shoulder and bounded for the roof hatch so fast Nyx suspected she feared Nyx would change her mind.

"Binyamin is the daughter of a family originally from Hafthah," Taite said. "Called the so Mahasin."

"Not Yazeed or Muhktar? Not a Drucian name either, maybe?"

"No, it's so Mahasin."

"Not just Mahasin?"

Taite peered at her. "How hung over are you?" he said.

"Still drunk," she said.

"It's so Mahasin," he said, "definitely a compound name. I checked twice to make sure I wasn't mixing them up with someone else. Rhys did the first research pass. I verified all of it."

"Strange to keep a breeding compound name over multiple generations," Nyx said, pouring more whisky into her buni. "Thought they would have dropped the middle part to hide that they all grew up in government care. Government kids are war fodder. If they wanted to build wealth and get investments, they should have dropped the 'so' part."

"Apparently the grandmother made her fortune treating compound diseases," Taite said. "She was the last compound kid in the family. The rest—the daughters, the grandchildren, were all raised at home."

"Looking to remember where she came from," Nyx said. "So they own these chemical plants like she says?"

"Six of them," Taite said. "Two were blown up in the last four months. Investigations pending, but they weren't categorized as terrorist attacks, so they're low on the list for the order keepers. Order keeper reports think it was an inside job. No footage of anyone going in or out of the plant within twelve hours of the blast. No human residue on the bomb."

"They haven't heard of gloves?"

Taite shrugged. "Report says this type of explosive required an organic trigger. But there was no record of human blood codes on the device at all."

"Shit," Nyx said, and now she opened the report: "They used organic burst triggers, then? Those are at least forty years old. Used mostly for mining."

"Why mining?"

"Something gets blown up that's not supposed to, it was useful to know which worker fucked up," Nyx said. "Also prevented them being stolen. Who'd want to leave their blood code all over it unless it was a suicide mission?"

"Looks like somebody figured out how to use them without bleeding all over them."

Nyx verified the type of device in the order keeper report, and frowned. She had been a sapper in her former military life, and the sort of criminal who had the audacity to use one of these and get away with it intrigued her. As did the woman who wouldn't put on boxing gloves, but walked onto the mat in a fighter's stance. She couldn't help but note that triggering a device like this remotely was nearly impossible unless it wasn't humans doing the triggering. That left dogs, cats, ravens, parrots, or maybe foxes. A bug could probably do it, too. Any skilled magician could summon a hornet swarm to set off the explosion. But again—every device would have had to be reprogrammed to trigger on contact with that particular organism. It would take a lot of skill to customize every device to react to something other than a human.

"You asked about sisters," Taite said, pointing to another section of the report. "Here's where things get good."

"They weren't fun before?"

"There are seven sisters," Taite said. "There's two compound breeders, both dead of yellow fever. One died in prison four years ago. Three dead at the front. That just leaves the one."

"Binyamin?"

"No," Taite said. "There was a Binyamin, but she was the one who died in prison."

"So we got a job from a dead woman," Nyx said. "That's a first." But not unexpected. She looked at the prison dates for Binyamin, the dead one, and shifted uncomfortably in her seat. The prison listed was in Batul. It was the same prison Nyx had spent a year in when she was convicted of doing black work—selling zygotes for cash.

"The living sister was—"

"An apprentice bel dame," Nyx said.

"Yeah. Good guess. Did I write that down?"

"No," Nyx said. She'd seen it when the woman who called herself Binyamin flinched when Nyx tried to hit her. Resisting the urge to block the blow would have been tough for a bel dame apprentice trained to defend herself. And a bel dame apprentice would slide easily and unconsciously into a fighting stance, too.

"So this woman who gave us the job and told us her name is Binyamin is a liar," Taite said. "Thing is, we don't have a name for the bel dame apprentice. It got scourged from the record when she enlisted. So whoever you dealt with is some nameless person."

"But she shares the surname?"

"Maybe," Taite said. "Seventh sister is adopted. So could be a so Mahasin, or not."

"Well shit," Nyx said.

"Maybe we should pass on this one. Feels weird, you know?"

"You have that bug I gave you from her?" Nyx asked.

"Downstairs."

"Tell it to go ping its owner," Nyx said. "We'll take the job."

Taite blinked at her. "Uh . . . really?"

"Did I stutter?"

"No, no," he said. "I just . . . I mean, why do all this work to figure out if the job is dodgy and then take it knowing it's dodgy?"

"'Cause I'm the boss," Nyx said.

She told herself she was taking it because of the type of device and the intrigue of an inside job perpetuated by a woman who had the gall to pretend she was someone she wasn't. It wasn't about her own sister, and doing something worth a damn for what remained of her toxic, fucked-up family. It wasn't because she understood vengeance, because any woman trying to fool Nyx into thinking she was someone else probably had a personal issue with something Nyx had done in her past. And it was a very long past.

Nyx closed the report.

As Taite turned to go, a low, mournful wail started up from the west. For a half moment she thought it was the call to prayer coming at some off time, but it came again, louder, and she recognized the whine of a burst siren.

"This fucking day," Nyx muttered. She heaved herself out of her seat and trotted down to the basement, passing Rhys at his workbench while he packed up his bugs. "They'll be fine," she told him, but he secreted them away into various pockets in his burnous regardless. Bugs were expensive, and she supposed he knew she wasn't going to spend more if they got bombed out.

When she went into the basement, ducking because of the low ceiling, Taite was already there, messing with the radio.

"Hopefully the burst siren is a false positive," he said. "Com chatter upstairs said there was heavy fighting in Aludra today, so there might be some miasma blowing in triggering the sirens. Oh, I sent your bug off to its owner already."

Nyx stuffed herself into a ratty overstuffed divan. It sat up against the wall of the big freezer where they kept bodies chilled on days the bounty reclamation office was closed. She rummaged in the cushions for a bottle. Found nothing. She pulled off her goggles and flung them beside her. The radio belched out a misty orange haze that began to solidify into some talking head from the local news.

The ground trembled. Nyx got up and went for the stairs, instinctively yelling, "Rhys!"

"What?" Rhys said as he clattered down the steps, yanking the hatch down behind him.

"You and those fucking bugs," she muttered, and sat back down. "Anneke already head out?"

"Like a shot," Rhys said. "Don't bother calling after her."

"Anneke would take a hit from a burst and just pick it back up again," Taite said, switching the radio past two daytime operas and a Kitab education show to arrive at the burst warning station.

Rhys stopped at the bottom of the stairs, gazing into the deep shadows under them. "How did this dead dog get down here?" he said.

A heavy whump sounded above them. Dust and dirt particles sifted into the stale air.

Nyx picked at a tear in the divan, curling the stuffing onto her finger. "Don't remember notes on dogs," she said, and laughed because that wasn't quite true. Any number of shapeshifters who could step into dog skins had been on the bounty boards before.

Taite settled against the wall next to the radio. "It must have come in the back and wandered in. You leave the basement hatch open?" he asked Rhys.

"Why would I?" Rhys said. He knelt beside the dog. Nyx could just make out the shape of it in the dim light. Rhys gently turned it over. Pointed. "There are six dead hornets under here. It triggered the intruder trap. This isn't a dog. Only a human would trigger the trap I set."

"Yeah, well, you're a shitty magician," Nyx said. "Maybe it's a mistake. Last thing we need today is a dead shapeshifter."

"We can have it tested," Rhys said

"Can't we just bury it?" Nyx said.

"Come on, Nyx," Taite said at the same time Rhys said, "No."

"All you men conspiring against me," Nyx said. "Remember I still have to re-up your contracts."

Another burst made the world tremble. Nyx leaned back into the divan and stared at the ceiling. "Fine," she said. "I'll report it after the siren's done."

Rhys gazed up at the trapdoor.

"What is it?" Nyx said.

"Not sure," he said. "But I think . . . I think someone is knocking on the door out there."

"They can wait for after the raid," Nyx said. She wished he would stop caring about things, or noticing them. Half the time she thought he'd do better half-drunk than she would. Good for his nerves.

"What if it's Anneke?" Taite said.

"She could palm herself in," Rhys said. "Nyx, I really think—"

"After the raid," Nyx said. "I don't want to open a door to anyone dumb enough to be out in a raid."

"It's probably one of our clients," Taite muttered.

Nyx said, "Serves them right on both counts, then."

"We can't just leave them out there," Rhys said.

"For fuck's sake!" Nyx said, pushing herself off the divan. "You so eager to help, why don't you go up there? But you won't, will you, because you're godly and righteous and it's easier to level guilt and blame than do a damned thing yourself, isn't it?"

She got up and pushed past Rhys, not wanting to see the look on his face. She knocked him out of the way with her shoulder and pounded back up the stairs.

Above, the world outside was eerily still except for the low

THE HEART IS EATEN LAST

wail of the sirens. She didn't like going out during raids. Not just for the obvious reason but because the world was so quiet it felt like being the last person alive. She wondered if that was what hell was like, wandering around on a deserted street, wondering if you were mad, if the war was all over and you were the last person standing.

She went right for the door. A heavy whumping sound came from the north, then the shock wave. It rattled the equipment on the work tables. Loose gun parts and dead bugs pattered all around her feet as she walked.

Nyx hitched one hand behind her, taking hold of the hilt of her scattergun, and opened the door wide with the other, ready to run off whatever dumb kid was looking for shelter. If it was a client, though, maybe she'd look heroic. Maybe they'd tip better next time.

A stout little woman wearing a hijab and an intricately embroidered violet housecoat raised her head, and Nyx knew her by the coat long before she caught sight of her pouting, squinty-eyed little face.

"Look what you've done, sister," Kine said as the sirens wailed. "I've come here all the way from the coast and gotten my best housecoat dirty. Now what's this you were saying about the Muhktars?"

Kine complicated things, in the way that only Kine could.

While the air sirens wailed, Kine followed Nyx to her office, and turned up her nose at the empty bottle and dusty interior.

"You *live* here?" Kine said.

"I do a lot of things here," Nyx said.

"It's worse than your last domicile." Kine kept her hands clasped in front of her, as if afraid that she'd get some contagion or disease if she touched anything. It was probably a good instinct.

"Why does my business concern you?" Nyx said.

"Those are dangerous families you mentioned," Kine said. Her gaze roved around the office now; at first Nyx figured she was still judgey about things, but the look was keener than that. She was clearly looking for foreign bugs, the type tailored by a magician to spy on people like Kine who had government clearance.

"Turns out the woman I'm working with isn't part of either family," Nyx said. "So it was all a false alarm."

Outside, the burst sirens gave one last mournful wail, then trailed off into silence. Nyx glanced into the outer room. The rest of the team would come up soon.

She opened her arms, trying to herd Kine back to the door. "Raid's over and I'm fine," Nyx said. "You should go back to the coast."

But Kine remained firm. She planted her feet and set her mouth and Nyx knew the only way she'd get her out was to move her bodily, which Nyx was getting ready to do.

"The Muhktars are powerful shapeshifters," Kine said. "Do you have shapeshifters in your employ who can best them? I can guarantee you don't, because you must have a license for a shapeshifter, and you've always been terribly cheap."

"Inexpensive, not cheap," Nyx said. "All my girlfriends will tell you."

Kine frowned.

"I told you," Nyx said, "we aren't dealing with the Muhktars." But her thoughts drifted back to the dead dog in her cellar. She had thought she had this bel dame apprentice figured out, but now she wasn't so sure. There were plenty of people who wanted vengeance against Nyx. But how did the dogs fit? Was she using them as reconnaissance, too, instead of bugs?

"Nyx?" Rhys's voice, from the workroom.

"In my office," she said.

Rhys came in, Taite just behind him. They stopped short on seeing Kine.

"Rhys, Taite," Nyx said, "this is my sister Kine. She works at the compounds on the coast. Big fancy government job."

Kine's eyes got big. She took a step back on seeing Rhys. "Rhys is not a Tirhani name," Kine said.

"It isn't Chenjan either," Nyx said, "but that's what he calls himself."

Kine stared at her. "This is too much," she said. "You're employing *Chenjans* now? Have you sunk so low?"

"I wasn't aware I could sink any lower in your regard," Nyx said. "I'm pretty pleased with myself now, actually."

"I didn't know you had a sister," Taite said.

"Just the one," Nyx said. "It's enough."

"So many men here," Kine muttered.

"Can I get you a drink before you leave?" Nyx asked. "Rhys makes stuff you'd drink. Tea, things like that."

"We should have lunch," Kine said. "It's the proper thing to do."

"I don't do lunch," Nyx said.

"We are sisters. We should go to lunch."

"She's your sister," Rhys said. "You really should go to lunch."

"See?" Kine said. "Even the Chenjan agrees with me." She sniffed.

Nyx glared at him. Taite snickered and popped back out of the room, clearly smart enough not to take sides. Unlike some other people.

"We'll get food on the way to dropping off the dead shifter," Nyx said. "All right? Rhys, help me bag up that dog."

It took a good half hour to get the dog bagged and usher Kine out of the storefront. Kine lingered near Rhys's prayer mat, making a little moue with her mouth that made Nyx fear she was actually going to try and start talking to him, and that wasn't going to go well.

Finally, the sack with the stiff dog over her shoulder, Nyx strode down the busy streets of Punjai with Kine at her side. She wasn't sure which was more of a liability—Kine or the dog. Kine kept pace with her, curling her nose at every man and uncovered woman they passed. Kine muttered about cancer and modesty, and how God had decreed women cover themselves to protect them from cancers, and why were all of these women so foolish and why were so many foreign men here, instead of fighting for God?

"Why aren't we taking the train?" Kine asked as they passed the gated entry for the overhead train. The door was heavily barred; scorch marks stained the face of it.

"Train hasn't worked in a decade," Nyx said. "Besides, the office isn't far."

The shifter licensing office was twelve blocks away. Nyx stepped nimbly over trash heaps and venom-addled junkies, massive bug carcasses and discarded food wrappers. By the time they reached the broad amber door of the office she had to admit she was pretty hungry after all.

She pushed to the head of the queue, ignoring the hot, startled stares and gaping mouths of the folks waiting ahead of her. Most of the people in line were foreigners, and men at that. They weren't in a place to complain at her barging in.

Nyx swung the dog carcass onto the table and waved over the paunchy old man behind the counter. He panted his way over, limping heavily on what was clearly a poorly made organic hybrid of a leg, the sort men got when they came back from the front when their families couldn't afford a proper magician to put a good one back on. He was missing most of the back of his head; it was slathered over in green bug secretions, and he wore what remained of his hair long to try and cover it. The deep grooves of his face were covered in stubble, at least in the places that weren't too scarred to prevent it.

"Can I help you, bel dame?"

She smirked at that, pleased to be mistaken for what she once was. There was a murmur in the crowd, most of whom were either shifters or mercenaries looking for shifters, likely, and several lanky, hard-bitten types took a step back. She liked the breathing room that being bad afforded her.

"Need this tested," she said. "Found it in my basement."

"Basement?" he said, sucking what remained of his front teeth. He pulled a syringe from the front of his apron and jabbed it into the dog's throat. Withdrawing it, he said, "One moment," and went into the back.

Kine leaned into her and said, low, "I believe there was a queue, Nyxnissa."

"You always did draw inside the lines," Nyx said. "What did that ever get you?"

"Prestigious, reliable, and cancer-free employment," she said.

"Better not say that too loud," Nyx said, leaning against the counter while the half dozen people in line pretended not to listen. "Men here'll eat you for something good as that. And you don't want to know what the *women* will do."

The man reappeared from the back. He put down a big book of green paper on the counter and opened it up with a sigh. "It's a shifter," he said. "We will need to log this death."

"Fuck," Nyx said. "How much is the fine?"

"You found it in your basement?" he said, peering at her.

"Listen," she said. "It triggered one of my magician's traps. I have a whole team who'll tell you the same. It's all legal."

"I'm sure," he said. She didn't like the way he mushed up his face, like he was just tolerating her answer, knowing the law was on her side as a Nasheenian woman, but she let it slide.

"Anyway," she said, "I'm in the market for a shifter anyway. You know anyone?"

The man raised his brows. "You've brought a dead shapeshifter here, which you admit was killed in your own basement, and want me, a shifter, to recommend a good shifter to you?"

"Yeah," Nyx said.

The man clucked his tongue and bundled the dog back into the sack, and walked away to the back room again.

Nyx glanced over at Kine. "What did I say?"

"Only what you always say."

Nyx looked around the room, sizing up the ropy mercenaries and foreign shifters. There were a couple tables at the front of the store where a big Mhorian, two skinny Drucians, and a one-armed Heidian were playing cards. A young Nasheenian sat alone near them, looking like she was halfway to drinking herself to death.

Nyx sat up on the counter and said. "Hey! I'm hiring shifters over on Hadya Street. Be good with a gun. Not squeamish. Reliable." She hopped off the counter and started toward the door.

"Fucking Nasheenians."

She turned to see who'd said it, but the card players were all staring hard at their cards, and the folks in line were staring straight ahead.

The Nasheenian kid was laughing, though. "Yes we are," she said. "We sure are."

"I pay cash," Nyx said, "or bugs, for contract bounty work. Your choice. The fucking is extra."

Kine made a little squealing sound at that, which made the whole trip worth it.

"Let's go to lunch," Nyx said.

Rhys never liked the jobs Nyx gave him, but he didn't like starving, either. He told himself, often, that he wasn't here because of the work. He was just biding his time until he got real employment. But no matter how many doors he palmed or letters he wrote to cities with more gainful employment, the answers he got back—when he got them—were resoundingly negative; sometimes violently so. He'd had no idea how many pejoratives Nasheenians had for men, and Chenjan men in particular, until he had started looking for a job.

But now, for the first time ever, he had a job offer in his pocket for a team other than Nyx's. It should have been the boon he was waiting for, but he'd held on to it now for two days. It was a job in the interior, working as a translator for the Nasheenian foreign affairs department. Why he hadn't drawn up his resignation the day he received the letter, he wasn't certain.

Rhys rubbed the paper of the invitation between his fingers in his pocket as he walked with Taite to the library at the center of town, though it wasn't a library anymore so much as it was a woman behind a heavy door who sat at a kiosk connecting Punjai to real archival collections in the interior. No one was fool enough to keep anything of value in the border towns, not when the Chenjans could spill over and occupy them at any moment. The last time Chenja had taken hold of the city was just fifteen years before. They'd gotten halfway to Mushtallah before they were turned back by a sea of magicians. His mentor, Yah Tayyib, had told him that story often. The subtext of it wasn't lost on Rhys. Rhys didn't want to forget which side he'd been born on; he considered Chenja the morally superior country, of course. But the Nasheenians didn't want him to forget where he came from, either.

So when he and Taite stepped up to the door of the library and a large woman knocked into Rhys so hard he fell, it was by no means an unexpected or unprecedented occurrence.

Rhys hit the ground hard. The woman leered over him, her great one-eyed face eclipsing the sun.

Taite babbled an apology.

"Watch your step, child," the woman said. "Don't go looking into matters that don't concern you or your employer. She should be in prison, and if she keeps on with this job she took, that's where she'll end up. Free advice."

Beside her was a big yellow dog; its head was as high as her waist. It growled at Rhys while wagging its tail, a strange mix of signals that he couldn't parse.

She pulled up the hood of her brown burnous and stepped over him, back into the busy street. The dog loped after her.

Taite helped Rhys up. "Nyx has a way of making friends," Taite said.

"Why does she choose these jobs instead of sticking with the bounty boards? At least with the bounty boards we have legal support and backup."

"She likes to live dangerously," Taite said.

"I don't," Rhys said. He pulled his hand from his pocket.

Taite laughed. "Then I don't know why you signed on with Nyx."

"Some days I don't either," Rhys said. Then, "I have another job offer."

Taite looked at him sharply. "Really?" he said.

"Is that odd?"

"No, just . . . well, I guess it is. Hard for foreign men to get jobs. I mean, I know. I've tried."

"It's for the government."

"Have you told Nyx yet?"

"No."

"Well, maybe wait to tell her until you're sure," Taite said. "She'll fire you on the spot."

They pushed inside the library and waited in the short line to speak to the librarian at the kiosk. They found the information they wanted fairly quickly, about the address linked to the bug Nyx had given Taite; she printed most of it out, which was expensive, but not as expensive as having it coded into a bug. That said, paper was easier to hack. Rhys hoped the one-eyed woman and her dog weren't just waiting around to jump him again.

They made it back to the storefront relatively unscathed, just in time for mid-afternoon prayer. Rhys left the papers on Nyx's desk and then unrolled his prayer rug as the call to prayer moved out over the city. Leaving Nyx's team should have been an easy decision, so why was he hesitating?

When he finished and stood he noted that Taite was watching some radio opera, chin in hand, while his com console ticked away at recording some other hunter's com channel that Nyx had put him on. She was always spying on former team members and stealing their jobs. Taite was Ras Tiegan, and there was no Ras Tiegan church in Punjai, but Rhys had seen him praying at night. They shared a god, but not a faith. Still, Taite was observant of his own beliefs. It was a good start.

"You ever been in love?" Taite asked Rhys.

Rhys rolled up his prayer rug, considering both the question and who was asking it. "With God, certainly," Rhys said.

"Everyone loves God," Taite said, "and God loves most of us back. But what about people? That's tougher."

"I suppose it is," Rhys said. "I put my trust in God for that."

Anneke pushed open the front door, arms brimming with packages that no doubt carried more weaponry than was needed for eight armies. Rhys went over to the hatch leading into the basement and pulled it open for her. She grunted and dropped her packages there, then started running them down to the basement one at a time.

"There's no rules to it, love," Taite said while two women declared their undying affection on the radio. "No sense. At least with God, you know what to do to keep his love, to make sure you're on his good side."

"You're too young for love anyhow," Rhys said. "A young man like you—"

"You aren't that much older," Taite said. "And anyway, in Ras Tieg I'd be married by now."

"Marriage and love can be different things."

Anneke popped her head up from the basement. "Sounds like something you read from a book," she said.

"Spare us your own treatise on love," Rhys said. "I expect you learned it from Nyx, and that means you'll turn something sacred into something—"

"Nyx would tell you love is wanting to fuck someone you can't," Anneke said.

"—coarse," Rhys finished, and grimaced.

Taite said, "Well, that explains why you don't have a lot of dates, Anneke."

"What do you know?" Anneke said. "Here's some advice Nyx gave me early on. I'll give it to you, kids. As long as you're in this business, don't fall for anyone. The more you care about a thing, the more it can be used against you. That counts for when you get out, too. People keep grudges a long time in this business."

Rhys said, "Well, I don't intend to do this long."

"That's what everyone says," Anneke said. She shrugged. "No offense."

"I'm not like you," Rhys said. "I'm going to have a family someday, and a respectable job again. This is temporary. We aren't all like you and Nyx."

"I'd like to be more like Nyx," Anneke said, "But I ain't. She may not live long, but she'll live good."

Someone knocked at the door.

"I'll get it," Rhys said quickly. He was ready to exit the conversation.

He opened the door just in time to see a blue-burnoused woman scuttle off down the street. A brown-papered package lay on the stoop.

Rhys bent to take the package. A thin, humming whine filled his head and thrummed deep within his bones. He froze.

"Don't move!" Anneke said.

He was half bent over, arm extended toward the package. The paper trembled. He let out a long, slow breath.

Anneke came up behind him, padding softly along the floor. She let out a low whistle. "You are so fucked," she said.

When Nyx got back from lunch, still snarling and spitting at some stupid thing Kine had said about modesty, only a little tipsy from a couple of beers, she found Rhys bowing over a bomb and a Nasheenian woman fighting off two dogs on the stoop. The scene was so strange that Nyx actually hesitated mid-step while her brain tried to put the scene together into a story that made sense.

In that moment of hesitation, she gave in and chose action over reason.

Nyx pulled her pistol and shot at the dogs. She didn't hit them, but the noise was enough to scare them off. The Nasheenian woman saw her with the pistol and reached for something. Nyx front kicked her in the chest. The woman was about Nyx's size, and she stumbled, but didn't go over.

"You stand down," Nyx said. "Don't cause trouble. I won't hurt you. Rhys! Don't you move."

She turned to Rhys while keeping the woman in her peripheral vision.

Big drops of sweat trickled from Rhys's face and plopped on the package below him.

She set her gun down on her right—far from the woman— and flattened herself on the ground in front of the package. She felt the twinge in the air, the same feeling that had probably saved Rhys from getting his face blown off. He wasn't a sapper, but any magician with half a brain would recognize the dissonance as some bug-triggered device.

Rhys was pretty, yes, but not stupid. "How long you been like this?" she said.

"An hour!" Anneke said from inside. "Sent Taite to get you."

"Didn't see him," Nyx said. She blew a bit of air at the underside of the package. Dust clung to the shiny resin that escaped the seams of the paper.

She tugged one of the needles from her hair—she kept three poisoned needles secured there as a matter of course— and used it to work the paper loose. A bead of Rhys's sweat plopped onto the paper above. She felt his breath. An hour in a bowed position like that was an impressive feat. She didn't consider how much longer he could hold it.

Nyx worked the paper back and peered inside. For once, no one was saying anything, and she found that very soothing.

The guts of the bomb were familiar: a cube of resin covered over in paper, and inside the resin, a series of organic filaments connected by orange thorn bugs engineered for exactly this purpose. Too much movement would trigger the filaments, which would cause the bugs to explode, throwing poisonous, buggy shrapnel for about ten paces in every direction.

She pushed the needle deep into the package and touched its poison tip to the little filaments, just enough to spread the poison from the needle to the filament. The organic tissue sucked it up. She waited, counting her breaths. If the bomb was made with the right mix of organics, the poison should do its job breaking down the filaments connecting the bugs in about fifty seconds. But that was a big if. She hadn't dealt with one of these in a while.

Nyx counted to sixty, then levered herself up slowly onto her hands and eased her body up over the package. She rolled her eyes at Rhys and said. "Straighten up and stand back."

If it went off, her body would take the brunt of it.

Rhys let out his breath and levered himself back. His whole body shook. How he'd held that position so long, she wasn't certain. He'd have done well under torture conditions.

Nyx waited, but felt no humming in the air, no taut snap that told her the mechanism inside had sensed any further movement. She sat back on her knees and picked up the package. Shook it.

Rhys and Anneke flinched inside the doorway.

"We're good," Nyx said. She pulled off her burnous and wrapped it around the package. It would need to be properly taken apart and disposed of. She glanced over at the Nasheenian woman who'd been tangling with the dogs. "So who the hell are you?"

"I'm here from Hadjara," she said. "You called her last night and she sent me."

Kine said, "Just how many people did you call when you were drunk last night, Nyxnissa?"

"I don't remember calling Hadjara," Nyx said.

The woman handed her a piece of paper, its edges already starting to flake away. Nyx opened it and read an address for a brothel on the other side of the city and a time listed that would put her there just after dark. At the bottom it read: *I have information about that apprentice you asked about.* As she finished reading it, the paper disintegrated more rapidly. She shook it, and it burst into a confetti of tattered brown fragments.

"I'm off," the woman said, eying Nyx's package.

"What?" Nyx said, hefting it at her. "You had enough fun?"

"Plenty, thank you," she said. "Call off those dogs next time."

"They aren't mine," Nyx said.

"Regardless," the woman said. She pulled up her hood and ducked back down the alley.

"Is this a usual practice?" Kine said. "Bombs on your doorstep, strange women arriving from alleys to battle with dogs?"

"Pretty much," Nyx said. "Let's get this sorted." She pushed inside. Rhys was already in the back, presumably sitting down or praying or whatever it was Rhys did after almost getting blown up. "It's gotten hot here," she said to Anneke as she walked to her office. "Let's pack up."

"Where?" she said.

"Right where they don't want us," Nyx said. "We're going to Binyamin's happy home in Alabbas. You got the address from examining the beetle, right?"

"But, uh, didn't they just try and kill us, boss?"

"Maybe yes, maybe no," Nyx said. "I have an idea she was gunning for all of you more than me."

Anneke said, "You think she was going to blow us up and frame you?"

"I'm thinking a lot of things right now," Nyx said. "And if she wants to fuck with us, I'm going to go fuck with her family."

"Nyxnissa," Kine said from the door of the office. "It sounds as if this is becoming a personal vendetta. Might I remind you this is just work. As you told me, it's not even work for a powerful family. Why not let it go?"

"She's trying to do me in," Nyx said. "You'd rather I sit here and get drunk?"

Kine pursed her mouth.

"Yeah," Nyx said. "Fuck these people. You know what happens when you get a reputation for getting walked over, Kine? No, you fucking don't. I do. Somebody fucks with you and your people, you fuck them up, or they will come at you again, and then your enemies hear about it, and then you've got a hundred other bounty hunters and women with grudges and dead brothers you brought in, and you're fucked. What protects me and my people is reputation. This is about reputation."

Nyx was shaking, and she paused to get control over herself. She knew this game. This was the prison game, and it had followed her own here now with Binyamin's sister whatever-her-name-was. She had fucked somebody up in prison, and now their family was trying to fuck up Nyx.

"Why not give it up?" Kine said. "Surely I can find you a position on the coast, perhaps as a janitor—"

"Fuck you," Nyx said. "A fucking *janitor*? Go fuck yourself. This is what I'm good at. You go home, Kine. Anneke, go find Taite and tell him we're moving out. I'll go shake Rhys out of his catshit mood and get him moving."

"Nyx—" Anneke said.

"You want another job? Another employer? I'll break your contract right now."

"Uh, no, boss," Anneke said. "Like you said, we need a shifter on the team first. Before Alabbas. Because, the dogs, you know."

"Fuck!" Nyx said.

Anneke held up her hands. "Don't blame me!"

Nyx knew the brothel address well, from the paper Hadjara had sent, because she used to do some black work for the women and men who worked there back in her pre-prison days, when she was ferrying stuff inside her womb from Punjai to Faleen and back.

She had dismantled the bomb and sent it to a friend from processing to see if she could find out who'd made it. Bomb-making was still a specialized profession, and sometimes bomb makers' styles were so distinctive that every bomb acted like a signature. Nyx had hesitated at the threshold to Rhys's room before she left, and decided not to go in. Let him cool off awhile. Taite had returned, and was on board with running a check-up on the bakkie and getting their supplies packed up.

"Remember to get Anneke to pack food," Nyx had told him, "not just guns."

Kine was tougher to get rid of. She'd ranted more about the powerful families of Alabbas until Nyx threatened to call in order keepers and tell them Kine was trespassing. That had earned Nyx a dark look, and she suspected Kine wasn't going to talk to her for a long time after this.

But there was more important shit on the line than her sister's approval. So now she trudged alone through the dark toward the warm, rosy glow of the brothel. She used the long walk—paired with a quick rickshaw ride that she haggled down to a reasonable fare—to try and remember when she had called Hadjara. She hadn't made many friends back when she was a bel dame. She'd tell anyone who asked that she hadn't fucking been there to make friends, but Hadjara had been young and funny and tolerant of Nyx's grim humor. It helped that Hadjara was just a clerk working in the bel dame offices, not a bel dame or apprentice. Nyx had found talking to her to be a useful palate cleanser after a long day of serious talk about the best way to bleed out a body. Sometimes you forgot you were a human when you were a bel dame.

Nyx knocked at the door at the top of the stairs. A slit in the door opened, and Nyx saw one grizzled old eye peering out.

"Fuck me," the woman on the other side said, and the door opened. A skinny, hunched old woman with a tangle of white hair stood on the other side. She carried a cane with a big red polished rock on the end and held up her arms to Nyx. "Thought you were long dead," the woman said.

"I'm tough to kill, Morda," Nyx said. "Is Hadjara here?"

"Sure," Morda said. "Come on in. Best place to find a woman to talk politics at without getting a bullet between the eyes." She pointed a finger at her own forehead. "In, in, let's go."

Nyx followed her inside.

The evening was still early, and there were only a few women at the bar. A young, beautiful Nasheenian man tended bar. He was most assuredly over sixteen, which raised Nyx's brows. She turned to look at Morda, who waved her fingers at Nyx. "Not full Nasheenian," Morda said. "He's a half-breed. I have papers. All very legal."

"Sure," Nyx said. "Whatever. I don't do that sort of work anymore anyway."

"Not unless contracted, eh?" Morda said. "Have a drink on us. I will get Hadjara."

Nyx ordered whisky from the boy at the bar. He had the sense to give her a double take. "Not here for you," she assured him. She could not help looking like what she was, or perhaps like what she had been. Boys always sensed it. It was why she so often had to go through their female kin to get to them back when she was a bel dame hunting down deserters like this one. Morda had good forgeries—she'd seen some of them—and she suspected this boy's was on par with that.

A man came in from the hall; a big Mhorian man with a mane of yellow dreadlocks and spidery blue tattoos running across his face. For a half moment Nyx wondered if he worked there, because it had been a long time since she took a man that big to bed, but he was shabbily dressed and didn't set his attention on her immediately. A patron, then.

She went back to her drink and was surprised when he sat down next to her instead of slinking out the back like most foreign men did at brothels, like talking and fucking was shameful.

"I heard you were looking for a shifter," he said. His accent was thick. If she had to guess, he hadn't been in Nasheen long.

"My shit isn't your business."

"I'm looking for work," he said. "I remember you from the shifter licensing office. Morda said you were all right."

She sized him up again. "Go to the storefront like anybody else if you want to interview for a job. The fuck you doing at a brothel?"

"I do work for Morda," he said. "She had me run an errand for Hadjara. She will give you a reference."

"You apply like anybody else," she said. "You ain't special."

He drank his beer all in one go. She watched him glug it down, imagined gripping that wide neck. She shook her head. She needed a fuck like she needed water right now, and fucking anyone would do, wouldn't it?

"I'm Khos," he said.

"I don't give a shit," she said.

His expression was oddly pained, but he shrugged and stood. He lumbered out the door, and she relaxed a little. Strange men soliciting work in brothels was the last thing she needed right now. But he was a shifter, yeah, and if Morda spoke for him he might be a good quick fix for Alabbas.

Morda came out with Hadjara, and Nyx stood. Hadjara had grown out her dark hair since Nyx had last seen her. It was braided close against her scalp. She was older, too; over thirty now, probably. Age suited her; the fine lines and deeper frown and harder edges that came with seeing too much shit under two suns gave her some character. She was a little too pretty for Nyx's taste, and a little too upbeat, but Nyx was reconsidering.

"Thanks, Morda," Hadjara said. "You want to find a room, Nyx? Had one set aside. Bar tab's on me."

"All right," Nyx said. The vibe in the brothel wasn't bad, but she was still concerned about her lack of memory.

"You know that shifter?" she asked Morda, jabbing her finger at the door. "The Mhorian?"

"Khos?" Morda said. "Yes, he does odd work for us. He was here to run a message for Hadjara. I told him to speak to you. Was that all right?"

"Might give me some warning."

Morda showed her teeth. "Don't tell me he intimidated you, Nyx."

"Not a fan of big men," Nyx said.

"I can attest that this particular man is well-equipped for a number of useful jobs," Morda said, and cackled. "From the look on your face, you could use more than talk tonight."

"Another time," Nyx said.

Nyx followed Hadjara to a private room at the back, equipped with plush divans, a big bed, open shower, and closet stuffed with illegal pamphlets and manifestos. Brothels were a hotbed of political activity in Nasheen, and more political parties and revolution-mongering probably went on there than fucking. Morda had told her a while back that early laws related to brothels made them exempt from government surveillance—an early attempt to curb a very lucrative bribery ring that had targeted male politicians before the war. No one had bothered to change the law in all that time—everyone being busy with other shit—and so brothels had become one of the safer places to talk about what sort of shit one was going to put down or blow up.

Nyx sat on a divan and put her feet up.

"Drink?" Hadjara said, moving to the ample liquor cabinet.

"You know I do," Nyx said. "But first tell me when exactly I called you."

"You didn't."

"That's both a relief and a signal I should probably shoot you."

Hadjara laughed. "We both know you can't hit anything, Nyx."

"So what is this about?"

"You've triggered a lot of discussion among the bel dame council," Hadjara said, pouring them both a whisky. She brought the glasses over. "And you did ask me to report to you if you came up in bel dame discussions."

"Friendly arrangement," Nyx said. "You do what you like."

"I like you," Hadjara said. "I wanted you to know."

Nyx balanced her drink on her knee and waited for Hadjara to drink first.

"So they going to kill me or what?"

"They're afraid to have you working for that family in Alabbas," Hadjara said. Her gaze moved to the door once, fast, then at the floor. That put Nyx on edge. "There was a bel dame apprentice associated with that family, and she had a very bad reputation. I looked her up for you."

"And I didn't even have to call," Nyx said dryly. "Hadjara, we haven't talked in a year, and you're stationed all the fuck away in Mushtallah. That means it took you at least a day to get here by train, which is also expensive. You could have sent a letter, even encoded a com to my com tech. Why a personal visit?"

Hadjara lifted her glass, and Nyx noted that her hand was trembling. "I'm sorry, Nyx."

"Goddammit," Nyx said. She pulled her pistol and leapt off the divan, putting the divan between her and the door. "At least tell me her name," she said. "The bel dame apprentice. The one trying to frame me for this catshit that's about to go down. One name before I kill you or they do."

Hadjara's eyes filled. Nyx heard footsteps pounding up the stairs.

"Rasim Muhktar," Hadjara said, and the door burst open.

Nyx shot first. But their aim was better. She ducked as they came in firing. They hit Hadjara in the head and chest.

Nyx scrambled across the floor to the big wardrobe stuffed with pamphlets, and pulled it down behind her for cover. It was heavy, and fell like a massive tree. The crash made the whole room shudder. Nyx glimpsed four women in the doorway, and let off another couple of rounds in their general direction. She glanced at the window. It was covered in paper, probably lined with an organic filter, too, to keep out bugs and noise at the very least—people at the worst.

She let off a few more shots that, predictably, hit nothing, and huddled behind the wardrobe for another breath. Two options—fight out through the front or take a chance that she could pass through the window without getting fried by it.

Getting shot hurt. But getting fried or—at the very least—stunned by the window filter had a far higher chance of ending her stand here quite permanently and negatively.

"Fuck it," she said, and pulled her scattergun from her back with one hand and her sword with the other. Swing and shoot.

She twisted her body so she was headed toward them shoulder-first, giving them the leanest target possible while firing her scattergun. One woman dropped. Another took cover in the hall. A bullet thudded into Nyx's right shoulder; another hissed past her ear. She felt a hot, burning pain and splash of warmth on her neck.

Nyx mashed the closest woman's face with a palm-heel strike and butted the other in the jaw with the end of her scattergun. Not satisfied that they were down quite to her liking, Nyx shot them both again and slogged toward the first one who'd gone down and lay clutching her gut and pissing in her own rapidly pooling blood.

"That was a friend of mine," Nyx said, and shot her in the face.

Nyx grabbed one of their guns; a much fancier one than she was used to, with at least ten more shots in it. The barrel was sleek, skinned in an organic sheath. It molded itself to her hand. She shot out into the hall, aiming high for the ceiling, and heard a shot in return from her left, giving away the location of the fourth and final woman.

Nyx rounded the corner, keeping close to the wall, and came around the corner into the main room just in time to see the woman sloughing off her clothes and starting to shift. Long strings of mucus bled from her eyes and mouth as her body folded in on itself; the hair on her arms and neck grew darker and longer as her face elongated.

Nyx shot her mid-shift. The twisted body dropped. Nyx surveyed the rest of the room. Blood smeared the floor. The glasses behind the bar were broken. But she saw no other bodies. Hopefully Morda and her crew had had time to hole up in their rooms.

She knelt next to the partially changed woman. The woman was huffing mucus now. Her ears were curled up, and the whites of her eyes had been nearly swallowed.

"I don't take kindly to people trying to kill me," Nyx said, "or killing my friends." She drove her sword through the woman's still mostly human hand, the fingers slightly truncated, the nails thicker and sharper now, but not fully dog yet.

The woman whined.

Nyx's ear was starting to burn in earnest now; her shoulder throbbed. She wondered how much of the ear she'd lost to the bullet, but didn't dare put her hand up to it yet. The wound in her shoulder was more serious, and bleeding profusely. The pain was starting to register properly, and she let her grip on the sword go lax.

"Here is what I promise," Nyx said. "I'm going to leave you here to bleed out or get chopped up by Morda and her crew, or even, if you're lucky, just tossed out the back where your friends will find you. I'm doing that because I want them to know that I'm coming for them, and that Nyxnissa so Dasheem takes no shit from anyone. You put a hit out on me, I hit back."

Nyx yanked her sword from the woman's hand and

sheathed the blade. She stood as blood drooled down her arm, and staggered to the door of the brothel, which still hung open. She clattered down the steps, scattergun still dangling from her one good hand. She tried to get a rickshaw, but none of them would stop for her. She supposed if she drove a rickshaw, she wouldn't stop for her either.

Her vision swam. She pushed her bad hand up through her shirt in some vain hope to ease up the flow of the blood. There was surely a hedge witch around here who could patch her up. Instead she stumbled into a bar and demanded a drink. When they didn't bring one, she hefted her scattergun at the barkeep. They passed over one whisky, then another, and she barely got down a third drink before the order keepers showed up and asked her to vacate the premises.

"You got no better shit to do?" Nyx yelled at the beefy women. "No bodies in a gutter somewhere? No burglaries? No brawls? You coming here to interrupt a bleeding woman trying to have a drink. You know who I am?" She waved the gun at them, oblivious to the weapons at their hips. Even drunk—especially drunk—she was more than confident she could take them.

Blackness rode the edges of her vision, and she blinked hard, shook her head. "I just need another drink," she said. She turned from them and banged her glass on the counter.

The bar woman took the glass with shaking hands and refilled it. Nyx heard the order keepers talking in low voices behind her. Let them try and remove her. Just try it.

"Excuse me, I work for her."

Nyx turned at the voice. She knew the accent. It was the fucking Mhorian man. For all his bulk, he came into the room with head bowed and shoulders hunched, his gaze on the floor, like he was just some penitent little fuck.

"The fuck do you want?" she said. She picked up her glass, but it tumbled from her fingers and shattered on the floor. "For fuck's sake," she muttered. She reached for it, and saw long streamers of blood flowing down her arm. Why was her wound bleeding so badly? It was just a scratch, nothing. Need to find a hedge witch and get fixed up, that's all.

She stared at the blood mixing with the whisky on the floor, and had a sudden jarring flashback to another bar, another night, somewhere on the Chenjan front. Nyx heaved back against the bar as her legs trembled. She vomited.

"I've got you," the Mhorian said, and took her by the shoulder. "I'll take her home," he said.

She punched him in the arm, but her strength was waning. She gazed at the vomit on the floor and wondered how so much blood had gotten into it.

"That woman is fucked," one of the order keepers said.

Nyx laughed. "You've no idea," she said.

"I'm taking you back to Hadya Street," the Mhorian man said. "Will you come with me? We'll go slow. Perhaps we'll find a rickshaw."

"We going to fuck?" she said, pawing at his face. She left bloody fingerprints on his cheek. His face was so serious.

"Maybe later," he said.

"I'm holding you to that," she said, and that was the last clear memory she had for some time.

Rhys had just settled in to sleep after evening prayer when someone banged on the door. He lay awake staring at the ceiling, waiting for Taite to get it. Anneke was out gambling, but he could hear the radio on in the workroom, and that meant Taite was still awake.

The pounding came again. Louder this time.

"Get the door," Rhys muttered. He had written his resignation letter for Nyx and left it in her office, but she wasn't home yet, and he wanted to be soundly asleep when she finally got home and read it. He wasn't sure how she would react. Would she throw him out right away, like Taite said? He had saved some money, and he might be able to float for a while until the government job sent him a train ticket and stipend.

The knocking went on and on. He heard a voice yelling now: a male voice, which was unusual.

Rhys sighed and rolled out of bed. He pulled on a burnous and went out into the workroom. The radio was still on, but Taite wasn't there. The trapdoor to the basement was open. Rhys called down. "Do you hear the door, Taite?"

"What?" Taite yelled.

Rhys said, "Never mind, I'll get it," and pulled his burnous close. The air got much cooler at night, and no one had bothered with a fire. Without him to nurse them all, this place would fall apart. Let it fall apart, he thought. Maybe the world will be a better place.

With Nyx and Anneke both out, he wasn't just going to open the door to anyone, not this time. He'd learned that lesson one too many times, most recently this morning when he was nearly blown up. Instead he pulled open the viewing port on the face of the door and stood just to the left of it as

Nyx had taught him, just in case somebody tried to shove a gun through it.

The dim orange light of the glowworm lantern above the door showed him a grim picture. A huge, moon-faced Mhorian man had one arm wrapped around Nyx's waist. She was covered in blood; half her ear was gone. Her eyes were glassy and the pupils were unevenly dilated.

Rhys threw open the door and helped the Mhorian bring her inside. "What happened?" he asked.

"She was shot," the Mhorian said. "I think it was a smart bug, not a regular bullet."

"Put her down here," Rhys said. "Shut the door."

The man laid Nyx down on the floor of the foyer. Rhys pulled up her bloody tunic to reveal the breast binding beneath. He ran his hands downwards from the wound until he reached the bottom of her rib cage, and felt a soft, niggling tremor in his hands. He told the bug inside her chest to stop its tunneling, and felt it respond.

After closing the door, the Mhorian knelt beside him. "You a magician?" he asked.

"Yes," Rhys said. "We need to get this bug out. It's done damage to her internal organs. I don't know how she's still standing."

"Heard she was a bel dame," the man said.

"Who are you, exactly?" Rhys said.

"Khos Khadija. Saw her in the bar. She had some trouble with order keepers."

"They did this?" Rhys couldn't imagine order keepers surviving an encounter with Nyx unless there was an army of them.

"No, long story. What can I do?"

"Go in the back, get some hot water from the tap. I'll need a knife. You'll find one in the kitchen back there."

"What's going on?" Taite said. He came in from the workroom, wiping his hands on a rag.

"I'll need red bug salve," Rhys said. "Make up that spider-mite tea."

"Shit," Taite said, dropping the rag. He ran back into the workroom.

Rhys tried to redirect the bug inside Nyx's rib cage to repair some damage while they waited, but whoever had programmed it was a far more powerful magician than he was.

Nyx was drooling blood and babbling nonsense about fields of body parts and black suns. He chanced a look at her face and a dagger of fear cut through his body. What if he lost her? What if she died right here under his care, after all she had done to keep him safe? For all the horror and madness she had exposed him to, she had taken him in when no one else would. He wanted her to tell him now it would be all right, and he hated himself for that.

"Concentrate," he muttered, and closed his eyes. He directed the bug to start pushing up through Nyx's abdomen, moving it past major organs. When he opened his eyes he could see it bulging there against her skin, slightly smaller than the bullet casing that it had ridden in on.

The Mhorian handed Rhys a knife and set a bowl of water next to him.

Rhys said, "Hold her down," and was suddenly glad to have this huge man here to hold Nyx because neither he nor Taite would have been able to do it.

Rhys sunk the knife into Nyx's belly. She thrashed and swore, though it was not his name she used. He heard a litany of names from her, and more creative curses than she had yet used.

Khos pressed her down with one hand on her good shoulder, the other on her opposite hip. Even injured, though, she was strong, and it almost wasn't enough. Rhys sliced open her skin and popped the bug out into his palm. It was a green-backed, wormy little thing with a mouth full of teeth. The mucus it secreted stung his skin, so he dropped it into the hot water.

Taite came in with the tea.

"Help me get her to drink it," Rhys said.

It took all three of them to get the tea down. Rhys suspected they would have had more luck if he dumped it into a whisky. Rhys took the salve from Taite and spread it over the wound he'd made, which began to sizzle and mend itself almost immediately. It was an expensive concoction he'd gotten from his mentor, Yah Tayyib, and worth using now. He cut open her tunic over the original bullet wound and put salve there, too, and slathered more onto her ear. She was still a mess, but she wasn't bleeding anymore.

"Can you pick her up?" Rhys asked Khos.

"Think she'll bite me?" Khos asked.

Rhys peered at Nyx's face. Her eyelids fluttered, and she was whispering something about taxes and bomb squads.

"Maybe we'll just try and walk her to her room," Rhys said.

Rhys on one side, Khos on the other, they half-walked, half-dragged Nyx to her cot at the back of her office and laid her down. She had lost a sandal somewhere, so Rhys took off the remaining one, and covered her in a light blanket. He moved to the brazier at the corner of the room and used a handful of bugs to start a fire.

When he turned around, he saw Khos sitting next to Nyx. She was snoring softly now.

"I'm Rhys," Rhys said to him, holding out a hand.

"Khos," the man said, taking his wrist.

"Yes, you told me." Rhys sat beside him. "You know Nyx."

"Only met her tonight," Khos said, "in a brothel."

Well, that explained a lot, Rhys thought. "You have a place to stay?" he asked. He'd been a foreign man in Nasheen long enough to know what the answer probably was.

"Sometimes," Khos said.

"You can stay the night," Rhys said. "Extra bed in the back. Taite's the kid at the com. Anneke is out tonight, but she does weapons, sniper work, that sort of thing."

"That's nice of you," Khos said. "Haven't met many nice people here."

"Well, I'm not Nasheenian," Rhys said.

Khos grinned. "I can see that." He nodded at Nyx. "She be all right?"

"Probably," Rhys said. He hesitated. "If she isn't, we'll all need to get out of here quickly. You understand?"

"Yeah," he said. "They'll blame us."

"Yes," Rhys said. "You want to clean up? Her blood's all over you."

Khos looked down at his large, bloody hands. Her blood was smeared across his face and tunic. "Thank you, yes," he said. "Back there?"

"Yeah, past the kitchen," Rhys said.

When Khos was gone Rhys lay down next to Nyx's cot and listened to her snore. He stared at the ceiling and clasped his hands over his stomach. He hated her, so why did it hurt to see her get what she deserved? This was the life she'd chosen. And she would keep choosing it. She would come home every day bloody and drunk and spouting nonsense. Resigning was the only way to be free of her. Distance was the only way he could get himself to stop caring. Otherwise he'd just be here day after day at her bedside, watching her destroy herself.

"Rhys?" Nyx reached down and took his hand.

Rhys didn't protest. He stared at her filthy, broken nails, the rough calluses, the smears of dried blood and the rough, lined skin and squeezed her hand back.

"Nyx," he said, and it was a sigh.

"I need to piss," she said.

He let go of her hand, and went to find her a bucket.

Nyx woke with a start, still reeling from a terrible dream about being eaten alive by maggots. She swung her legs out of the cot and dry-heaved. She saw a neat bedroll on the floor beside her, and had a dim memory of Rhys lying next to her all night. She stumbled to her desk. Her arm ached, and she stank terribly. She rubbed at her eyes and then dug through her desk drawers.

"There's no whisky in there," Rhys said from the doorway. He held a plate of fried plantains that smelled great.

"Catshit," she said.

He set the tray down on her cot. "I'll get you tea."

"Buni, at least, for fuck's sake."

"Thank you," he said.

"For what?" she said. Her head felt stuffed with honey. Her mouth felt like she'd set it on fire sometime the night before.

"For not letting me get blown up yesterday," he said. "You remember?"

She shrugged. "I need a magician."

"I'll get the buni," he said, and she saw his face fall as he turned, and she resolved not to look at him again. What, was she supposed to say thanks to him, too, for . . . whatever? She was his fucking employer. It was in his best interest to keep her alive.

She noticed a sealed letter on her desk and opened it. "What's this?"

He glanced back. "Nothing, don't—" He reached for the letter. She held it away from him, squinting at the text.

"It's . . . a resignation letter," Rhys said.

"The fuck? We're leaving for Alabbas today. I need a magician."

"Let me get the buni. We can talk." He hurried out of the room before she could say more.

Nyx rubbed her face. Her memories of the night before were bubbling up, hot and sticky things that came in dim flashes. Blood, bodies, liquor. Always the same.

Rhys brought her a cup of buni and asked her sit on the cot so he could rub more salve into her wound.

"Can do it myself," she muttered, but drinking the buni sounded better than wiping stinking salve on herself, so she let him do it.

She winced as he unwrapped her crusted bandages. The skin was scabbed over. He rubbed more salve onto the wound and started putting on a clean bandage.

"So you leaving me?" she said.

"What happened to you last night?" he said.

"That wasn't what I asked you."

He knotted her bandage and frowned at her. It wasn't often he'd sit this close to her. Their knees touched.

"I can't watch you kill yourself," Rhys said.

"That's not what—"

"How drunk were you, to not remember if you called someone or not? So drunk you fell into a very stupid and obvious trap and nearly got yourself killed, is that right? Good guess?"

"Didn't know you cared," she said, rolling her shoulder.

He packed what remained of the bandage back into the medical pouch. "I don't care, Nyx. Do what you want. It's your awful life."

"Then get the fuck out of here," she said. "Live on the fucking street for all I fucking care."

"You make everything awful," he said. "Every hand someone holds out, you chop it off."

"You hold out enough hands, you get them chopped off," she said. "Maybe you'll learn that someday."

"I saved your life last night, Nyx."

She picked up her plate of fried plantains and set it on her lap. She used both hands to take the buni from the floor and drank it down in one go. "Buni's good," she said.

He waited.

"I know what you did," she said. "Know it'd be easier for

you all to let me go, right? But you gotta get this, Rhys. If I let these people go, other people are going to come. This isn't going to end until I end it in Alabbas. They will come for me. They will come for you, too, no matter where you go. Sorry, but that's what it is. I've pissed on people in my time, and if they see weakness, they'll kill all of us."

"I believe you," he said. "I'll go to Alabbas, but that's it."

She poked at her food. "We're better together, Rhys."

"I don't believe that," he said. "I don't think you believe it either."

He went to the door.

"That Mhorian still here?" she asked.

"Sleeping in the back," Rhys said.

"I'm going to shower off," she said. "Send him in in twenty?"

Rhys nodded, and left her.

Nyx ate the plantains and stumbled her way to the washroom, passing Anneke as she came out.

"You look like shit," Anneke said.

"Thanks," Nyx said. "Bakkie packed?"

"Yeah. And I won six notes at flush last night."

"Great," Nyx said, and shut the bathroom door. She rinsed off using a hose attached to the sink and watched the dirty water whirl through the drain at the center of the washroom.

When she was more or less clean—or cleaner, at least—she knotted on a new dhoti and pulled a tunic over her breast binding. She didn't feel like going through the bother of changing that one just yet.

She pushed back into her office and saw the Mhorian was already there, standing in front of her desk with his hands clasped in front of him like he'd come to the front of the class to be scolded. He gazed up at her with winter-blue eyes, his face nearly lost in the mop of his dreads.

Nyx had met a good number of shifters she didn't like, but none this . . . big. Big men always made her wonder about the fullness of the rest of their package, but they generally disappointed her. A thick, confident woman with a prized, custom dildo was a far better bet if that was how she felt like playing it. The fact that she was thinking about dildos made her realize she was feeling a lot better.

"Have a seat," Nyx said.

Khos trundled into the chair across from her desk. He was so large he dwarfed the chair. It creaked under his weight.

"Why do you need a shifter?" he asked.

"Why do you need a job?"

He huffed at her; it put her in mind of a frustrated dog, which she supposed was a fair comparison.

"I need a dog shifter," she said. "You look the part, but I need to verify you can shift into a dog. Yeah?"

"I can," he said.

"You can fight?"

"I can. Trained as a brawler."

"What, like a gladiator?"

"Something like that."

"Good shot?"

"Reasonable," he said. "Not a sniper, but I'm good with weapons. Not blades, but bullets."

Nyx drummed her fingers on her desk. "I don't get it," she said, leaning toward him. "You're Mhorian. Why leave a peaceful country and come out here and wallow in all this war and shit?"

His grim expression didn't change, but he considered the question for a long moment. Then, "I wanted to go somewhere where the pain outside matched what I felt here," he said, and touched his heart. "A country at war with itself seemed like the best option."

Nyx snorted. "I get that," she said. "I don't need to know all about your shit though, understand? You keep the past in the past."

"All right," he said.

She stood. "You're hired. I'll have Rhys write up a short-term contract. If you make it through this job alive maybe we'll make this a regular thing. We're headed to Alabbas, so go out and get anything you need to pack up for a trip. You have an hour."

He nodded and walked right back out the front door. She stayed there a long moment looking after him. She liked that, unlike Rhys, he hadn't pointed out that he'd saved her life. He didn't ask for a thank-you. He just did his fucking job and didn't try and collect points for it.

"Anneke!" she yelled.

"Yeah, boss!" she called back from the workroom.

"Don't forget to pack the whisky!"

"Already done, boss!"

Alabbas was a dirty city, dry and rotted like a mite-infested foot left too long in the sun. It was a company town, its inhabitants stuck working for the big factories on the south side of the city. The air had a briny smell to it, and Nyx noted contagion sensors ringing the whole city. Mostly she saw those on the edges of the front and up north to warn people of miasmas caused by wild bug swarms and contagions. Out here they were most likely an early warning system for a factory that had an explosion. Not that it was likely to help them much this close to a blown out building.

They'd passed the burned-out wreck of just such an unlucky factory on the way in. Nyx had managed to stuff the whole team into the bakkie, but had to have Khos shift to do it. He rode beside her up front, sitting between her and Rhys; he was a panting, good-natured buffer between them, and Nyx couldn't help patting his fluffy dog head a few times on the way up.

Taite and Anneke rode in the back with the trunk open, using respirators to breathe through the dust kicked up by the bakkie. They stayed cool with organic blankets that wicked away their body heat.

Rhys didn't speak a word to her the whole way, which was quite a feat, because it took five days to drive all the way south to Alabbas and the address they'd pulled from the bug. By the time they all got there Taite and Anneke were bickering, Khos spent most of his time napping, and Rhys mostly just glared at her.

Nyx didn't feel like defending her decisions any more than she already had. It was looking less and less like she'd get paid for this job, which was quickly turning into a vendetta, and she knew it.

Once they got holed up inside a seedy company-owned hotel, she splurged on three rooms because she wanted one all to herself so she could piss and sleep without listening to someone whining or enduring Rhys's odious stare.

She sent Taite out to do reconnaissance on the so Mahasin house to gather intelligence and put Khos on dog duty. "They're running with dogs," she told him. "I want you to find out if they're feral or shifters. I have a good idea of how they're triggering these bombs."

"What's a Muhktar doing with so Mahasins?" Taite said, shaking his head.

"Adopted, remember? Who the fuck knows how families work out here. Maybe she got sold to them. Maybe she just likes them better. Small town politics are tricky, though, so don't step into any shit."

She sent Anneke out to collect local gossip and found that Rhys had already left to find some food before she could give him instructions. Well, fuck him, she thought, and went back to her room and napped for almost six hours.

When she woke, Khos was looming over her in the blue light of the second dusk.

"The fuck?" she said.

"Found the dogs," he said. "They aren't at the address you sent Taite to. I sent him to where the dogs are instead."

"You did what?"

"I thought—"

"I don't pay you to think," Nyx said. "Just report. Where is he now?"

"I'll take you there," he said. "Rhys is with him."

"Lot of fucking uppity assholes on this team," she said, and rolled out of bed.

"Most boring part of the job," Taite said, munching from his bag of crisps in the front seat of the bakkie. The bakkie was parked outside a big walled house where half a dozen dogs slept out on the sidewalk in front of the garden gate. They were all rangy little mutts that looked like littermates.

"But it's a great way to learn a lot without getting a bullet," Nyx said from the seat beside him. Khos had shifted again, and was already out on the street, sniffing in gutters. It surprised her the other dogs hadn't tried to attack him. She took the pack of crisps from Taite and grabbed a fistful. She hadn't eaten since they got to Alabbas. "They come out yet today?"

"Only to feed the dogs."

"What, these strays?" She offered the crisps packet to Rhys beside her, but he ignored her. Whatever.

"Yeah, there are more in the courtyard. The two kids come out, the twins, and they feed the dogs. Address says this is a Muhktar house. Just so you know."

"Twins, huh? What do they feed them?"

"I dunno. Table scraps? They like dogs, I guess. I heard more inside, when I did the walk by. Khos thinks there are at least eight more dogs inside."

"They raise them to eat them?" she said. "Some got to be shifters."

"I think . . . I think they keep them as pets?"

"Bizarre."

Taite shrugged. "Everybody's different. They just seem too friendly with them to eat them, but who knows? I used to name the ditch bugs we raised before we ate them."

A woman came out of the house, wrapped in a heavy burnous. "Here we go," Nyx said. "You know that one?"

Taite squinted. "Can't tell. You?"

"Naw," she said. "How many you figure are left in there? People, I mean. Not dogs."

"Don't know," he said. "That's the third woman who's left, and I've only ever seen those three—her and the twins. But I'd think they'd leave someone with the dogs."

"May be time to go in," she said. "Real polite-like."

"That's it? No plan or anything?"

"What, you wanted to wait for an invitation?"

"Damn, Nyx, but—"

"I said I'd be polite."

She pulled out her pistol, slid out of the bakkie. She bet they'd only leave a couple young kids, maybe, or some teen apprentices, to watch the dogs. Maybe a dowdy old matriarch. She could handle that many.

Nyx tried the door first the old-fashioned way to verify it wasn't unlocked. She had tried busting in her fair share of doors that turned out to be open because someone had just popped out; not often, but enough to check. She waved for Rhys, but it was Taite that got out.

"No," she said, "Rhys. What, you going to talk it open?"

Rhys came out and sidled up to her along the doorway. "If we're arrested for this," he said, "I want your guarantee of protection."

"So, it speaks," Nyx said, watching the street behind him. "You want my protection in prison? They don't much like me in prison."

"So I keep hearing," he said. He pulled a long black bug

from the sleeve of his robe and set it onto the great outer gear of the door. It was a clunky old pre-war thing. The bug skittered up into the gears of the mechanism. Rhys murmured something she couldn't make out, and the door clicked open.

Nyx pressed into the room, gun raised. She wasn't a great shot with a pistol, but the ammunition for it was cheaper than what she put in her scattergun. She snorted dusty air and padded into the dim room, noting the two doors inside: one into the courtyard, one into something that might be a kitchen.

A little Ras Tiegan girl stood there holding a bowl of pastry. Her mouth hung open when she saw Nyx. Nyx was dressed in her dirty dhoti, tattered breast binding, and a faded burnous with months of dirt caked up along the hem. Her braids were coming undone and she hadn't washed anything but her face since they had arrived in Alabbas two days before.

The girl wore the tricorn-shaped hijab the Ras Tiegans called a wimple, gazed out at Nyx with big eyes. She was probably about Taite's age, and if Nyx guessed right, had spent her whole life either at home with her mother or right here serving the people in this big house.

"I'm here to see the head of the house," Nyx said. "You tell her the bel dame council has words for her."

"I'm sorry," the girl said, staring hard at Nyx's feet, "the head of the house is not home."

"Then you won't mind if I look around," Nyx said.

Nyx strode past her and into the living area. She kept her pistol out while her eyes adjusted to the bright light streaming in through the windows that faced the central courtyard.

Two figures stood there, deep in conversation. They were older women, maybe in their forties—or fifties, if they spent a lot of time indoors.

"What is—" said the one on the left. She was taller, soft in the face, and heavy about the hips and bust.

Her leaner companion said, "Jaquelin, who did you let in here? Where are you?"

"No," said the plump one, and put a hand on the other's wrist. "We are not enemies!" the woman said. "You're here for my daughter, aren't you? You're here for Rasim. There have been others."

"Less polite, I bet," Nyx said.

The woman looked at Nyx's pistol.

"Yes, less polite."

"Others?" Nyx said. "Bel dames?"

"Bel dames, order keepers, foreign agents, mercenaries like you. She has nothing to do with us."

"You know she's blowing up your factories?"

"We . . . suspected, yes. We have tried to take care of that. She was resentful of her . . . other family. This is a family affair."

"You put people on her?"

"Yes, we put out a contract for her."

"She's taken up another name, another identity. Binyamin so Mahasin. That's how she's evading your mercs."

The leaner woman swore softly under her breath. "The audacity—"

"I see," said the other.

"You don't," Nyx said. "She's using your Muhktar dogs to blow up your Muhktar factories. She train them?"

"Yes, she always loved them."

"Where is she?"

"You've done everything she expected, you know. She wanted you here."

"I get that," Nyx said. "I'm here. So where is she?"

Rhys waited quietly just behind her; she was aware of his presence, and so were the women. He had pushed back his burnous so the hilts of his pistols were visible. He wouldn't kill them, and she was a bad shot, but they didn't know that.

"She doesn't care for us," the lean one said, shrilly. "Killing us won't change her mind. You won't—"

"I don't want you," Nyx said. She gestured to the courtyard. "I want the dogs."

"What?" Rhys said.

The women glanced at one another. "Take them," the plump woman said.

"What the hell are we doing with a half-dozen dogs?" Taite said, closing the door of their hotel room on the barking, jumping pack of them.

"She's using the dogs to deliver the bombs," Nyx said. "That's why we don't see them on any of the recordings. It's the fucking dogs."

"Those are well-trained dogs," Taite said. "I can't even get a dog to sit. Not unless—"

"It's certainly more likely they're shifters," Nyx said. "Though somebody good with a dog could certainly train one to do something like that. But shifters would be easier. Less messy." She glanced at Khos, who had shifted back into his human form, and was eating a fistful of spicy tofu. "I need you to figure out which ones are dogs and which ones are really shifters. I want information from them."

Khos shrugged. "When they get hungry, they'll shift. It's a defense mechanism. If you get too weak to hold form, you shift back to human."

"How long?" Nyx said.

"Three days? About that," Khos said.

"You don't intend to leave these dogs in here without any food for three days, do you?" Taite said. "They'll eat each other!"

"You got a better idea, smart kid?" Nyx said.

"I could shoot 'em," Anneke said. "Shifters always try to shift back when you shoot 'em."

"Pleasant group you have here," Khos muttered.

"Can you get it out of them any sooner?" Nyx said. "You got a humane way to do it, big man, you've got your shot."

He huffed at her and looked from her to Anneke and back. "All right," he said. He opened the door to the barking pack and slammed it behind him.

"Big job to give someone we just met," Taite said.

"What, you want to do it?" Nyx said. "You go walk right in."

"You don't have to be mean about it."

"How long have you been in Nasheen? Of course I have to be mean about it."

She pushed past him and went back to her room. She found Rhys waiting at the door.

"Fuck, what—" she began.

Then she saw he held something in his hand. She stopped still in the hall.

"What the hell is that?" she said.

"It's . . . a heart," he said. He held it out in front of him. His whole body was taut. His face was grim. The heart was as big as his fist, bloody and still bleeding. For a half moment she thought she was dreaming or having some kind of flashback.

"Whose . . . heart?" she asked, because it seemed like the most logical thing to ask.

"She said it was mine."

"Who said?"

"The woman who was here."

"Are you hurt?"

"No," he said, but his tone was still distant, disaffected.

"Then how can it be yours?" Nyx said. Her hand moved back toward her scattergun, almost unconsciously.

"I . . . don't know," he said. "This woman . . . she was . . . it's like I knew her from somewhere."

"Yeah, well, I thought I did, too," Nyx said. She followed the line of the corridor with her gaze, but saw no one else there. Finally within arm's distance of Rhys, she took the heart into her hand.

Nyx considered it a moment, then bit into the tough meat of it and chewed thoughtfully. Swallowed.

She put the heart back into Rhys's hand and then wiped her bloody hand on her tunic. "It's a dog's heart," she said. "Human tastes different. You're fine." She opened her door. He stared after her, still unmoving.

Nyx sighed. "Listen," she said, "if you are going to last this mission, you need to understand something about how people win. You don't hit someone in the face. You demoralize them first. She comes back, you shoot her. Get some sleep."

"But . . . she knows where we are."

"Of course she does. We have her dogs. Her family was right—she wanted us here. I have my guesses on why, and we're going to undermine her."

"How do I know that?"

"You don't," she said.

"What . . . what do I do with this?"

"Cook it up with some onions and gravy," she said.

He curled his lip at her, and that's when she knew he'd be all right. "I don't eat meat, Nyx."

"Good night, Rhys." She closed the door.

The privies on the floor were shared, but her room had its own sink. She went to it now and washed her hands. Stared at her bloody mouth in the mirror. She bared her bloody teeth and grimaced at her own reflection.

After rinsing out her mouth, Nyx assembled all of her weapons. She didn't sleep that night. Instead, she brought Anneke in and laid out the plan.

"Rasim needs to think I turned on you," Nyx said.

Anneke crossed her arms and spit sen in the sink. "Why'd you turn on us?"

"I did some bad things in prison," Nyx said. "Shit my team shouldn't know about. You know what I'm talking about."

Anneke's arms were covered in prison tattoos. She nodded. "Yeah, I get it."

"Once Khos gets the location of the next factory they're blowing up and where she'll be after, we pack up like we're going to stop them together, get it?"

"Keep going."

"You set up on the roof. Need you to hit Khos and Taite

with tranquilizer darts. I'll take Rhys. Tranquilizers will mess with his talent. Don't want to shut him out in case we need that later. I only need a half hour."

"Half hour to do what?"

"Taite would say I'm confessing some sins," Nyx said. "But it's between me and her. Not you and the boys. I know you get that. They won't."

Anneke chewed her lip. "Don't like this one, boss."

"Half an hour, Anneke. Then you bring the boys in and we haul her in. All right?"

A knock on the door. Nyx answered. It was Khos. "Got the factory location," Khos said. "They're blowing it up tomorrow afternoon when everyone's at end-of-week prayer."

"Tell me you've got more than that."

He showed his teeth. "She's in a big old grain silo just north of the burned out factory. It's just her and half a dozen shifters."

"Let's go fuck some stuff up then," Nyx said.

And all that left Nyx here, holding a scattergun to Rhys's chest. The look he gave her as her finger squeezed the trigger was one she'd seen on the faces of a hundred dead boys. It was one she'd never wanted to see on his face, but she preferred it to the yearning look he'd given her earlier. She didn't know what to do with that look. She knew what to do with this one.

She squeezed the trigger.

The blast took Rhys off his feet. He slammed onto the

rooftop. She crossed to him in two long strides and knelt beside him. She pressed her cheek to his and whispered. "Stay still. They're watching. They need to think I believed you."

He wheezed for air. She placed her fingertips on his chest. She had loaded the scattergun with soft organic pellets, the sort that the military used for training exercises. They burst on impact, leaving no residue or shrapnel, but they could bruise and even break ribs. She had a feeling she'd been close enough to break a couple of Rhys's ribs.

But that was better than killing him.

She holstered her scattergun and headed back down the stairs. She needed him to lie still for a half hour, hopefully more.

Nyx got to the bottom of the stairs, where Anneke sat with the bodies of Taite and Khos, sniper rifle on her knee.

"Get this buttoned up quick, boss," Anneke said.

"Half an hour," Nyx said. "Then you come in with guns blazing."

"Would prefer that the other way around."

"Gotta end this," Nyx said.

Anneke nodded.

Nyx put her respirator in her mouth and took off running in the direction of the grain silo, two kilometers away. It was a hot run, but she was twenty-seven and good on her feet, still. She yanked out her scattergun as she came into the shadow of the silo and sucked down a bulb of water.

A small square, like a dog door, was carved into the silo. She squeezed in, just barely getting her ass through, and muscled her way up the stairs. She went up and up, past a room teeming with dogs all panting over a water trough.

Nyx kept her weight on the outside of her feet and breathed shallowly until she was up and out of their perception.

She found Rasim in a converted office. She sat at the table with a gun in her hand already pointed at Nyx. Her hair hung in a long braid down her back, and she'd swapped out her clothes for sensible tunic and trousers and boots.

"Liked your hair better in Punjai," Nyx said.

"I knew you were here," Rasim said.

"Clearly," Nyx said. "I knew you wanted me here. I figured the best way to get revenge on a woman even bel dames won't touch is to frame me for something pretty dishonorable, like blowing up Nasheenian weapons factories."

"When did you know?"

"Sparring."

"I thought so."

"So now what?" Nyx said. "You want to give me the speech?"

"What speech?"

"A speech all the angry women like you give when I kill your sisters or your brothers or your daughters or your sons. Some angry, frothy rant about how unfair it all is, and how you loved them so much. I gave you some time, see. It's just us. You can spew away."

Rasim smiled thinly. "You know why I didn't finish my bel dame training?"

"Because you knew what we'd be?"

"No," she said, "because my sister died in a prison brawl. Binyamin was always tougher than me. But she got mashed in the head. It wasn't even you who did it."

"I get it," Nyx said. "Somebody else got to you. Who wants me framed for this? How much they pay you?"

"It's too late for that," Rasim said.

"You're a good girl," Nyx said. "Doesn't have to end this way."

"I'm going to be rich," Rasim said, "and you'll be back in prison. I think it's a fine way to end things."

"Why the dogs?"

"Because I love them," she said. "Does it need to be more complicated than that?"

"They're just animals."

"Shifters can become dogs," she said. "Are they more animal in form, or should we treat them as humans? What if they shifted and did not have the energy to shift back? Lots of shifters choose to live their lives as dogs. Besides, they're untraceable. And every one of them will be happy to point to you as the one who directed them to blow this all up."

"You have the others rigged?"

She nodded. "All the plants that are left will blow up in . . . oh, two hours, maybe. Not much more than that. What will you do about it?"

"Tell them you did it," Nyx said. She let out a long breath. Binyamin hadn't been the woman in prison she'd thought she'd been, then. She hadn't been the woman Nyx needed to repent for, just someone caught in the crossfire.

Rasim raised her gun.

"Anyone ever tell you bel dames are hard to kill?" Nyx said.

"You aren't a bel dame."

"No," Nyx said, "but unlike you, I used to be. And they taught me something there."

"What's that?"

"Don't talk too long," Nyx said.

The bullet took Rasim between the shoulder blades. She slammed into the table.

Nyx hustled in and bound her hands behind her with sticky bands from her pack.

"Anneke?" Nyx yelled. No answer. If it was Anneke, she was early.

Nyx looked around the edges of the room. It wasn't sealed up top. Someone could have squatted on the floor above and gotten a shot through the gap between the floor and the wall.

Rasim whined. The bullet hadn't hit anything vital; looked like it just missed her spine, too. "Lucky girl," Nyx said.

"Anneke?" Nyx called.

"Here, boss," Anneke said. She slithered down from the floor above, coming in from some retrofitted venting shaft. Her gun was slung over her shoulder.

"You're early," Nyx said.

"Couldn't help firing after that line," Anneke said. "Too perfect. You know, better early than late."

"Where are the boys?"

"Downstairs clearing out the dogs," she said.

"Early," Nyx muttered.

"You get what you wanted?" Anneke said.

"Pretty much," Nyx said. "Not what I thought it was."

"Good, then," Anneke said.

Nyx took Rasim by the hair. "We need to diffuse those bombs, Rasim. Where's the codes?"

"I don't have them," she said. "You know how they work? They need to be sealed in living flesh to survive. More than a few moments outside of living tissue, and they disintegrate. It's why shifters make such good triggers."

"I got it," Nyx said. "Where are they?" She pointed the scattergun at her chest. "I'm happy to cut you up into pieces to find them. We were nice with the first bullet."

"They're not inside me," she said.

Nyx heard noise on the stairs. Khos, Taite, and Rhys walked up. Nyx didn't look at Rhys. She expected the bakkie ride over hadn't been very comfortable with bruised ribs.

"Then I'll cut up all your friends," Nyx told Rasim.

"No," she said. "They're inside *your* friend."

"What?"

Rasim bent her head to Khos. "Your friend, who met our friend Hadjara for a discreet transaction."

Khos's eyes widened. "What's she saying?"

"You a dog runner?" Nyx said.

"A what?" he said.

"Where is it on him?" Nyx said.

"He won't live through you taking it out," Rasim said. "It's wrapped around his heart."

The heart. That's what she was doing, fucking with them and the heart. "Yeah?" Nyx said. "The fuck do I care about one dog? Lot more people going to die if he lives."

"Now, wait—" Khos said.

"Who will die, Nyxnissa?" Rasim said. "The factories are empty. We only destroy empty factories. What you're saying is the life of one man is worth less than the weapons that will go on to kill thousands, hundreds of thousands, of men. Is that true?"

Nyx spit sen. "I fucking hate revolutionaries," she said. "I liked this better when you were just getting paid to frame me."

"Could we get back to talking about this thing in my heart?" Khos said, voice rising. "Hadjara said that injection was—"

"What, something easily removable?" Rasim said. "It's up to the two of you now. You want to stop the destruction of a few weapons? You get out your knife and you kill this man."

Nyx pulled a big knife from the sheathe at her hip. "You forget who I am? What I do?"

"Not at all," Rasim said. "I trained to do what you do, remember?"

"And gave it up," Nyx said. "You quit because you have no stomach for blood. When you figured out the sort of sacrifices you have to make, you turned coward. It wasn't about losing your sister at all."

"Was it cowardly?" Rasim said. "Is it cowardly to do what the system expects of you, or cowardly to go along with it?"

"You tell me," Nyx said, "you're the one framing an innocent person for blowing up factories."

"Oh, you're not innocent, Nyxnissa so Dasheem."

"Get her out of here," Nyx said to Anneke.

"Sure thing, boss," Anneke said, and tugged at Rasim's restraints. "You want me to kill her?"

"Not until I have the code," Nyx said.

"Now, wait a minute—" Khos said, holding up his big hands.

When Rasim and Anneke left the room, Nyx hefted her blade.

"Nyx," Rhys said, quietly, but she pretended not to hear him.

Khos scrambled back, hands still raised, until he pressed against the wall. Odd thing, she thought, that a man so big retreated without a serious tussle.

"They're just weapons," Khos said. "You wouldn't kill me on her word. Hadjara had me run a job, a simple ferrying job. I thought I'd finished it before we left Punjai."

"I'm doing a job, too," she said.

"You don't need to do this," Rhys said. He did not move from where he stood, but his voice rolled over her, warm and smooth as silk.

"I took a job," she said. "I finish my jobs."

"It's not a note," Rhys said, "and you aren't being paid for it. It's just weapons, Nyx. She was a liar trying to frame you for this!"

"The weapons support the war. The war is Nasheen."

"Nasheen is more than the war," Rhys said.

Khos's eyes were big. His gaze moved rapidly from Rhys to Nyx and back again.

Her fist tightened on the blade. "I have a job," she said.

"You never took the job," Rhys said. He came up beside her, speaking softly. "We can walk away. It's not our fight. We don't owe it anything. So some factories blow up. What's that matter?"

She twisted the knife at Rhys and lunged for his throat. She pressed the blade there. "Chenjan," she spat. "You would say some catshit thing like that. Make us vulnerable. Move in with some army."

"I'm not your enemy," Rhys said.

"The whole world's my enemy," she said.

"I'm not," he said. He swallowed, and she saw his skin ripple against the blade.

How many dark throats like his had she cut? Dozens, certainly. Hundreds? No, she was not at the front that long. But a lot. Too many. He was just another body. Another bag of Chenjan blood. Like Khos, he was a foreign man, and foreign men were disposable. No one would miss them. She'd be doing the world a favor. Her head swam. Flashbacks. Irrational behavior. Fuck, was she losing her shit again? Deep breath. Count back. Where the fuck was she?

"Nyx?"

She snarled something at him, she wasn't even sure what, and pressed her forearm against his chest, pinning him to the wall.

His gaze darted to Khos, and Nyx said, "You think about moving, dog-man, and I'll castrate you."

"Nyx," Rhys said, "it's not a job. There's no honor in it."

She huffed out a long breath.

Too many throats.

My life for a thousand, she had sworn. Not a thousand lives for mine.

Nyx released him. Her body surged with adrenaline. She let out another breath, and turned so neither man could see her hand tremble as she sheathed her knife. She hocked the rest of her sen onto the floor.

"Fuck this place," she said. "I have shit to do." She smoothed back her hair and wiped the sweat from her face. She glanced back at the men, irritated. "Are you coming or not?"

She did not look at their faces, because she did not want to know what was there.

They returned Rasim to her family with little fanfare.

"You had a bounty on her, right?" Nyx said. "I want the

bounty, and a land grant for a house in Mushirah, and you can do what the fuck you want with her and I won't tell anyone she's responsible for blowing up those six factories that are filling the sky with shit right now."

The Muhktars were indeed a powerful family. They paid her and had the land grant notarized the next day. The money was far more than Nyx had expected, and she divided it up among the team that night over fried rotis and sugar soda two towns over where the air was clearer.

Anneke whooped and hollered at her cut and stuffed it into her breast binding and rocketed off to the nearest card hall.

"We leave at dawn!" Nyx said, and Anneke waved at her.

Taite went up to bed at the hotel. "Might as well get some sleep before she comes back," he said.

Nyx had gotten three rooms again, and she left Khos and Rhys at the café downstairs to be grumpy by themselves. She was tired of their moods. Men were so emotional.

She bathed and threw herself into bed, but every time she closed her eyes, she saw that beating heart in Rhys's hands, and she remembered that it had been far too large for a dog's heart, and it had not tasted like a dog's heart at all.

She remembered holding her knife to Rhys's throat for no reason. She remembered losing her shit at them in some hot, stifling silo that felt like the desert. The whole world felt like the front. She could never scrub away the front. It followed her, buried deep in her heart.

"That woman was going to kill me," Khos said.

Rhys stared into his bowl of gravied yams. The first big sun was setting, and he closed his eyes and tried to enjoy the last of its heat on his face. Life always felt more precious right after you almost lost it. "Nyx kills a lot of people," Rhys said.

Khos leaned toward him, bushy brows furrowed. "Why did you speak for me?" Khos said. "Is it really because you're Chenjan, because this would help the war?"

"Why does everyone think I do things because I'm Chenjan?" Rhys said. "Did you trust that Hadjara woman because you're Mhorian?"

Khos straightened. "Well, yes," he said. "Women only lie about politics." He poked at his food. "I didn't realize this was so political."

"You have a lot to learn about Nasheen," Rhys said.

"I am new here, that's true," Khos said.

Rhys considered asking him what he was running from, but that would end with Khos asking Rhys the same question, and he didn't want to answer that. He was starting to understand why Nyx didn't ask her team a lot of questions.

"No matter what Nyx says or does," Rhys said, "just remember she's always out for herself. If you remember she's always thinking about herself, you can convince her to act morally, sometimes."

"She really was going to kill me."

"She'll do anything to finish a job," Rhys said. "We're all expendable."

Khos sipped his tea. The way he held the cup was surprisingly delicate, for such a large man. Rhys wasn't sure why he expected a man that size to go around crushing things, but he did. Maybe it had been so long since he saw a man who clearly wasn't starving or mistreated or broken that he'd forgotten what was possible.

"I will consider all you've said," Khos said.

Back at the storefront in Punjai, Nyx sat up on the roof with Anneke drinking whisky and throwing rocks at parrots. The little parrots were commonly used as spies by those too cheap to buy bugs.

"Too many men on this team," Anneke said, pouring herself another glass. The day was just starting to cool as the first sun rode low over the horizon, burning it a rapturous orange. "Shit gets too emotional. Wah-wah, I don't eat meat. Wah-wah, don't cut out my heart."

Nyx shrugged. "Cheaper than hiring women."

"True, true," Anneke said. "I sure ain't cheap."

"War's not going to go well for Nasheen next few years," Nyx said.

"What, 'cause of the factories?" Anneke said, and snorted. "Filthy Tirhanis will be happy to fill more orders. Southern factories mostly supply Ras Tieg."

"What's Ras Tieg have to fight?" Nyx said.

Anneke peered at her. "You ever talk to Taite?"

"No," Nyx said.

"They don't like shifters there," Anneke said. "Some kind of religious war over it. So in the end we put more money in Tirhani pockets, and saved some Ras Tiegan shifters, maybe."

Or maybe they were supplying the other side there? Who knows? What I'm saying is, I don't stay up at night thinking about it."

"You think I do?"

Anneke shrugged. "You say you don't, but you piss a lot about it. It was a bad job. I like to just forget about bad jobs."

"Pour me another drink."

"Sure, boss."

Nyx threw a rock at a parrot, and missed. "Goddamn, I can't even fucking throw straight."

"We ain't none of us perfect," Anneke said. She sucked at her drink. "You think that Chenjan will stay?"

"Rhys can come or go, I don't fucking care. He can't fucking make up his mind."

"Someday you're going to kill that Chenjan," Anneke said, "and it'll be meaner'n what you do to all those other people you fuck."

"It'll be fine," Nyx said. "Someday I'll just eat him right up, and we'll get over it. He'll leave then for sure."

"You be nice now," Anneke said, slyly. "You take out his heart first."

"No," Nyx said finishing her drink. "I'll eat his heart last."

A few hours later, drunk and thinking far too much about fucking, Nyx knocked on Rhys's door.

She wasn't exactly sure what she was going to ask him for. Reading, maybe? He hadn't read to her in a while. Reading that would lead to fucking. Fucking, then reading. Then he could leave the team. After she fucked him. Like normal people did.

When he didn't answer, she knocked again. "Hey, open up!" she said.

The door opened. She found herself staring at a broad, pale chest crisscrossed in blue tattoos. She followed the map of the muscled chest up and up to Khos's broad face and grinned.

"Well," she said.

"Well," he said. He held a bottle of beer in one hand, and she saw a box of empties by his bed.

"You . . . up to anything?" she said.

"You came here for a drink?" he said. "You seem to have had some already."

"Oh, I had my eye on coming down here before the drinking," she said. "You?"

"You did promise the fucking would come later."

"Could come a few times, really," Nyx said.

He opened the door wider. She took the beer from his hand and kicked the door closed behind them.

It had been far too fucking long since she fucked someone.

She finished the beer and tossed the bottle into the box with the others and pulled at his trousers. He took her face in his hands and kissed her so passionately that a wave of desire shook her body. She wrapped her legs around him and he carried her to the bed where they proceeded to fuck like two very drunk and very hungry people.

He was warm and tasted good and kissed her like a man who breathed women, dreamed of women, found bliss in the arms of women. And for Nyx, who had never known bliss or surrender with or toward anyone or anything, seeing him submit to sensation—to lust, desire—was one of the most intensely erotic things she had ever witnessed.

She had been only half joking about coming a few times, especially considering how drunk she was, but he was eager and perfectly skillful, and the second time she came she thought she was dreaming this whole thing because she wasn't stupid enough to fuck anyone on her team, was she? And wasn't she looking for Rhys?

They lay tangled together in the sheets, sweaty and semi-delirious with drink and sated lust, and she traced the fine blue tattoos running up his legs.

"You want to know about them?" he asked softly as he tangled his fingers in her unraveling braids.

The fear started then, riding up over her satisfaction, sinking deep in the pit of her stomach. She drew her hand away. "No," she said.

Nyx slid out of bed.

"Is something wrong?" he said.

"No," she said. "You were fine."

"Is this about him?"

"Who?"

"You certainly know who."

She pulled on her dhoti and braided back her mussed hair. She either wanted more to drink or wanted to get to bed. Probably both. Stupid mistake, fucking a guy she'd signed a contract with.

"You should see the way you two look at each other," Khos said.

"We don't look at each other," Nyx said. "He's just a kid."

"A pretty kid, by anybody's standard. And if even I can see that, I imagine you sure can."

"Well, no amount of looking is going to make any difference. He's still God full. And I'm still godless."

"Maybe you should find God again."

"Maybe he should become godless."

"You compromise for no one."

"No."

"That's a lonely place to be."

"You trying to open me up? You're nobody special."

"Haven't I already opened you up?" he said, and she hated the way he said it, propped up there on one elbow, because he was gentle and beautiful and he had also been a dog runner who now had bomb codes wrapped around his heart, and she broke everything she touched, even things that were already broken.

"The cunt is not the heart," she said, standing, "though a lot of people get the two confused."

She went to the door and yanked it open.

Rhys resolved to find Nyx and say his peace. If he was leaving, he wanted her to know why. He wanted her to know that if she really cared about him like she pretended, then they shouldn't work for each other. They should figure something else out. Maybe there was something to work out.

He found Anneke passed out in her room, and Taite listening to the radio. "You know where Nyx is?" Rhys asked.

"Probably ask Khos," Taite said.

Rhys didn't ask why it was Khos would know. He went right to Khos's door, which had led to a storage closet not long before. Everything that used to be in the closet was still stacked outside of it.

Rhys heard voices inside. He raised his hand to knock.

The door opened, and Nyx stood in front of him, braids tangled, tunic in hand, wearing only her dhoti and breast binding. Beside her, Khos sat on his bed, naked.

Rhys opened his mouth, unsure of what to say.

"The fuck?" Nyx said.

They stared at each other. Rhys tried not to stare at Khos. He stared at Nyx's bared abdomen instead. "I . . ." Rhys began. He dropped his hand. "I was . . . looking for you. Thought . . . Khos had seen you, maybe."

"Well, you were right," Nyx said. Her face flushed, or it looked like it did. The light was dim, and he couldn't be sure. She shut the door behind her. "What did you want?"

Rhys cleared his throat. "Nothing," he said.

"It had to be something. You didn't come all the way down here for nothing."

"Just . . ." He gazed at the door again. He was a fool, in fact. A fool to think she was anything but what she said she was. "Nothing, just wanted you to know I was staying on the team," he said. "I talked with Anneke and she thinks the government job might be dodgy. Something to lure foreign men to the interior."

"I'm sure she's right," Nyx said. "You're staying, then."

"Yes," he said, "why not? Nothing has changed." He turned to go.

"Rhys?"

He did not look back at her, but he stopped, listening.

She came up beside him. "Early day tomorrow. Back to work, all right?" she said. "Need to meet you in the bakkie at the second dawn, and we'll head over to the Cage to pick up some jobs, sound good?"

"Good, all right," Rhys said. He went back to his room and shut the door. Pulled off his burnous. His shoes. His tunic. Unbuckled his guns. Took off his belt. Stripped to his small-clothes, and then he just lay there in bed alone, remembering when she took his hand. Remembering how she had fired that gun into his chest. Remembered how he had felt when he was with her, despite or because of all that, and tried to imagine how he would feel without that sense of being safe and protected, even in the company of a woman willing to break his ribs to serve her own ends.

He didn't know why he stayed. Didn't know why he couldn't go. He put his hand over his heart, and wished he could tear it out.

The next morning, Nyx left the storefront to see Rhys waiting for her in the bakkie as the big orange demon of the second sun lit up over the horizon. Nyx had swilled half a carafe of buni—no whisky—after getting out of bed. Now she slid into the seat up front next to him. When he glanced at her, it was with contempt and disgust, and she was all right with that. She knew what to do with it. It was the needy, heartfelt kind of emotion like the looks Khos had given her after they fucked that left her cold. It made her want to run. Maybe it made

Rhys want to run, too, which is why he wasn't now. He hated her enough to stay. So she would take his contempt and his disgust, and bundle it up tight and close.

He gazed out over the hazy city, contemplating the world outside his window. The world without her face in it.

"Finally ready?" he said.

"Born that way," Nyx said.

"Born drunk, more likely."

"You can be both," she said.

She started up the bakkie. It coughed yellow smoke and beetles out its back end. Nyx turned on the juice. "These fucking beetles are starving."

"Heart full of beetles," he said.

"If only," she said, and drove them to their next job.

SOULBOUND

"Whoever destroys a soul, it is considered as if he
destroyed an entire world. And whoever saves a life,
it is considered as if he saved an entire world."
—Babylonian Talmud Sanhedrin 37a

NYX HAD BEEN FALLING APART since the magicians put her back
together again sometime after the war. Now, at thirty, staring
down the barrel of an acid gun, she figured she was about to
break apart for good. She'd heard that lots of people found
God again when looking that hard at death, but mostly she
felt relief. At thirty, Nyx was lucky to be alive, let alone facing
a messy death at the end of a gun.

The kid holding the gun was fresh from the front, so
fresh it looked like she still had all of her original fingers.
The dusty corridor of the hotel was tight. The girl had swung
up the gun just as Nyx came up from murdering one of
the hotel's security guards. Nyx let her gaze tarry on those
smooth fingers, fascinated with the final details of her own
death.

But the fingers gave the girl away: too straight, unblemished,
not a callous or crack or dirty fingernail. Those weren't the

hands of a kid who'd spent time with weapons in trenches. They weren't the hands of a kid who knew how to handle a big girl gun. Nyx followed the line of the fingers up to the trigger device, and the little round safety plug that was still inserted just behind it.

"Bloody amateur," Nyx said, and lunged.

The girl fumbled with the gun, frantically clicking the locked trigger. Nyx ripped the weapon away and bashed her on the side of the head with it. The girl stumbled against the bullet-riddled wall of the hallway and sat hard on her rump.

The door to the stairwell behind the girl popped open. Anneke burst in, rifle first. She brought with her the stink of gun oil and citronella. Anneke was a wiry, fearsome little woman with a face like a hammer. She was nearly as dark as a Chenjan, but far less modest, geared up in her dhoti and breast binding—though she really didn't need one—and little else. Her lips were smeared red with sen, and when she spoke, she showed crimson-stained teeth, like some demon from a Chenjan parable.

"Lotta fucking stairs, boss," Anneke said, huffing hard.

"You seen any more of her team down there?" Nyx asked. "We've got four more notes to fill."

"Naw, just the one in the morgue."

"Where's Khos?"

"Got tied up at the morgue with Rhys."

"Are you fucking kidding me?"

"Rhys said, uh, autopsies take time."

"She had a gun at my head."

"Bad place for it," Anneke said, "hardest place on the skull, there." Anneke spit on the floor next to the girl. The sputum was bloody red with sen. She nudged the girl with her boot. The girl squinted up at Anneke, vomited, and promptly passed out.

Nyx might have hit her too hard. Could have been Nyx down there on the floor, bloody and vomiting her guts out. If only.

"You sure this is the girl on the note?" Anneke said, picking at her teeth. "Real raw to pull a gun and not a swarm, you know? I mean, if she's a magician like she's supposed to be."

Nyx knelt beside the girl and pulled up the sleeves of her tunic. Both forearms bore thorny black tattoos that marked her as a member of the rogue Death Magicians. Nyx pushed back the dark mat of hair on the girl's head and found the shiny scar on her forehead where she must have had the other marks removed.

"Didn't have much time for conversation," Nyx said, "but the markings are right."

"Let's throw her in the trunk and eat," Anneke said. "I'm starving."

"Morgue first, then food."

"Story of my life, boss." Anneke slung her rifle over her shoulder and moved to do the same with the girl, but Nyx stopped her.

"Let me search her," Nyx said. She rifled through the woman's burnous and came out with a couple of notes, two death beetle larvae in matchboxes, and a pamphlet advertising the theatrical production of *The Horned Magician in Mushtallah* at the brothel next door. Nyx pocketed the cash and frowned at the rest. Part of her wanted to know what the kid was up to, but most of her just wanted to get paid and move on. She wasn't being paid to solve some mystery. She was being paid for a head. Several of them.

The girl was still out. Nyx figured any brain injury wouldn't be permanent. Probably. Once she turned the girl over, the junk in her pockets was somebody else's concern.

"Load her up," Nyx said.

Anneke hefted the girl up over her skinny shoulders and hauled her downstairs. Nyx followed, shoving the girl's contraband into the sack at her hip that she usually used for carting around heads. Girl should be thankful that the government paid more for her alive than dead. The Death Magicians were up to all kinds of scary shit. The Queen wanted her piece of that before she burned them all alive or whatever it was the government did to rogue magicians. Unlike bel dames—the elite assassins the government hired out—magicians were still largely policed by government agencies. She was fine not knowing what the government did to them after she brought them in.

Anneke rolled up their catch into a cooling blanket and then secured her in the trunk. Nyx strolled across the dusty street to the morgue just as mid-afternoon prayer began at the mosque at the edge of town. This was Shibaz, a northern border town. The call this far out from the big cities was a lot nicer. In Amtullah and places like that on the interior, dozens of mosques competed with one another, each starting the prayer just ahead of or behind the mosque down the street, until all you could hear was discordant warbling.

Nyx scanned the horizon. Six missing magicians could do a lot of damage on the interior, which begged the question as to why they had come all the way out here. The note she'd picked up made it sound like they were running illegal contraband—poison agents, shit like that. The border was a good place for that, she knew. She used to run her own illegal shit around the border towns, back before she got caught. Prison hadn't been all that inspiring. Mercenary work was more legal, but didn't pay as well. At least sometimes the view was good.

The smudge of low mountains to the north hinted at something other than desert out there, but Nyx knew better. By all counts, the northern desert went on and on, more wild and contaminated than anything south of here. She hoped she never had a reason to go any further north than this shitwater for whatever remained of her life. Thirty was such a great age for dying, really, before any of this shit could catch up to her. Maybe this job would do her in, finally. Rounding up a gang of rogue magicians with just one mediocre magician, a moralist shapeshifter, felon sniper, and snot-nosed kid of a com tech was pretty much doomed to fail. But weren't they always doomed to fail? It's what made it so exhilarating when they survived the day. Or the hour. The minute, really. This was why she drank so much.

"What you frowning at?" Anneke asked as they crossed the dusty street. The air smelled like wood smoke and brine—not a natural combination out here. It was most likely something left over from a spent burst heaved over from the Chenjan side of the front.

"Thinking about our odds," Nyx said.

"We can just take her and go back," Anneke said. "Figure her dead friend in the morgue, plus her, that's a good pay day."

"Naw," Nyx said. "Too easy."

"How much trouble we get into 'cause we're bored, boss?"

"A fucking lot," Nyx said.

"I do like trouble," Anneke said.

The local morgue was in the basement of the general store, a not uncommon combination in these little towns. Signs outside the store proudly proclaimed that they also offered moneylending, tattoo, and discount inoculation services. All three of those were either illegal or highly regulated services, which had signaled to Nyx that the owner would be more than happy to let them into the morgue to examine unclaimed bodies—for a fee. Which is, of course, what she'd done.

Nyx walked past the grocery clerk, who studiously pretended to be engrossed in the misty yakking projections oozing from the radio. Nyx descended the steps into the basement, Anneke close at her heels, and ducked to clear the low beam at the end of the stairs. She slid through a transparent filter, noticeable only because it made her skin prickle. Once through it, the smell of death clogged her nostrils, a smell so heavy that it felt like a physical force. The filter was an expensive thing for the shop owner to invest in, but clearly necessary to keep the patrons upstairs from fleeing en masse.

Khos, her shapeshifter, stood over the sink at the back, pressed back his mane of yellow dreads as he dry-heaved. Three bodies lay on stone slabs behind him. One of the bodies was relatively fresh, but the other was pretty far gone. Jars of mostly human organs lined the walls, just as they would in a magician's operating theater, and Nyx wondered if they did illegal tissue repair here as well. Should have that up on the door, too.

Rhys, Nyx's magician, was elbow deep in a pretty fresh corpse at the center of the room. Next to him was a skinny woman with tangled hair, the current clerk on duty. She gnawed at her nails while watching him work. Nyx had paid her five notes to get access down here. The clerk wasn't the owner, though, and getting caught down here could get messy.

"You got the goods?" Nyx said.

Rhys didn't look up, but the clerk did. She spit bits of her nails across the body. "I need you gone in an hour. I keep telling this fucker—" she sputtered.

"He's *my* fucker," Nyx said, "not yours. He answers to me. And I told him to stay until he found what that dead magician was smuggling in that meat suit of hers. My note is for the girl and her friends and the goods they're carrying. If they dropped the goods, I need to know."

"Here it is," Rhys said. The clerk took a step back as Rhys pulled a slimy black blob from the body's chest cavity.

"Bag it," Nyx said.

"I need to neutralize it."

"Can it travel without doing that?"

"Certainly, but there's a chance it could burst and give us all . . . whatever this is. You want to risk that?" His gaze met hers, all big eyes and long lashes, daring her to risk it so he could get all self-righteous about it.

"Do it," Nyx said.

A knocking sound came from the direction of the stairs.

"Now the fuck what?" Nyx said, turning. "This place is fucking closed until further—"

Nyx saw the big glowing barrel of a buzz gun pass over the threshold of the doorway. She didn't wait to see who wielded it. She'd already had enough of gun barrels in her face today. She pulled her pistol, let off two wild shots in the direction of the interloper, and rolled behind the nearest slab.

"Let it alone!" the woman on the stairs yelled. "Don't touch another body!"

Nyx chanced a look around the slab, gun first. The woman on the stairs was young, with the elaborate locs and dress of a Mhorian, but her bold features and complexion were Nasheenian. She was a skinny young thing, all sharp angles and elbows. The lack of flesh made her fearful expression that much more intense. Another fucking scared kid with a gun. Nyx was used to grizzled war vets and tough old cats here at the edge. What the fuck were all these kids doing out here? Back in her day . . .

"Drop that!" the woman said again, to Rhys.

Rhys raised his hands. The black bag of contraband rested on the body's bloodless hip.

"I've got a note on this body and its goods!" Nyx said. She hoped that would swing the barrel her way, but the woman kept it fixed at Rhys. Buzz guns were nasty things. They packed a big, poisonous punch. At this range, at Rhys's weight, the chances of him surviving a single blast without immediately rolling him into a magician's gym were slim.

While the barrel's trajectory didn't shift, the woman did spare a glance Nyx's way. Nyx considered tossing off a few more shots, but even at this distance she wasn't liable to hit anything. At best, she'd just be making a bigger distraction, and that hadn't worked so far.

"This is a government note," Nyx lied. It sort of was, kind of. It was a mercenary note, not a bel dame note, but it was close enough. She had been a government-sponsored bel dame once, running down deserters and other criminals for the government, but that hadn't lasted. She wasn't so good at rules. But this kid didn't need to know that. "You interfere, you go to prison. I've been to prison. It's not fun. What do you think they'd make of a kid like you?"

That swung the barrel.

Well, shit, Nyx thought, I need to try words more often.

The girl hefted the buzz gun Nyx's way, and stared straight down over the top of the barrel at her. Nyx flashed her teeth. Flexed her fingers on the hilt of her pistol. Anneke and Khos were better shots than her, but neither had moved as fast as Nyx had in bringing out a weapon, and that meant she was the only one in the party currently armed.

"I'm twenty-six," the woman said, and Nyx had a moment of dissonance at that. She looked nearly a decade younger.

"What," Nyx said, "you some rich kid? What the fuck are you doing down here mucking around in flesh? Go back and sit behind your filter and fuck your cousins."

"Could we lower the guns and talk, maybe?" Rhys said. He still had his gore-covered hands in the air.

"No," Nyx and the woman said at the same time.

"Put up your hands," the woman said to Nyx.

"I'm Rhys," Rhys said. "This is Khos, Anneke, Nyx, and over here is Khalida. But you know her, right? We're not here to cause trouble." Nyx snorted, and he glared at her. "I can show you the note for this woman, and others," Rhys said. "This is all perfectly legal and none of us wants you to get into trouble."

"There's been an outbreak," the woman said.

"Of what type?" Rhys said.

"Sin," she said.

Nyx sighed. "Oh, fuck, not another crazy—"

Rhys talked over her. "Sin?"

"I'm Abdiel," she said. "I'm doing . . . it's important research on the seat of the soul. These people are dying of sin. I need to study them so I can help others."

"You think this bag inside of her is . . . sin?" Rhys said.

"It's organic," she said. "It's native to the body. I was doing research here. Khalida seemed all right with that, but I suppose you paid more."

"Why the fuck is some Mhorian in a border town researching sin?" Nyx said.

"It's called the luz," Abdiel said. "It's supposed to be located somewhere in the spine. About the size of an almond. This is my life's work. I'm very close to a breakthrough."

"That's big enough that it should already be found," Nyx said. "Maybe it's not a bag of sin in there, just black market goods like it says on their notes. Maybe talk to your Mhorian elders and get another project."

"Dissection isn't permitted in Mhoria," Khos said. He was still painfully pale from all of his dry-heaving.

"What?" Nyx said. "Not even on dead people?"

Khos said, "No, not even on . . . dead people."

"So you're grave robbing for theology, then?" Nyx said.

"That's a big word for you, Nyx," Rhys said dryly.

"Fuck you," she said, then, to Abdiel, "The dead get burned up here for a reason. You can't keep them overnight. Bad shit happens. This one should have been burned already. It'll be walking in an hour."

"I assure you I dismember them in a way that makes it nearly impossible for them to become reanimated," Abdiel said.

"Nearly isn't good enough," Nyx said. Her hand was getting slick with sweat, but she dared not release her grip on the pistol.

"The government doesn't like my research," Abdiel said. "The Nasheenians find it quite valuable, but in Mhoria it's . . . repugnant. They say one should simply believe that the luz exists, though it is only theoretical. Belief should be enough. But I find there are too many questions left unanswered in the holy book. And it is such an easy question to answer! Much easier than many other riddles."

"What's the Mhorian holy book?" Nyx asked.

"The Sifarim," Khos said. "Collectively, that's what they're called. There are eight. For some people there are ten. My father really only considered four of them to be canonical. It . . . depends on who you ask."

"Yeah, all right, enough about books," Nyx said. "I don't know why I bothered asking."

"You say you have . . . other warrants," Abdiel said.

"Notes, yeah," Nyx said. "Looking for four more people involved in this racket. Not a sin racket. Well, I guess technically they have probably sinned, but it's not strictly sin I care about."

"You have a dead end," Abdiel said. "I can take you to where I collected this body. There were more, but . . . I wouldn't be able to study them all before they became reanimated. They may be the ones you're tracking. We could help each other."

"Why not go back alone?"

"Because it's ten kilometers west," she said, "and I don't

have transport. If you take me there, I could get them with just enough time to study them before I needed to dispose of them."

Nyx curled her lip. "The front," she said. "You found them at the front."

"They were caught in a border town," Abdiel said. "It's under Chenjan control now. That's why I need your help to get back."

"You have a government sponsor for this work?" Nyx said.

Abdiel shook her head. "I . . . this is a personal project."

"Fuck and fire," Nyx said, "I don't believe in a soul, or cutting up bodies for no good reason. You aren't even saving their parts for anything. You're worse than a magician. You nuts?"

"I'm perfectly sane," Abdiel said. "What do you care, though, about my purpose or my mental health, if I can get you what you want? That's what you are, you said. A mercenary."

Rhys interrupted, thankfully. "Could we put the guns down now?" he said.

"Her first," Abdiel said.

Nyx slid her pistol across the floor. She had another just like it on her other hip, and a scattergun strapped across her back, hidden by the length of her brown burnous, but it made it look like she was ready to play nice. The gesture didn't generally work with other mercenaries or bel dames, but dumb kids fell for it every time.

Abdiel took a step back into the stairwell. Nyx got up, hands raised.

"So," Nyx said, "you ready to trust a bunch of bloodthirsty mercenaries?"

"Not you," Abdiel said, and she gestured to Khos with the gun. "Him."

The gun went off.

The expression on Abdiel's face when the gun roared was almost as startled as Nyx's. A massive glowing arc of fiery shrapnel scraped through the air as the thunderous boom of the gun shook every body in the room. The stink of ozone and burnt lemon made Nyx's eyes water. The kick of the gun took Abdiel off her feet. She landed hard against the stairs and let out a shriek.

Nyx dove for Abdiel. She ripped the gun from Abdiel's hands and disarmed it, removing the internal and external trigger mechanisms. A deep, yowling cry reverberated through the room. Nyx's gut clenched, and she broke out in a cold sweat.

Khos was keening.

Anneke slid up next to Nyx, rifle out. Nyx put her hand up and batted the barrel away. "Just watch her," Nyx said, raising her voice over the sound of Khos's pain. "Make sure she doesn't do anything else stupid."

Nyx went over to where Khos lay in a pool of blood and piss. He was a big man, and his writhing had left smears of runny crimson all over the grimy floor. The blazing shrapnel from the buzz gun had torn open his left side, shredding his left arm and seeding it with green, gooey spores that were rapidly sinking their tendrils into his flesh.

Rhys knelt over Khos, one hand on Khos's right shoulder, the other hovering over the wound. "He's going necrotic," Rhys said.

"No shit," Nyx said. "Can you fix it?"

"Not on my own. I need to evacuate him."

Nyx glanced back at Anneke, and the little cowering clerk, Khalida, who had positioned herself under the sink, making herself as small as possible. Good plan on her part.

"I need a three-person team to retrieve those bodies," Nyx said to Rhys. Khos was still yowling, but she tuned it out. She had gotten very good at tuning out cries of distress. "You drive him over to the squat where Taite is and have Taite drive him to Kashan. They've got a good magician's gym there run by a woman named Tabriza. She owes me a favor."

"Taite's just a kid," Rhys said. "You can't put him in a bakkie with Khos like this. Who will keep this wound stable? I'll go with Khos."

"I need a magician," Nyx said.

"Nyx—"

"You're always saying my name when you talk to me, like I don't know it. You work for me, not Khos."

Khos jerked on the floor, flailing his bad arm. Blood spurted.

Rhys pulled off his burnous. "Help me get this around him," he said to Nyx, and she did.

Khos was both heavy and strong, a bitter combination in his current state. He took a swing at Nyx with his good arm, meaty and clumsy, and she easily ducked it. Anneke came over to help, but Nyx waved her back. "I need you to clear the way up there," Nyx said. "Take point. I don't want to be ambushed by magicians." Then, "Abbi," Nyx said. "A little help. You, too, Khalida. Make yourself useful, you little shit."

Anneke loped up the steps to clear their way.

Nyx could have dragged Khos's deadweight up the steps,

but fighting him while he bled and howled was a little much for her to tackle on her own. Nyx wrapped her arm around him and pulled his good one over her shoulder. Foamy blood oozed from his wounds and spattered his mouth. He heaved, spewing vomit that reeked of rancid milk. How he still had anything in his stomach was anyone's guess. He jerked in her arms.

"Little help!" Nyx said, again, and Abdiel and Khalida finally came up behind and gripped him as he keeled over. Abdiel was shaking like a thorn bug. Nyx figured cutting up bodies all day required a different sort of stomach than hauling around live, bloody ones.

The five of them hauled Khos up the stairs and loaded him into the bakkie half a block away. It was the longest half block Nyx had walked in some time. She kept hearing the whine of artillery. She scanned the sky, saw nothing, figured it was phantoms again. She sometimes saw boys with their faces mashed in, and a bloody river spouting from her own arm while a magician sobbed and told her how sorry he was, so sorry, but she had to be rebuilt . . . Ghosts from some other time, some other life, dusty as funeral ashes.

"Drive," Nyx told Rhys, and slammed the bakkie door. She leaned into the open window, said, "And you come back quick. We've got four more notes to bring in. You got it?"

He said nothing, but the look he gave her was ice. He pressed the juice pedal, and the bakkie barked away into the street.

Nyx sat down on the curb. Anneke took position next to her. They were both covered in sticky blood, rancid puke, and the little green spores that had settled into Khos's open wounds. Nyx wanted a bath and a whisky and a fuck, not necessarily in that order.

"Think he'll make it?" Anneke said.

"Shifters are cheap," Nyx said, but her memory disgorged an image of Khos between her legs, his big hands on her ass, and she had to fill her mind again with his souring body, resigning herself to the likelihood of his death. Plenty of people on her teams died. Plenty of people she had fucked died. This was Nasheen. This was what it was to be alive in this place, in this time. You accepted it or you went crack fucking mad and died an old woman in the desert, babbling to her ghosts. "I don't care," Nyx said. She pushed herself to her feet and pointed at Abdiel. "When Rhys gets back, we're going hunting."

But Rhys didn't come back.

Taite did.

When Taite walked into the front of the general store where they were all eating, Nyx threw a pan full of yams at him. He ducked. The clay pan broke neatly into two big pieces, spraying mashed yam all over the store counter. Abdiel clapped her hands over her mouth and tumbled out of her seat. Khalida, the little clerk, shrieked. Anneke kept eating, undeterred, her rifle leaning against the table at her elbow.

"Bloody hell!" Taite said.

"It sure will be if Rhys isn't behind you," Nyx said.

"He's taking Khos to a magician's theater. He's half dead. Did you see him?"

"I saw him," Nyx said. "Fuck." She sat back down at the stained table at the back of the store, rattling the rest of the cookware. Anneke put out a hand to steady the pot of softened dog meat.

"You saw what happened to Khos and you're still running this note?" Taite said. Taite was a skinny, pock-marked kid, all knees and elbows, not much out of his teens. He was supposed to be her com tech, kept safe behind a com console where he could spy on and transmit messages sent by bug pheromones, beetles, and other secretions. This wasn't a great place for him. She had absolutely no use for a com tech on the battlefield. He'd get shot immediately. But once again, Rhys was fucking up and giving her no choice. She needed to fire the little shit magician and get somebody who would fucking listen.

"Don't ask questions right now," Nyx said. "You have the bakkie? You bring guns and com equipment?"

"Yes, but Khos—"

"Stay focused, Taite."

"A team member is down, I—"

"He's being treated," Nyx said. "We carry the fuck on. There are four death magicians out there and this little fuck over here knows where they fucking are. So shut up and make yourself useful. You'll drive. And you," Nyx said, jabbing her finger at Abdiel. "You ride up front with me."

They all piled into the bakkie, minus Khalida, who slammed and locked the door the moment they were all in the street.

"That was not fair payment!" Khalida wailed after them. "Not for what I went through!"

"You're lucky you lived," Nyx shouted back, because she couldn't stand ungrateful people.

"West," Abdiel said from her place up front, squeezed between Taite and Nyx on the torn front seat. Bullets slid around on the floor with a couple of food wrappers and half a can of lubricant.

"That narrows it down," Nyx said.

Anneke slammed the door in the back and set her rifle beside her.

"Drive," Nyx said.

Taite fumbled with the starter. Nyx tapped her fingers on the dash while he sweated it out. Finally, she snapped, "Get in the back. I'll fucking drive."

He ducked out and slid into the back next to Anneke, her rifle now set between them. Nyx hit the juice and they were off, spewing dust and dead bugs behind them.

Taite crowded up behind Nyx. She felt his hot breath on her neck as he said, "So what the hell are we doing?"

"Hunting sin," Nyx said.

"The seat of the soul," Abdiel said.

"She says there are other bodies out there," Nyx said. "Probably our magicians. Already dead, even."

"West is the front, though," Taite said. "Bloody piss, this is the third suicide mission in as many months. Some of us like being alive."

"Real perceptive crew I have here," Nyx said. She tapped the steering wheel and reached for the radio. The radio hissed and spit watery yellow images of talking heads, then cut out. Just her luck.

"Shit," Taite said. "Rhys didn't say it was the front. That's why he didn't come. You know he's probably not on the right side of Chenja."

"Yeah, well, we sure as fuck aren't either," Nyx said.

"We got any liquor?" Anneke asked.

"Under your seat," Nyx said. It was half the reason she couldn't wait to get back on the road. Anneke yanked out the bottle, took a swig, and handed it over to Nyx.

Nyx drank, and passed it back. Something whined overhead, and Nyx peered out over the street. She swerved around a dead dog and turned out past a big sign that said, *Seven kilometers to contested territory. Go with God.*

No other place to go out there than with God, Nyx thought.

"Why are you looking for souls?" Taite said, still leaning up on the back of the front seat.

"It's my vocation," Abdiel said. She played with the edge of her yellow Mhorian robe, which was frayed and dusty. "My research, in Mhoria, is on the soul, and where it resides in our bodies. But as your . . . your Mhorian man said, they don't allow autopsies in Mhoria. They do in Nasheen, though, of course. So I came here to complete my research." She reached into her robe and pulled out a little book. Nyx glanced over at it as Abdiel thumbed it open. Inside were detailed drawings of dissected bodies. Spines featured prominently.

"So have you found the soul?" Taite asked. He pointed at one of the spines. "It's there in the spine?"

"Well . . . there are some . . . differences, between Nasheenians and Mhorians."

Nyx snorted. "Is that so? You think you haven't found this place where the soul is because Nasheenians don't have souls, is that it? Blaming us because you believed some rumor in your holy book?"

"That's not what I said."

"That's what I heard," Nyx said.

"Let's be logical," Abdiel said. She tucked her book away again. "All of our holy writings discuss the presence of the house of the soul, the luz. It's thought it may be at the base of the spine. In a similar area where you pulled out those black bags of toxins. I think the two are related."

"Those were just border cats," Nyx said, "you know, people who smuggle things in their bodies. People doing black work. I've done work like that. It's got nothing to do with clearing sin out of the soul, or whatever mystical organ you think houses the soul. If it did, you'd have found this lux or whatever—"

"Luz," Abdiel said.

"Right," Nyx said, "you'd have found it right there, or Rhys would have. But you haven't. So it's just a story."

"It's not that crazy," Taite said. "Ras Tiegans have been looking for where the soul is housed for a long time. I mean, no one's found it, obviously. But lots of people still talk about it. The heart, the brain, and there are all sorts of other organs that we don't even know much about. Why couldn't they house the soul?"

"Because if you took them out," Nyx said, "that person would be soulless. Better question is, what makes somebody soulless? How do you say I've got a soul and you don't?"

"Or the other way around," Taite murmured.

"We're all from different worlds, originally," Abdiel said. "Certainly we are all very different looking people, with very different views of the world. Why is it so strange to posit that our anatomy is different? The skeletal structure of Drucians is highly abnormal—"

"What, are we comparing them to you, or Nasheenians?" Nyx said. "First Families, or grunts? Like, what's your definition of normal? Man, woman, somebody in between? You tell me. I'll need a pretty firm definition that'll probably only fit five people anyway."

"For a grunt, as you say," Abdiel said, "you get very tangled up in specifics. What do you care about my research? You said you only care about the bodies."

"I've seen how First Families use the idea of good breeding to justify sending us all off to war," Nyx said, "to get ground up by the machine while their smooth-faced kids lounge around at home eating figs. So yeah, I know your kind."

"*My* kind?"

"The kind that needs to justify all the shit they do. At least I'm honest. I kill people for money. I don't pretend it's something prettier, like looking for a fucking soul. You go cutting out parts of people to see if they have any soul left, you pretend it's a noble cause. But it's no nobler than mine. You're just a butcher."

Taite leaned over to Anneke. Nyx watched him in the rear-view mirror.

"Half a note says Nyx sleeps with her," Taite said.

"I'm not taking that bet," Anneke said, taking another pull on the whisky bottle.

"Oh, shut your shit," Nyx said.

———

The season was spring, but most of the rain out here in the central desert came in the fall, not the spring. That meant it was bearably warm but parched-mouth dry. When dusk hit the dry air was going to get bitterly cold, and Nyx didn't want to be out here when that happened. She watched the horizon while Abdiel nattered on about her research, eagerly answering Taite's questions. The People of the Book always had more things in common than not. Nyx wondered when they would all just give up and admit that. Too easy, really. There were certainly plenty of people she would never forgive for old ills, no matter how much it would benefit her. Because fuck those people.

Anneke had her gun propped up on her lap now, whisky bottle between her legs, window rolled down, doing her own surveillance in the back. The desert scrub turned to pitted dunes as massive as First Family housing complexes. Fragments of burnt-out old cities and abandoned weapons, ancient contagion sensors, and mangled military vehicles lay scattered across the contested ground. Nyx had yet to see a military blockade, but there could be rogue squads hiding out behind any of these dunes.

"I love the desert here," Abdiel said. "The dunes are like mountains."

"I like an unobstructed view of where the fuck I'm going," Nyx said. She chewed at the dry, ragged skin of her lips, wishing she had more sen to dull the increasing sense of unease she was getting this close to a hot zone.

"This turn, up here," Abdiel said. Nyx saw smoke in the distance for the first time, little fingers curling skyward. The tracks here along the road were fresher, and there were signs of recent fighting. The air smelled of burnt copper and saffron, and that got her skin crawling. They were still a good way off from the official front, but this was heavily contested territory. As she turned off the track she slowed down and finally stopped once she saw the black smear of the village in the distance. Little settlements like this were routinely gutted and overrun every five or six years. The sort of people who came back and resettled tended to be those who traded in guns and illegal genetic material, as well as the very poor and the very desperate. The magicians had likely been here to make some kind of contact where they could turn over the toxic bags in their guts for cash, or whatever else they wanted.

"We're walking the rest of the way," Nyx said, cutting the juice to the bugs.

"But—" Abdiel began.

"If this town was taken, the road's likely mined now," Nyx said. "Even if it isn't, you know, better safe than splattered on the road." She glanced back at Taite. "See, now? Not so suicidal."

"You just don't want to go out stupid," Taite said.

He wasn't wrong about that.

Nyx popped open the trunk, half expecting to see her captured magician friend asphyxiated in there, forgotten, but Rhys hadn't fucked her over completely. He'd removed their captive and stuffed the trunk full of guns, bursts, water, and other desert gear. Maybe she wouldn't fire him just yet. She could be merciful when it suited her.

Nyx tossed Anneke a bandolier of additional ammo and refilled her pistols. She hefted a big acid gun and gave Taite a shotgun.

"What should I use?" Abdiel asked.

"Your wits," Nyx said, and shut the trunk. She didn't need another team member obliterated by Abdiel's poor trigger control.

Nyx put Anneke on point. She was little and had better vision and better aim than Nyx. Nyx came next, and had Taite take the rear, behind Abdiel.

"Try to stay about fifteen paces apart," Nyx said. "That way if we hit a mine it won't take us all out."

"That's reassuring," Taite said.

"Should be," Nyx said.

When it came to roadside bombs, there were signs to look for. Sometimes you'd see kids out there watching the roads who'd stick their fingers in their ears when you got close to a mined section, anticipating a blast. Chenjans liked to stick bombs inside piles of dead Nasheenians, so anybody trying to do body retrieval would get taken out, too. Magicians who triggered bombs generally had to have line of sight, so she scanned for robed figures with hands outstretched or lips moving, staring far too hard at their current position.

But it was eerily quiet out here. Even as they advanced on the village and the acrid smell of smoke got thicker, Nyx heard and saw very little. The suns were still up, but the first sunset wasn't more than an hour away. She really didn't want to lose the light.

"My sister served so I didn't have to," Abdiel said.

Her voice sounded loud in the quiet, making Nyx start. "What the fuck?" Nyx hissed. "Figured you were raised in Mhoria. And what the fuck does that have to do with shit now?"

Abdiel lowered her voice. "My father is Mhorian," she said. "We were born here, but went to school there, and of course, my studies extended much longer than my sister's, but only because she took my place here. I could have been extradited and made to serve. I'm just saying this because . . . you should know I haven't done this before. I mean, I just drove out here on a tip. I didn't think about bombs or anything."

"You didn't have to tell me," Nyx said. "Your poor gun safety already gave away how much experience you have."

"She was serving the last year of her service when she died," Abdiel said. "A year I should have served."

"Never feel bad about other people's choices," Nyx said. She thought of Khos, screaming, half his body torn in two, and flashed back to sitting astride him again, fucking him like it was the end of the world for them both, coddled by the fuzzy warmth of too much liquor. He spit blood, she was covered in blood . . .

Nyx inhaled sharply and kicked herself back, narrowing her vision at the next curve in the road. Sometimes what was real and what was memory all got tangled up together, like living your whole life at once. Fucking Khos had been months ago, but she hadn't fucked anyone since, and her mind tore at the memory like a rabid dog now that he was most likely dying. Maybe she would fuck Abdiel after all, just to put some other memory over that one.

"She sacrificed herself," Abdiel said, "so that I could be some great tissue mechanic or organic philosopher. But I'm failing at that, too, aren't I?"

"I'm not a fucking head magician," Nyx said. "Cry about your problems to someone else. I have my own. And I have

four bodies to bring in. Your sister didn't sacrifice herself
for shit." She paused, listening to the wind over the dunes
to either side of them. "When you're out there, if you're a
woman, you talk about what you'll do when you get back. She
was planning a life, after."

"That doesn't make me feel better."

"It wasn't meant to. It's selfish to make somebody's life or
death about you. It was her life. Let her have lived it as she
chose."

Anneke raised a fist and halted.

Nyx waved her hand at Taite and Abdiel. "Hush now," she
said.

"What you got?" Nyx said.

"Bodies," Anneke said. "She was right about the fucking
bodies."

There were a lot of fucking bodies. Nyx had seen her fair
share, but this was . . . a lot. Likely the whole village and all
of its assorted mercenaries and criminals and poor refugees.
When she'd been at the front she had heard about purges like
this committed by both sides, but never seen it in person so
soon after it happened. The bones were usually well bleached
by the time she came through with her unit of sappers. The
stench of death was so strong it made her eyes water. The
only relief they had was that the wind was blowing the other
way.

"This many dead when you came out here?" Nyx asked,
poking at a corpse with her foot. She stood at the base of the

pile of bodies, which were stacked half as high as the nearest dune, almost twice her height. The heads and cocks were piled separately in two other piles. It had taken her a while to realize what the cock pile was at all, it was already so riddled with beetles and blood worms. She had a hard time imagining there were enough cocks in this village to make a pile, but from the looks of some of the gleaming green suits tangled in the heap, there were soldiers in there, too. Plenty of cocks on Nasheenian soldiers.

"Yes," Abdiel said. "That's why I thought, maybe, the rest of your bodies were here. The Chenjans must have come through here and just . . . killed everyone"

"What the fuck were you doing out here?" Nyx said.

"I told you, I—"

"You could get bodies anywhere."

"You know that isn't true," Abdiel said. "Nasheen has strict protocol around body disposal, as you said. I had no choice but to come out here and take unclaimed dead—"

"Of course they were fucking unclaimed," Nyx said, "everybody they ever fucking knew is dead *here*! You came in before Nasheenian body crews could retrieve and decontaminate these people. You're a fucking body snatcher. That's fucked up."

"You, too, collect bodies for a living," Abdiel said, and sniffed. "I don't see what we do as being terribly different."

"She has a point," Taite said.

"It's different," Nyx said.

"I dunno, boss," Anneke said. For the first time, Nyx noticed that Anneke had brought the whisky bottle with her. Anneke chugged at it now and returned it to a loop at her belt. Was Nyx the only one taking this shit seriously?

"Oh, shut up," Nyx said. "Taite, help me dig through these. You remember the marks?"

Taite wrinkled his nose. "Yeah, I remember."

"Stay on watch, Anneke," Nyx said. She pointed up to a far dune. "I want you on point up there. Something happens to us, you go back to town and get reinforcements."

"Uh . . . like who, boss?" Anneke said.

"Anyone not drunk," Nyx said.

Nyx yanked off her burnous, got to work as Anneke trudged up behind a far dune and settled in. The bodies had been there awhile, dead as long as the one back at the morgue, but these had been out in the sun longer. Skin sloughed off bone. Scalps were starting to pool out behind the heads they'd once been attached to. And the bugs—so many writhing, chittering masses of bugs that Nyx was surprised there was any flesh left at all. How long had they been there? A couple days, more? There were maggots, so it had to be a few days, at least. She knew far more about the lifecycle of most bugs than she cared to admit. If Rhys had been here he could have waved the bugs away and told them to go eat each other or something.

"Got one," Taite said. He pushed over a corpse and hauled out another one beneath it.

Nyx waded over and checked the tattoos. "Yeah, that's one," Nyx said.

"Can I open it first?" Abdiel said. Her eagerness creeped Nyx out, but she nodded.

"Just don't spray any of that black goo on us."

Abdiel knelt next to the body. She unrolled a mat of tools that Nyx had taken to be a bedroll, revealing incredibly expensive metal scalpels and saws.

"Your parents rich?" Nyx said.

"My work pays well," she said.

"So you do sell off the bodies when you're done," Nyx said.

"We all have to make a living."

Nyx snorted and went back to work. Could all four really have ended up here? "The fuck they doing out here?" she muttered, and shook her head. This was a retrieval, nothing more. Whatever these death magicians had cooked up, it wasn't her job to solve it. Some days that fact couldn't dissuade her from peering into it, but today she didn't find the mystery that tantalizing. She just wanted the bodies and a bath. Instead, her old bel dame training kept pulling at her, long after they had thrown her out. But butchers didn't need to know the reasons behind things. Butchers just needed to do their jobs.

"This fucking job," Nyx muttered.

"Isn't two enough?" Taite said.

Abdiel slit open the body in front of her. Nyx was breathing through her mouth already, but gagged all the same. She turned back to the pile, and gagged again. Shit, she was going soft.

A heavy masculine voice barked from behind her, "Put your trust in God."

The accent was Chenjan.

Nyx slowly raised her hands. She spread her fingers, to show she had nothing concealed between them, and turned.

Abdiel squealed and dropped her scalpel. Her hands came up a lot faster. Taite popped his head up over the pile and froze.

A six-person Chenjan squad had come up behind them from the direction of one of the mortared houses. Nyx cursed herself for not clearing any of the remaining structures before they started on the bodies. Rookie mistake. She blamed liquor and dead bodies and Rhys. Always blame Rhys. The squad members were dressed in organic suits that blended with the sand. If Nyx looked too close, the bodies blurred with the scenery and made her eyes hurt.

"State your purpose," the man said. Chenjan man. Nyx wanted to bash in his face and make him bleed. She'd done the same to hundreds of men just like him. Anneke had a rifle, which would have been useful for taking out one or two targets, but she wasn't going to be able to snipe six of them before they blew Nyx and Taite and Abdiel away. Nyx hoped Anneke was already crawling back toward the road.

"Just a little friendly grave robbing," Nyx said.

The Chenjan men advanced. "On your knees," the man said again. As he got closer, Nyx could see some of his face. Young kids, all, not more than twenty if a day.

"Gotta ask nice," Nyx said.

He tried to butt her in the head with his gun, but she dodged it. He swept her legs out from under her instead, and she let him, because fighting him when his friends were all out of her range with guns trained on her wasn't smart even for her.

Taite had his hands in the air now, too. He looked like he might shit his pants. He may already have. Stupid kid to bring to the front. This was among her stupidest ideas, and she was paying for it now.

"We're going to disarm you," the man said.

"Sure thing," Nyx said. They could certainly try.

The men removed all of Nyx's visible weapons, even the poisoned needles in her hair, which impressed her. But they missed the razorblades hidden in her sandals. Only bel dames ever found those, and occasionally some of the palace security techs.

The men marched Nyx, Taite, and Abdiel to a bunker back out behind a mass of ruined structures. The ceiling was caving in the back, and the whole thing was riddled with bullet holes. Nyx thought it might have been an old munitions storage building. Now it smelled like this lot had been pissing and shitting in it for days.

"Stay quiet," the Chenjan man said. He was still the only one who had spoken to them. The others could be golems, for all Nyx knew.

They shut them up in the back in a closet or smaller storage area of some kind. The air was warm and close. The darkness was shot through with light from stray bullet holes that had penetrated the mud-brick exterior.

"Will they kill us?" Abdiel whispered.

Nyx ignored her. She paced the cramped space—six paces by four paces—looking for a way out. "Here," she said, pointing to a crumbled bit of the wall at the back. "This place was hit a couple of times. It's not structurally sound here."

"So?" Taite said.

"Dig," Nyx said.

He did, and so did Abdiel. When they had a bit cleared away, Nyx crouched down to help. But there were two big solid beams of bug secretions that framed the mud-brick filling, and the narrow opening was only big enough for Taite. By then it was full dark, and Nyx was sweating over how long it would take the Chenjans to realize who the fuck she was and come out and kill her. Or, worse, take her back into Chenja with them. All this trouble over a couple months' worth of rent. Shit.

"Go," Nyx told Taite. "Two kilometers further west, there's usually a Nasheenian station."

"Everything is dead out here," Taite said. "You don't know they're out there. When was the last time you were at the front?"

"There's always a Nasheenian post nearby," Nyx said, which was mostly true. "You just tell them 'my life for a thousand,' and you tell them where to make the strike."

"A strike? Are you kidding?" Taite said. "They're as likely to kill you as save you!"

Abdiel grabbed at her arm. "Don't call a strike," she said. "The bodies. They will ruin the bodies."

"Fuck the bodies," Nyx said. "We're all going to be fucking bodies unless we get out of here. You need to know when to cut your losses in a run like this. We're cutting our losses." Then, to Taite, "Go before they come back."

She only had to ask twice more. Taite squeezed through the opening and lit off across the dark desert.

Flare away, Nyx thought. That was it. That was all she had to play. Nyx slumped against the side of the bunker and put her head in her hands. Rhys should have been out here with them. She should have insisted. No magician, no shifter, just her and this dumb bedazzled academic and Taite, who couldn't slap his ass with both hands outside a com room.

Abdiel said, "You think they'll listen to him, if he finds them? The Nasheenians?"

"Who knows?" Nyx said. "He's a foreign man. I wouldn't listen to him."

"Then what's the point?"

"One of us lives," Nyx said.

Abdiel narrowed her eyes. "You care about that? Other people living?"

"Why wouldn't I?"

"The way you treated that other man . . . The Mhorian man."

"I had a job to do then. Now I'm just cutting losses."

Abdiel didn't seem to have anything to say to that. Nyx settled in to get some sleep. The Chenjan squad would need to get orders on what to do with them, torture or hold them, so they had some time.

"Do you think," Abdiel said, and Nyx sighed because shit, this might be her last night to get any sleep ever at all, "that Mhorian man . . . what's his name?"

"Khos," Nyx said.

"He's part of your team?"

"Yeah."

"You are not bound to him?'

"No."

"You don't care for him?"

"No, clearly."

"You—"

"You seriously want to try and hook up with the man you probably killed?"

"Are you certain—"

"Listen, woman, you can fuck him and eat him for all I care," Nyx said. As if this whole job could get any stranger. "I've got shit to do. Let's stay focused, get some sleep. They'll most likely torture and kill us after morning prayer."

"This was all my idea," she said, hugging her knees to her chest. "It's my fault we're all going to die here."

"For fuck's sake," Nyx said. "Stop making this all about you again. I needed what I needed. You needed what you needed. That's it."

"There was no sin in that body," Abdiel said.

"What?"

"The one I looked at before the Chenjans came. No bag of sin."

"I told you it was just a toxin."

"I'll find the luz," Abdiel said.

"I'm sure Khos can help you find it," Nyx said. "He knows where plenty of things are." If he was still alive. She rubbed her eyes. She was thinking about fucking him again, which wasn't productive. She tried to think about fucking somebody else, but it always ended up being someone on her team, so she thought of Radeyah, dear sweet Radeyah, her lover from back in Mushirah, and her nimble tongue, and that was enough to take her off to sleep.

The thumping of heavy burst fire outside was enough to take her right back out of it.

Abdiel hugged the ground. She was talking in Mhorian, reciting something like a prayer.

Nyx jumped up and went to the door. Tried to listen. Nothing. She put herself flat against the wall beside it and waited.

One of the Chenjans burst in, gun already drawn, more rookie moves, shit, and Nyx hammered the gun from his hands and beat him in the face with it. She shot the man behind him and pushed her way topside.

Abdiel squealed behind her, but Nyx wasn't paying attention. She didn't need Abdiel anymore and she could fall over and die for all Nyx cared. Nyx had the bodies and the shit inside of them. She didn't need answers. She was a fucking mercenary, and it was time to act the part.

Nyx fought her way up, shooting the two Chenjan officers at the top of the formation in rapid succession. Above her, the sky was alive with red and yellow and violet bursts, great sparkling streamers of light that cast dangerous gases and contagions all around the field. Nyx had been inoculated against all Nasheenian contagions. The likelihood that any of them would slow her down was very low, but she couldn't say that about anybody else on the field. When the magicians put her back together again, they cured a lot of shit. Maybe even cured her of a soul. Who knew?

She scrambled back down the formation and sprinted across the debris of the town streets toward the bakkie. The light from the bursts was enough to maneuver by. She heard screaming behind her, but she did not turn. She ran. She ran and she ran while the sky exploded behind her. She was heedless of everything but her own breath, the pounding of her feet, heedless of mines or other squads or even her own team. Let it all burn behind her.

Nyx slid to a halt near the bakkie and tore open the door. The trunk had been rifled, but she didn't bother checking it to see what was left. Speed was more important than firepower right now. She started the bakkie up and hit the juice, and powered it up to the pile of bodies, not caring about the mines anymore. Just the bodies. Always, the bodies.

By the time she staggered out of the cab, Abdiel had

reached the body pile. She was huffing her guts out, coughing great foamy gouts of spit and bile and other, less savory things.

"Nyx," she huffed. "Nyx . . ."

Nyx hauled the partially autopsied body into the trunk, smearing mortifying flesh and bugs. She went for the next one just as Abdiel fell over next to the bakkie. Nyx grabbed the other body and stuffed it into the trunk. Pair that with the live one back at the storefront with Rhys and the one in the morgue and that wasn't a bad day's work. She could pay the rent and move on to the next job. Might not be clean, but it was a living.

Nyx yanked open the door to the bakkie and then slid inside.

Abdiel reached a hand to her. Her face was illuminated in a brilliant blue burst of light. Nyx gazed down at her and for one searing moment Abdiel was not some stranger, but her sister, Kine, grasping for her hand after falling into an abandoned well. How long ago had that been? Twenty-five years? Longer. Her mind was dredging it all up now at the worst possible moment. She needed action. She couldn't stay stuck in some dead past.

"You aren't my sister!" Nyx screamed at Abdiel. The bursts pounded overhead. "You aren't real! You aren't a person!"

"Nyx!" Abdiel gasped.

Nyx pounded on the steering wheel and screamed in frustration. She screamed at Abdiel, and Rhys, and Chenjans in general. Most of all, she screamed at the war, and what it had turned them all into.

"Goddammit!" Nyx yelled. She opened the door, grabbed

Abdiel under the arms, and pulled her into the bakkie beside her.

Then Nyx hit the juice again and powered away from the contaminated village, heading out toward the west, the front, and the Nasheenian squad she had promised Taite would be out there.

She found Taite four kilometers later, huffing his way along the road, sweaty and exhausted. Nyx unlocked the back door.

"Good job," she said.

"What?" he said, heaving himself inside. He fumbled under the seat for a water bulb.

"The bursts," she said.

"I didn't find anyone," Taite said. "I was coming back to try and rescue you myself."

"Well," Nyx said, "glad that wasn't how it went down."

She spun the bakkie into reverse and did a wide turn. She slammed two of the four pedals, filling the cistern with so much juice that a lot of live bugs spit out the back end along with the dead ones. It had been Nyx's lucky day—bursts from some other raid had given her the cover she needed to bag her catch.

They drove in near silence for some time, listening only to the whir of the bugs in the cistern and Abdiel's hacking.

Nyx leaned out the window and yelled for Anneke as they wound closer to the border. Anneke would stay out of sight of the road, but not far from it.

A figure leapt out of a dune ahead of them, and Nyx slammed on the brakes.

Taite opened the door, and Anneke got in. She was dusty

and thirsty. Her bottle was empty. She dug around in the back for water. "Fuck of a run, boss," Anneke said.

Nyx powered the bakkie down the road. "Got lucky," she said.

"Good thing," Anneke said. "Shit, I was making shit time. You'd be dead."

"I know," Nyx said. She wondered if that'd be better.

Abdiel spit up blood and shrieked.

"She all right?" Taite asked.

"No," Nyx said. "She'll need a magician."

"Can Rhys do it?"

"Yeah," she said.

"That's a long drive," Taite said.

"It's a long night," Nyx said.

Nyx drove and drove, until the light in the sky was only a memory, a flashing at the edges of her vision, like every other piece of her past.

"I don't understand," Abdiel said.

They sat in the back of Nyx's storefront back in Mushmura. Khos was still healing up with real magicians, and they wouldn't be able to pick him up for another day or two. The bodies they'd recovered from the little shit town were laid out on the floor. Abdiel was sitting upright on a cot, holding a foamy cup of green bug juice in her hand. She had gotten some color back in her face, but her hands still shook. Rhys leaned in the doorway at the front of the store, arms crossed, pistols visible. Nyx liked it when she could see the bone hilts of those pistols. It reminded her he was only completely useless when it pleased him. As it was, she wanted to slap the shit out of him.

Abdiel stared across the floor at the open chest cavity of the body she had partially autopsied. "I wanted it to be more than that," she said. "There needs to be more than this, doesn't there? But all these spines are clean. No luz. How could so many get it all so wrong?"

"Maybe the soul's just somewhere else," Nyx said.

Rhys tried to catch her eye, but Nyx turned away from him and pulled on her burnous.

"I need some air," Nyx said, but Rhys followed her out to the porch. They had settled in here for another night and a day, and it was dusk again. She hadn't slept in all that time. Two days now, without sleeping? She'd lost count. Maybe that was what all the hallucinating was about. Why the past was clawing at her more than usual.

Rhys stood beside her, so close she could feel the heat of him. She wanted to take his arm and bury her face in his chest and breathe in the scent of him for the rest of the night. "I couldn't believe what I heard in there," he said.

"Yeah, djinn are real," Nyx said. "So were the Seven Sleepers, and also that guy with the green teeth I dreamed about last night."

"Were you trying to soothe her? 'Maybe the soul's just somewhere else'? Really? You?" His tone was far too full of mirth.

"I don't believe anymore, Rhys. Big empty place where God used to be—in me and in the world. But I remember what it was like. Not my place to take it away from some kid. The world does that well enough on its own."

"God doesn't go away," Rhys said, "even if you do."

"Oh, spare me the shit," she said, but her heart wasn't in it.

"You wouldn't take God from her, but you try and take him from me?"

"Rhys," she said, and she turned so their arms touched. "I take the piss with you, but when have I ever told you to leave God like I did?"

He stared at her with his big, dark eyes, and for a long moment she let herself get lost there. Then the fear cut through her. The fear that if she didn't look away now, and shit on him, that he'd look at her the way Khos did, and then she really would have to leave him and his God in a ditch somewhere the same way she was willing to leave Khos. And then how would Rhys look at her, after she let him think she had a soul and then broke his heart?

So she looked away. The evening was cool and dry, and Nyx felt invincible. The world felt a little brighter. She stepped lighter, here. Breathed deeper. Fuck, she felt so good after a close job where she'd almost bitten it. So fucking alive.

The call to prayer sounded. She shifted away from Rhys, so she could no longer feel his heat.

Saved by prayer. Always, prayer.

Nyx left Rhys at prayer and went to join Taite out in the back where he sat hunched up on a tattered wicker chair as the bloody purple-red of the day's first sunset smeared the sky. He turned one of his little saint statues over and over in his hands. Nyx didn't know which one it was—they all looked the same to her.

Nyx slumped into the seat next to him as the call to evening prayer sounded across the valley below. She tucked a little sen into her mouth from the bag at her hip. She still needed a fucking bath.

"Solid job," she said. "They're sending in somebody to pick up those bodies tonight. Get rid of that smell. I'll have Anneke wash out the bakkie in the morning. You'll get a good cut for this job."

"Every day we don't die is good I guess."

"You don't sound like it."

He rubbed the saint's face; the features had been smoothed into obscurity some time ago. To her eye, the head was a lumpy yam. "We all know Rhys is the only person on this team you give a shit about," he said.

"Where'd that come from?"

"I tell myself that's all right," he said. He kept his gaze fixed on the sky, and spit the words like he was at some Ras Tiegan confession. "It's all right because shit, when I worked for your old boss there wasn't a single one of us he'd sacrifice anything for. We were all alike, to a guy like that. But I won't lie, Nyx. It gets to me. It gets to me that I could live with you all these years like we're some fucked-up family and you'd just leave me to die on some rooftop somewhere if you thought I'd inconvenience a job."

"Never pretended to be anything but what I am," Nyx said. And she wanted to add, "not like you," but that felt too much like digging into his past, and she'd sworn not to do that with anyone on her team. She cast about for some whisky, but it was all still inside, and she'd have to get up and miss the bleeding sunset. "We're all mercenaries," Nyx said, instead. "You just as much as anyone." Then, before he could whine anymore, she yelled, "Anneke!" back into the house. "Get me a drink!"

Taite finally turned to her. "She's at the shooting range," he said. "You can't just drink everything away."

She pointed at his little statue. "You numb all this catshit with your little toys. I numb it with booze. No different."

"Whatever, Nyx," Taite said. He stood. "I wish … No, never mind. I just. I get what Rhys has against you, sometimes. I mean, I like my job. But . . . I get it."

Taite pushed inside.

"Fuck you, too," Nyx said, softly. To herself. To the wind. To a world that didn't fucking care.

Nyx was already drunk by the time she stumbled down the low hill behind the storefront and joined Anneke at the shooting range. It was almost midnight prayer. The whisky bottle between them was three-quarters empty. Anneke was still putting pithy little holes in the targets at the other end of the field while Nyx shot off her pistols wildly, hooting and hollering, stomping at the ground like a woman on fire. Maybe she was.

Anneke shot off another round. Nyx snatched up the bottle and threw herself on the cool ground, and gazed up into the black patch in the sky, the great darkness of the celestial plain where no stars were visible. She drank, and gritted her teeth, and wondered at the fact that she was still alive. It felt so fucking good.

"I don't think I have a soul," Nyx said.

"Eh?" Anneke said. Another shot, two more, then six in quick succession.

"No soul," Nyx said. "I got rebuilt, after the front. You know that. The magicians rebuilt me."

"Sure," Anneke said.

"Catshit. You didn't."

"Sure I did," Anneke said. "Your eyes are off."

"What?"

"Your eyes are two different colors," Anneke said. "I mean, other shit, too. You're mean and crazy. But mostly, you got two eyes it's clear ain't yours. Other parts, too."

"You say that like you ain't mean and crazy, too."

"Didn't say I ain't."

"You get rebuilt?"

"Naw," Anneke said. She brought her gun over to a stone slab near the little gun house. Far off, a brilliant amber burst went off. Some skirmish at the front. But the booze had numbed up Nyx enough that she barely registered it. "But I get what you mean, about having no soul. The war steals a little from all of us, you know. Leaves that big patch of empty."

Nyx pointed up at the darkness. "Like that."

"Sure," Anneke said. "Like that. You gonna shoot, or you gonna drink?"

"Both," Nyx said. She closed her eyes and soaked in the heat still lingering on the sand. "Ain't nothing like the feeling of being alive after you almost died, you know?"

"I know," Anneke said. "You get addicted to it."

"That why you run with me? You sick on it, too?"

"Why you even need to ask, boss? Sounds pretty close to asking about dead shit."

"No dead shit," Nyx said, and pushed herself up. She took a slug from the bottle, then handed it back to Anneke. Nyx pulled her pistol again and took another couple wild shots at the sandbag targets out there.

"Someday I'm going to teach you to shoot," Anneke said.

"What'd be the fun in that?" Nyx said. "I can't be fucking perfect at *everything.*"

Anneke cackled like it was the funniest thing she'd ever heard. Nyx couldn't imagine why.

Another burst broke along the horizon—deep purple, tinged in orange stars. It was beautiful. Everything was so goddamn beautiful, with or without a soul, with or without God at your hip.

Nyx took another shot.

CROSSROADS AT JANNAH

"The world is a prison for the believer and a paradise for the unbeliever."
—*Ṣaḥīḥ Muslim* 2956

THE FIGURE IN THE DOORWAY was missing half her face and most of her left arm, which had been replaced with a green glowing claw with a texture and sheen that reminded Nyx of a scorpion. More impressive was the bowed length of metal that served as the woman's left leg. What made it impressive was the fact that the woman hadn't been jumped in the street while she waited in the doorway, and been divested of her conspicuous wealth. No doubt anyone who considered stealing the pure metal had second thoughts on seeing the woman's shredded face. Nyx certainly wouldn't have tangled with her, and Nyx had been hunting down deserters, wrangling with gene pirates, and boxing with mullahs for half of her life. The one remaining eye that the woman turned upon Nyx was steely, cold, set back in the ravaged flesh of the face.

"You're Nyxnissa so Dasheem," the woman said.

"That's what the sign says."

"Not technically, no," the woman said, and sat down on the rickety chair across from Nyx's desk. The day was hot, and she was perspiring heavily. She pulled out a sweat rag and wiped it across her face, then tucked it back into her burnous. She wore a breast binding and loose pair of trousers. Her gut was the sort acquired over long nights of drinking to excess, which paired well with the broken veins across her nose.

Nyx took the hint and pulled out a bottle of whisky from the drawer at her left and poured them both a drink.

"Ah!" the woman said, smacking her lips. "I am Hafeez Arwa. You come well recommended as a woman good at finding things."

"Folks with problems always seem to find me."

"You do run a problem-solving business."

"Never thought of it as anything so refined."

"It's all in how you spin it," she said, polished off the drink.

Nyx capped the bottle and cocked her head at Hafeez. "Let's talk business before you polish off the rest."

"I need to find a data lake," Hafeez said.

Nyx let that idea roll around in her head a minute. Maybe the heat was getting to her, too. Her magician, Rhys, and her com tech, Taite, had retreated into the basement to escape the heat. She was starting to wonder if she should have done the same. She'd have missed this visitor, and her drink would be a lot colder. "A lake . . ." Nyx said, testing it out, "full of data. Right."

Hafeez plumbed the depths of one of her burnous pockets with her pincer arm and came up with a handful of beetle casings. She spilled them onto the table like dice. "I get you're used to finding bodies," Hafeez said. "This time, the bodies are the bugs that used to store information."

Nyx picked up one of the transparent rectangular cases. Inside was a shiny yellow beetle surrounded by threads of silky organic filament. "I know what they are," she said. "My com tech stores all recorded conversations on them. And I've seen them plenty in interrogation rooms when we're pulling up recordings."

"Ever wonder what happens to them when they're no longer needed?"

Nyx snorted. "Not once."

Hafeez said, "Most are destroyed properly, put in bins of acid that dissolve the casing and everything inside. But that's expensive. Others simply feed them to bugs tailored to the purpose. They're a form of flesh beetles, and they'll simply consume and excrete what's left."

"So what happens to the rest? Sticky fingers?"

"Laziness," Hafeez said. She tapped her glass on the table, but Nyx didn't think it was a conscious gesture. "There are firms that say they will collect your old casings and destroy them en masse. They haul them out into the desert and bury them in acidic lakes. Because there are so many casings, it takes a long time for them to break down. There are people, like myself, who take advantage of this. We go data fishing, scooping up casings from this acidic slurry to see if they can be salvaged or repaired and the data subsequently retrieved."

"I take it this isn't exactly legal."

"Ah, well," Hafeez said, swiping her claw in front of her as if turning off a radio image, "is that enough for another drink?"

Nyx obliged. She found the woman strangely likeable.

Surprising, because Nyx didn't like most people. Hafeez reminded her of an old commander of hers, from the front, right before she was blown up for the third and final time.

"Good, good," Hafeez said, smacking her lips. She went slower with the second drink. She collected up all of the casings and dumped them back into her pocket. Then she reached into her breast binding and pulled out a slippery casing, holding it out to Nyx. "Your people can use this to find the others from the same facility," she said. "I know it can be done, as I have hired private contractors before who do such work. I've even done it myself, of course, but . . . I need you to go to the data lake and pull out everything that came from the same place this casing did, in whatever condition it's in. Then return it to me."

Nyx took the casing from her. It was a pretty little thing, she supposed, a captured blue beetle suspended in fluid and trapped by a casing made of transparent bug secretions; little bubbles of air made dewy patterns on the beetle's spidery legs, and beaded the looping threads of the yellow filament that encircled it.

"You not going to tell me where it's from?" Nyx asked.

"Better you not know," Hafeez said. "The less a contractor such as yourself knows, the better. All you need to know is that I want others from the same place. Easy enough. In and out."

"If it was easy, you wouldn't hire me."

"Not so," Hafeez said, and she smiled like a particularly pleased cat, "easy is fine, it's the . . . questionable legality that isn't."

"How much it pay?"

Hafeez said, "A thousand notes."

"I could get more for that metal leg of yours."

"I'd like to see you try," Hafeez said, and she chuckled, sending her belly rolling.

"You serve at the front?" Nyx asked.

"This?" Hafeez said, waving her claw at her mangled face. "Ho-ho, no, but that's a pretty story, isn't it? This was an occupational hazard. But it did keep me from the front lines. I pushed a lot of papers with this limb!" She chuckled some more.

"I'll talk to my com tech," Nyx said. "If he can do what you think he can, then we'll put something together, and I'll have you sign a contract. I want half in advance. If he can't do it, no deal. I don't contract out anything on my team. I can tell you right now that he's probably not going to like this job at all."

"Fair enough," Hafeez said, "you can find me at that curry-stinking hotel, that Mont-plier place, until next week. The job must be done, the data turned over, before prayer day next week. Otherwise, I have no use for it, yes?"

"Sure," Nyx said.

Hafeez stood. Her metal leg creaked.

Nyx considered that leg for a long moment, wondering how spry this old woman really was. Hafeez caught her looking, and tapped at the leg. "You try me," Hafeez said. "You'll sleep better."

"I'll sleep a long time," Nyx said.

"Exactly that."

"I love it!" Taite said.

"Well, shit," Nyx said.

Taite bounced back on his heels. He was a spry, pock-marked kid, too young to go to the front even if they drafted half-Ras Tiegans like him, which they didn't. His dark hair needed a cut, and hung into his face in greasy tangles. A cut and a wash, Nyx amended.

She had joined him and her magician, Rhys, in the base-ment. Rhys was going through afternoon prayer, forehead to his prayer mat, murmuring his prayers to the north. Down here, the air certainly felt better, but smelled like a barracks. The freezer behind Taite's workbench where they kept bodies they were bringing in on bounty was empty, and had been for three weeks.

"We need the notes," Nyx said, "so I guess I should be happy you can pull it off, eh?"

"We'd make more money off that woman's metal leg than the job," Taite said.

"You're free to try and get it off her," Nyx said. "I think she'd cut off your head, and she most certainly wouldn't use my services anymore. Thing is, Taite, you go murdering your clients and word gets around and all the sudden you don't have any clients anymore. Got that? Cause, effect. You're a com tech. You should get that."

"Sure, sure," Taite said, rolling his eyes.

"You roll those eyes at me again and I'll cut them out," Nyx said.

"You say the nicest things," Rhys said as he rolled up his prayer mat.

"And then your tongue," she said, but her heart wasn't in it.

Rhys stood, and she let herself watch him do it. He was a lean man, tall, about her height. The pretty in him was always tough to quantify; some combination of beauty and humility that was difficult to find. He shaved his head, which she hated, but it did emphasize his features: the pouty lower lip, the long, slender nose, the broad cheekbones, and the dark eyes that did not meet her gaze now, but remained on the floor, as they usually did when she wasn't wearing anything but her breast binding and dhoti. Even her feet were bare.

"If you can fish out what she needs," Nyx said, "all I need to do is get us in there."

"Easier said than done," Taite said. "Those data lakes are heavily monitored, even one that's shabby."

"Let's hope for a shabby one," Nyx said. "It's fasting season, you know, time of miracles."

"I don't think that's the expression I'd use," Rhys said.

Nyx ignored him; when it suited her, she pretended he was a buzzing insect without a stinger, which wasn't far off from the truth, she supposed.

Taite flipped the casing over in his hand. "I can figure out where the data was created using the com," he said. "Once we know that, we'll need to figure out where that place sends its casings to be destroyed. Then fish it out."

"Easy," Nyx said, warming to the idea.

Rhys shook his head. "Another easy little adventure, is it?"

"Aren't they always?" Nyx said.

Rhys sweltered in the front seat of the bakkie, wondering how he'd gotten himself a starring role in yet another one of Nyx's dangerous schemes. Taite sat next to him, tilting the buzzing fan of beetles that provided the only moving air in the bakkie closer to him. They had rolled down the windows, but the air outside was so still it put Rhys into a trance if he allowed himself to tune out to his surroundings for any length of time.

Outside, the blue-tinged cargo bakkie they had been waiting for all day finally rolled up outside the security gates of the building.

"You realize we need to get inside," Taite said, face inches away from the beating wings of the beetles.

"Why?" Rhys said. "The name of the place is on the trunk. We'll look them up at the public com." He let out a little wisp of a command to the beetles to slow their wings. Simple tasks with common bugs weren't easy for him, but they were possible, and it did amuse him to see the look on Taite's face.

Taite shook the cage of beetles. "I think they're broken," he said. He raised his head and met Rhys's look.

Rhys burst out laughing.

"You shit," Taite said, and grinned back. He huffed the cage at Rhys.

Rhys caught it. He waved his hand over the cage, sending out a little threaded signal to the bugs, and they began their fanning once again. "It does give me an idea," Rhys said, "if you want to get inside and impress Nyx with all your fancy investigative work."

"Something even *you* can do?" Taite said.

"Indeed," Rhys said, "even *I* can do it."

Rhys exited the stifling bakkie and opened up the trunk where they kept weapons and gear like specs, cooling blankets, water, food, and antidotes to common contagions. Taite joined him, rubbing his hands together.

"Are we going to stage a break-in?"

Rhys raised a brow. "I'm not Nyx." He picked up a pair of specs. "We're going to be an honest pair of com tech repair people. You've done it before, right?"

"I've contracted at places like this, sure," Taite said. "Let's do it."

Taite piled cooling blankets into Rhys's arms and put the cage of beetles on top. He grabbed a mess of identification papers from a locked box under the trunk liner, and pulled out one of his old batches from his time, as he put it, "honing my skills under some tables."

Rhys sent a quick communication to Nyx via a red beetle swarm to let her know they were proceeding inside. He decided it was best not to wait for an answer and hear all about her thoughts on their plan's success.

They strode up to the front doors of the facility, which bore a great flickering sign composed entirely of red midges:

ARWA WAR BONDS

Taite wandered up to the front counter. The sound of trickling water filled the space; water moved through the walls, cooling the whole building. Rhys wasn't able to hear what Taite said because a massive woman was making her way toward him, and he responded by making his way as quickly as possible *away* from her.

"You, hey!" she said, and that's when Rhys started to run. He couldn't say why he ran. He was conditioned to it, now.

When women in Nasheen went after you, you ran until your legs gave out or your lungs burst.

"Rhys!" Taite yelled, bolting after him.

Rhys ran up the great stone stairwell, pushing past women in white-and-yellow outfits and perfectly folded hijabs. He sprinted down a long hallway.

Taite barreled after him, breath coming hard and fast, already winded. "Where the fuck—" Taite began.

Rhys followed the pull of the insects. Insects crowded in a few places, but the one he was looking for was . . . there. He pushed up a panel in the wall, and a malodorous stench wafted out, part dog shit, part vomit, part death. Garbage left the building. Garbage would get him out.

"Go," Rhys said, gesturing to the pit of stench.

Taite gazed back at the corridor. The big woman was getting closer, and she had brought friends. "I should have just stolen the leg," he said, and jumped into the garbage chute.

Rhys tumbled after him, regretting it even as he hauled himself inside. He slammed the chute shut behind him and lost his grip, falling after Taite into the darkness. He landed with a soft, wet plop and promptly began to sink into the filth, like quicksand.

"This is shit!" Taite said. "Waste of time, again. Nyx is going to have it out with us over this." The darkness was absolute. Rhys batted his hand in the direction of Taite's voice, but only smacked his hand against soiled papers and refuse and old, melting furniture made of bug secretions that was slowly being reclaimed by the mire.

Rhys searched for a swarm. He sensed one flying midge, a handful of cockroaches, mayflies, lice, gnats, flies, and smaller, stranger things. Finally he locked on a small swarm of red beetles, one just released from a communication, and called them.

They buzzed just overhead. Rhys gasped at them, "Garbage chute. Follow the swarm back. Haste?" And let them go.

Rhys waited awhile before trying to make his own way up, but the chute was too slippery. Sitting at the end of it did get him out of the pit, but that was a temporary respite. Everything stank.

"Found some other chutes over here!" Taite said. They mucked about in the darkness for some time, but there was no way back up.

After a while, tired and hungry and thirsty, they both went quiet.

"She won't come," Rhys said, finally.

"She will," Taite said, "but only because you're here."

A shaft of light appeared at the far end of the pit. Rhys squinted, shielding his eyes. A rope tumbled down.

"Hey down there!" Anneke's voice.

Rhys followed Taite up to the edge of the chute, navigating the churn. Taite grabbed the rope, went up first, then Rhys. When Rhys broke the surface, he found that they were outside the walls of the compound, in some kind of courtyard. Nyx and Anneke stood there wearing the white-and-yellow uniforms of the facility, complete with hijabs.

"Should have thought of that," Rhys said.

"Should have," Nyx said, spitting sen. Her teeth were blood-red with it. "You'd look pretty in a hijab." She wrinkled her nose, and said to Taite, "You got no excuse not to take a wash, now. Shit, kids."

Nyx stood out on the sidewalk of her storefront, waiting for Anneke. Rhys was next to her, smelling sweet as a spring breeze on the interior. He had a massive map tucked under one arm, and he still would not look at her after his rescue from the garbage.

"I can't imagine it's so easy to hijack a cargo bakkie," he said, with a little sniff.

"Certainly tougher than getting the name off of one," Nyx said, "but the complexity of a task really depends on who's doing it, right?"

"Fuck you, Nyx," Taite said from behind her, and she grinned.

Her Mhorian shapeshifter, Khos, sat in a bakkie idling in the street, smoking from an oversize pipe. It was a habit he had picked up at some tea house, and whatever it was he smoked had a bitter, acrid tang to it that hurt her eyes. He had tied up his mass of yellow dreads with a red scarf, a style she found even more conspicuous than the Mhorian dreads alone. He dressed like a practical Nasheenian, at least, in a dhoti and burnous, a couple of bandoliers around his neck, a pistol at his hip. He was a big man: big head, big hands, and as Nyx knew, lots of other important things, too. She was musing about that as Anneke drove up in the blue-banded cargo bakkie, honking the horn like a fucking maniac.

Anneke leaned out the side of the cargo bakkie, shotgun first, and Nyx had to just take a minute and rub her own head at the crazy of her team. At least Anneke got things done, even if they were often done extravagantly.

Anneke parked and jumped out of the cab. She was little and lean, wiry, all muscle and reflex, nearly as dark as a Chenjan. She had hacked her hair short, and it stuck out in all directions, obscuring her face and hampering her vision, so she nearly knocked into Nyx with her gun.

"Good, great," Nyx said, batting away the stock of the shotgun. "Let's all get the fuck in before we wake up half the neighborhood."

They all piled into the back of the cargo carrier, just a framed hauling bed that had been tented over in muslin and painted and waterproofed. The tented roof would be shit in an accident, but it shielded them and their cargo from prying eyes. Anneke had kept the existing data canister pickups in the back, and acquired two uniforms. Nyx didn't ask what had happened to the people who'd had the uniforms before her. Maybe she'd swiped them from a laundry somewhere. Anneke was resourceful.

Nyx peeled off her clothes and yanked on one of the blue-and-yellow uniforms. It was too small in the ass and the hips. She kept on her own sandals, not only because nobody they would encounter was likely to see her feet, but also because she kept razor blades hidden in the soles of them.

Taite, too, dressed in a uniform, which was too long and baggy on him, and slipped up front into the passenger seat. A Nasheenian woman and a foreign man driving one of these cargo bakkies wouldn't be questioned. Anyone else on the team, and they were inviting way too many extra stops.

Nyx settled in up front and waved back at Khos. He tapped

the horn, and Nyx turned on the juice to the bug cistern and cranked them back out of the alley and onto the deserted street.

Anneke peeked in from the back, parting the muslin curtain that shielded the back from the cab. Her face and the barrel of her gun were lined up side by side. She was grinning like a fucking maniac.

"Super excited about this one, boss," she said. "Never been to a data lake. Should I bring some swimming gear?"

"Too late to go back for it," Nyx said. "Rhys!"

"North until Adnan Street!" he yelled from the back.

"Good!" Nyx said. "You cozy back there?"

"No!" he said.

"Good!" she said, and grinned. She liked it when her plans panned out.

The security detail stopped them twelve miles from the location of the data lake facility.

Nyx slowed down when she saw the traffic ahead of them queuing up at the checkpoint. "I need a way around!" she yelled at Rhys.

"There's no way around," he said, and poked his head through the curtain. His eyes widened at the checkpoint. "This is . . . not optimal."

"Not at all," Nyx said. "Any ideas, Taite?"

Taite shifted in his seat. "Our papers aren't going to stand up to close scrutiny," he said.

"It's not military," Nyx said, squinting. "Looks like order keepers. Routine, then."

"I don't like this, boss," Anneke said.

When Nyx glanced back, Anneke wasn't visible, but the barrel of the gun was. "Goddammit, Anneke, put that shit away," Nyx said.

"What are you going to do?" Taite said, quietly.

"Let me think," Nyx said. They rolled forward with the queue as the bakkies ahead of them were released.

"Are they searching any?" Anneke said.

"One of them," Nyx said. It was hot up in the cab now that they weren't moving fast. The air was dead still. She watched the order keepers direct three women from a bakkie two up from them and pop open the trunk. One rolled under the bakkie. She didn't see any magicians helping out. It had to be routine. What a fucking time to get caught in some random security check. She had bad papers, a stolen cargo bakkie, a Chenjan in the back, and a half-Chenjan woman with a shotgun, too, and some half–Ras Tiegan with a questionable record when it came to com hacking. There were lots of cards she could play with them—they were just order keepers, not bel dames, not military—but that also meant it would take longer to get through the protocols with them. Order keepers didn't know her the way bel dames or military did. Order keepers hated people like her.

"Boss," Anneke whispered.

"Shut up," Nyx said. "I'm thinking."

The bakkie ahead of them moved up alongside the two order keepers. The driver held out her papers. She was waved through fast, long before Nyx had any sort of real plan in place. Faintly, Nyx heard Anneke muttering something in the back.

Nyx pulled up alongside the order keepers. They were lean women, both in their early thirties, hair shorn short. The one nearest the cab door looked tired and bored, but the one behind her was clearly fired up on her own importance. Anneke's muttering had gotten louder, and Nyx prepared to drown it out by bellowing.

Nyx fixed both order keepers with a broad grin and handed them her forged passbook for the rig and her identity. "Hot as hell out here, eh?" Nyx said. "Sorry they got you doing this shit. You come down from the north? Know how the weather is up there? Roads further north?"

"I don't," the woman with Nyx's papers said, peering at them. The sun rode high over the woman's shoulder.

Nyx persisted. "Back behind us, the road was washed out. Saw some folks who—"

"What are you carrying?" the woman asked.

A yell from the back, more muttering, louder this time. Goddammit Anneke, Nyx thought. Keep your goddamn cool. Had Anneke taken a stimulant or something?

"Huh? Oh, recycling data casings. Anwar. The war bonds place. Confidential stuff headed to a data lake."

"Open up the back, please," the woman said, handing Nyx back the passbook.

Nyx forced her grin into a grimace. "Oh sure, sure, just have to check with the boss. Confidential stuff."

"Open it," the woman behind said, and she pulled her pistol.

Nyx held up her hands. "Sure, sure, we'll open the back. No problem. No—"

The shotgun blast was deafening. A wave of sound cracked

the air, right behind Nyx's head. Her ears rang, the tinkling of a bell tone, high and warbling.

Screaming, behind her, *"Fuuuuuuuuuuuuuck. Fuuuuuuuck."*

Nyx stared at where the woman with the pistol had been. She was on the ground now, a pile of muddy meat, and there was coppery wetness all over Nyx's face; she tasted it on her lips, rolled her tongue over it.

The other order keeper was fumbling at her belt for her own pistol, panic-stricken face fixed on Nyx.

"Don't pull," Nyx said, and her own voice sounded muted, far away. "Don't pull it. Stand down."

Nyx opened the cab door, huffing herself out. She stumbled over the body of the order keeper. She reached for the other one, but the panicked order keeper was getting her bearings now, her resolve hardening, and Nyx knew, knew then, and in that moment, the woman didn't look thirty, but twenty, and it was all over, it was all about to be over. Coppery blood. Taste of death.

"Hush," Nyx said, as the pistol came up. Nyx neatly relieved her of it, yanking it cleanly from her hands, turning her own pistol back on her. "Hush now," Nyx said. "Over now," and Nyx pulled the trigger. Clean shot through the head, tiny hole in the front, splattering out the back.

"Hush now," Nyx said, and then muted stillness, the high ringing in her ears, the tone.

"Nyx! Nyx!" Her name.

She turned, pistol up, finger on the trigger, aiming to fire. She squeezed.

"Fuck!" Khos yelled.

He had run out from the bakkie, leaving it idling behind

them. The bullet missed him; Nyx wasn't a great shot at range, and went clean through the tented backing of the cargo bed.

Khos had his arms over his head, for all the good that would do, Nyx thought, and dropped the pistol.

She moved automatically. Hit him on the shoulder. "Get in. Follow," she said, yelling because she couldn't hear anything properly, still. "Gotta dump the cargo bakkie."

She turned, then looked back, said, "The bodies. Keep the bodies." She always needed bodies. Might as well take these, too.

There were two more bakkies coming down the road, hurtling toward the checkpoint. They didn't have much time. It was possible they had already been seen.

Nyx and Khos loaded both bodies into the trunk of the bakkie. Nyx kicked through the checkpoint until she found the fat round form of a dragonfly. It tried to fly away, but she mashed it with her fist and threw it in the trunk with the rest. It was the only recording bug she found. It was possible it had already sent the images it had seen somewhere else, but these were usually only pulled up after the fact.

Nyx slid into the driver's seat. Everyone inside was yelling. Anneke was screaming in the back, wailing like she was dying, "Let me up! Let me up! I didn't mean to! I'm all right!"

Taite was talking, too fast, too low, she didn't catch the words. She turned up the juice to the cistern and drove.

Nyx drove and drove, turning down little-used roads, country highways, dusty backwaters, until they came to some burnt-out wreck of what had once been a waystation. The others had calmed down by then, silent and numb, and some of her hearing was back. The first sun had already gone down, so they were bathed only in the deep blue light of the second sun, already headed back under the horizon with its sister.

Nyx got out of the cab. "Wipe it down," she said. "No blood. No hair. Nothing. Keep the uniforms, our gear. Get into the bakkie. We'll have to dump the bakkie, too, eventually."

"We need to do something," Taite said. "Those were order keepers." He hunched next to the side of the cargo tent, right near the bullet hole. "They didn't do anything to us. That was murder, Nyx."

"Fuck you!" Anneke said. She pushed more sen into her mouth, though it was clear she already had a lot of it.

"We're not sending Anneke back to prison," Nyx said. "Shit happens."

Khos kicked at the dirt. "Nyx, I—"

"I didn't ask for your opinion," Nyx said.

Rhys, softly, "Is this data worth innocent people's lives?"

"Is living worth your life? Is dying? Life doesn't mean anything," Nyx said.

"This is catshit," Taite said.

"Suck it up," Nyx said. "We dump the cargo bakkie here. Get real friendly again, folks, because we need to share our own bakkie until we can dump that somewhere, too."

Khos drove this time. Nyx rode up front with him, and Rhys, Taite, and Anneke sat in the back. Nyx had taken away Anneke's shotgun and put it in the trunk with the bodies. Whatever Anneke had been on, she was coming down from; she had the shakes bad, and they had to stop twice to let her vomit.

The road was soothing in the dark, and Nyx took some pleasure from that. The air cooled fast at night in the desert, and it felt good after the cloying heat of the day. They holed up at a falling-down way house across from a battered cantina, both of which smelled like urine, but they were the only buildings for as far as any of them could see, and that was something.

"Plan's fucked," Nyx said, eating a roti while sitting on the edge of one of the two slender beds. The blankets felt gritty, just like the floor. She crunched grit between her teeth. "Let's inventory what we've got. Taite?"

He sat back on his heels against the far wall, wrapped in a blanket. Rhys was rolling out his prayer mat in anticipation of evening prayer, and Anneke was kneeling beside him.

"The uniforms," Taite said, "some junk data casings from the cargo bakkie. Our weapons. Two dead order keepers."

"I think we should abandon the job," Rhys said. He knelt on his prayer mat, facing away from Nyx. "It's just a data retrieval job. We're not saving a child or even hunting down someone who killed someone else. We don't even know what it is."

The call to prayer sounded, tinny and warbling, from the cantina next door. It only got through a few lines before the muezzin gave in, maybe because he was asleep, or vomiting, or just because she figured nobody was listening, but Rhys and Anneke went through their prayers.

"He's not wrong," Khos said. He lay full length on the other bed, though Nyx was going to tell him to move to the floor soon. "Two people are dead. Order keepers, yes, not bel dames or military, but we aren't exactly tough to spot."

"This isn't a discussion about going back," Nyx said. "That's not a topic. This isn't a democracy. I'm not a fucking Hedian or progressive Tirhani or some fuck. We are discussing the plan we need to come up with to finish the job that we contracted for."

"We should have just stolen her leg," Taite said.

"Fuck you and the fucking leg," Nyx said.

Silence descended as they listened to Anneke and Rhys finish their prayers. Nyx fixed her look on the windows, which they had covered over in bedsheets. The windows here weren't filtered, not out here to hell and gone, but simply patterned carvings to reduce the amount of sunlight that suffused the room.

Rhys finished his prayers and rolled up his mat. "I'm not going any further," he announced, as if he were some fucking mullah with a fucking spine.

"You walk out like you did on that last job," Nyx said, "and I'll fire you right now and take away your little passbook. Then what happens to you when you try and walk the fuck out of here, in this shitty little border town? The women here will skin you alive."

"Could we try and be constructive?" Khos said. "I want to get to sleep sometime tonight."

"The road was the safest way in," Taite said curtly. "There's too much security outside the main road. You don't take any route to a data lake that isn't an authorized one."

"Why can't we go in on foot?" Khos asked.

"There are layers to the security onsite," Taite said. "You've got concentric and even overlapping forms of security. There's a toxic layer of gas on the very edges of the compound. Then you've got the wasp swarms that patrol in random patterns. There are plenty of other layers they change all the time, bugs coded to eat you, paralyze you, and what have you. Then there's the acid lake itself, and the human security teams, which patrol every thirty minutes. The only way in is with a cargo bakkie that can get through the areas already designated for the cargo bakkies. That's the safest route."

"So we'll tell them we were hijacked," Nyx said. "We've got enough blood and shit on these uniforms now to look the part. We say we were hijacked and just walk down the cargo bakkie road."

"That won't hold up," Taite said. "Our identification papers didn't even hold up to order keepers. With the cargo bakkie, we'd have a chance they wouldn't look too close. Without it, they'll scrutinize everything we do."

"It'll hold up if we sell it," Nyx said. "Really sell it."

"I already know I won't like this," Khos said.

Nyx jabbed a finger at him. "You, Anneke, and Rhys pose as hijackers. Me and Taite will stay in uniform. You push us along ahead of you as hostages. They sure as fuck won't take the time to look at our papers during a standoff."

"And how exactly," Rhys said, "are you going to get us to the data lake? They'll deploy every one of their security people and all of the facility's features to take us down."

"You leave that to me," Nyx said.

"Yeah," Khos said, "I'm definitely not going to like this."

Nyx expected the compound to be something extravagant, but of course, the less conspicuous it was, the better. They stole a new bakkie at a little town thirty kilometers from the site and drove to within two kilometers to survey the site. Big cargo bakkies arrived irregularly. Nyx sat up on a rise overlooking the road and only saw one in the hour she spent gazing through her specs.

"We could have kept the old bakkie, with this plan," Khos said as she walked back down to the bakkie where he waited, puffing away at his ridiculous pipe.

"I was a sapper during the war," Nyx said.

"Yeah, you never fail to mention that," Khos said.

"And I figured out all sorts of shit about a person after they blew something up," she continued. "The less we leave behind, the better."

"Not convinced of this plan," Khos said.

"You're only saying that because you loved the other one, and it was shit."

"I did love the other one," he said, "and it was shit."

Nyx went to the trunk where Anneke was gearing up and started equipping her own weapons. Taite and Rhys were huddled under the ruin of some old building, sharing a bulb of water in the scant shade.

"Sorry about what happened, boss," Anneke said, not looking at her.

"Shit does happen," Nyx said.

"Thought she looked like someone I knew in prison," Anneke said.

"I get it," Nyx said. "Being high as fuck didn't help, either."

"Sorry, boss. Won't happen again."

"No," Nyx said, "it won't. Or we're done. No catshit. We're done."

"I hear you, boss," Anneke said.

They piled into the bakkie and drove right up to the compound gate. When they were within range, Nyx and Taite got out, hands up. The others stayed in the bakkie; Nyx figured they would be easier targets in the open if there were snipers posted, even though Taite figured that wasn't likely.

"Open up!" Nyx said. "These guys hijacked our cargo bakkie. Stole a lot of data."

Khos let off a couple of rounds into the air, for emphasis.

There was a flurry of confused activity in the station. A swarm of red beetles left the station and headed off deeper into the facility. It was dusk again, moving to dark, and Nyx stood out there in the heat and felt the night come over them, waiting on the shit-eaters to get their shit together.

The bakkie door slammed behind her. Khos came up behind Nyx and wrapped an arm around her and put the pistol to her head, yelled up at the guards. "You want to see me kill them right here? Open the fucking gate or you'll have two bodies out here!"

That did it.

The gate opened, and they went through.

Khos held Nyx firmly against him; he was a hot, solid presence, and the stink of him was heady and not unpleasant, like an earthy whisky barrel. She wanted to fuck him again, which she was sure he knew. But then, it was natural to want to fuck somebody you worked with all the time. She'd wanted to fuck everyone on her team at one state of drunkenness or another. And flirting with death was the best drunk of all.

Taite, Anneke, and Rhys got out of the bakkie. Khos moved away from Nyx, and she turned back and gave Rhys a little salute.

Then they all scattered.

The explosion was impressive, even by Nyx's standards. She had packed the bakkie with explosives from a cache set out fifty kilometers away by an old acquaintance of hers, one she would owe big some other time. As it went up, Nyx dove into the ditch along the side of the road, crawling as fast as she could, hunkered low to the ground to avoid any lingering toxic gas from the first circle of the data lake's defenses.

The bodies from the trunk would mingle with the mess from the bakkie and the leavings from the explosives themselves, creating a morass of shit for these people to wade through for days, let alone the hour or so Nyx needed to fish the fucking data lake.

She met up with Rhys and Taite, just ahead of her, both crawling and coughing as the force of the blast pushed the toxic gas back their way. Nyx caught the hint of lavender in the air, and shuddered. "Stay low," she said.

Anneke and Khos would double back and meet them on the other side of the data lake, using the distraction of the explosion to cut through the fence and wait for them in a second getaway vehicle. Nyx was really glad she'd gotten half her fee up front, because expenses on this job were piling up.

Dusk turned quickly to full night. Rhys led the way, intuiting it with bugs or some shit.

"The swarms," Rhys said, after a long period of silence, and Nyx chanced a gaze up at the tall, willowy structures ahead of them.

"Trees?" Taite said.

"Those aren't trees," Nyx said.

They were buzzing swarms of flesh beetles, all organized into massive, clawlike shapes. They made a whispery sound, all their bodies moving and clacking over one another.

"Single file after me," Rhys whispered.

They crawled after him, Taite in the middle and Nyx coming up last.

"What about hornets?" she called.

"Those are out, too," Rhys said. "I'm trying to warn them off. The explosion has confused them. The effect may wear off soon, though.

"Ah!" Rhys said.

"What is it?"

"Stuck," he said.

It was nearly pitch black. The light they did have came from far behind them, in the still-burning car. Emergency vehicles had arrived, and there were at least half a dozen boots on the ground. They didn't have much time before the distraction became a real problem.

Nyx moved ahead. The ground here was getting muddy. She felt down the edge of Rhys's leg and unhooked his trousers from a jutting bit of metal.

"There you go," Nyx said.

"Great, ah—" and Nyx thought Rhys swore, but that couldn't be right.

He tumbled past her, sliding down the bank ahead of them. Nyx grabbed him, yanking him to a halt. The end of his burnous tumbled ahead of him, sinking into a muddy morass of water.

"Lake!" Rhys said, and pulled his burnous out. It hadn't melted, but it was certainly destressed.

Clouds rolled over the sky, giving them glimpses of the moons, which shed a brief glimmer of light over the broad, flat plane of the data lake. It was a soupy mess, like vomit, not a lake, but Nyx supposed that "data vomit" didn't sound as nice when you were marketing your trash service.

"I'm going to act as lookout," Nyx said, "up above the bank. They're going to get their shit together and send out a party to look here for us soon. We've got ten minutes. Do your shit and then let's get out of here."

"Ten minutes my ass," Taite grumbled once Nyx was out of earshot, but Rhys wasn't so sure they even had ten.

"Do it, deploy it," Rhys said. He stayed away from the swarms, most still moving in scattershot patterns around them.

Taite shrugged off his pack and pulled out a complex web of data beetles in perfect casings that they had custom made after their dip in the garbage chute. Rhys understood the principals behind it, as it was tailored to speak to the other types of casings that shared the same organic chemistry.

Rhys watched Taite toss it out into the lake like a net. It sank into the slurry. Taite kept hold of one end; soft blue lights flickered up the filaments as little bits of organic code sparked connections.

"Hey, hold this for a minute," Taite said, and before Rhys could reply, Taite put it into his hand and was scrambling further down the bank.

"What are you doing?" Rhys hissed. "We have five minutes!"

"That was metal back there!" Taite said. "There's some chips down here. All sorts of stuff ends up here. Just a little bonus. Hold on. It's two minutes!"

Behind them, the swinging arc of patrol lights cut through the darkness. Rhys ducked, instinctively.

"Hey hey!" Nyx called down at them. "Hurry up!"

Rhys peered at the net. He wasn't sure when it was done. He was just going to have to yank it out and they would run out with what they had.

"Rhys!"

"We're coming, Nyx, for—"

A swarm. He felt it, suddenly upon them, and he cried out, too late, "Taite!"

Taite screamed. If the search party wasn't out for them before, it was headed their way now.

Rhys dropped the data net and ran to Taite, sending out spidery commands to the swarm to disperse. It buzzed angrily at him. He stood over Taite as Taite's body jerked and shuddered. Rhys spread out both hands, focusing all of his energy on the swarm, compelling it to move on, to fracture, to break. It pushed toward him, the buzzing louder now, more menacing.

"Break," he murmured, "break."

The swarm thrummed, and he felt the shift in their path as they swarmed past him and over him, headed back to the site of the explosions.

Rhys grabbed Taite and hauled him up. Taite jerked forward, tongue lolling. "Help me, Taite," Rhys said. "Try." Rhys heaved Taite back up the bank, scrambling to the top where Nyx waited, half crouched, partially outlined by the still-roaring explosion. He wondered, again, what sort of accelerant she had used.

"You're just in time," Nyx said. "Can see the patrol lights coming." Her gaze swept the pair of them.

"He's paralyzed," Rhys said. "Take him."

Nyx didn't move. "Where the fuck is the data?" she said.

"I left it," Rhys said. "I knew we were out of time. Let's go. The patrol."

"Oh, fuck you," Nyx said. "You left the data? You should have brought me the goddamn data and then gone back for him, you lazy, cowardly fuck."

"I'm cowardly? No," Rhys said. He could see the lights coming, fast: flame flies. "If you're so brave, you go back for them. I'm not risking another—"

She pushed past him, knocking him so hard he dropped Taite and tumbled onto the sand after him. "Curse you, Nyx!" Rhys spat.

"Already fucked!" Nyx called over her shoulder, and disappeared over the dune.

Nyx slid down the bank and ran to the edge of the acid sea. The lights of the data net blinked at her as they continued to drift down, down . . . Rhys had just let the whole fucking thing go, just dropped it. All this catshit, and he had dropped it. For what?

She ran, and kept running, because in her head she heard him, again, and heard herself, calling him a coward. Fuck it.

Nyx ran into the acid sea and grabbed the netting into her

arms and hauled it back out. The slap of the acid was sharp, a burn that seared the skin of her legs and arms; little droplets wet her face, making burn marks, no doubt, and she slogged back up onto the bank with the net and the little casings that had adhered to the ones in the net. She bundled them up even as she rubbed soil onto her burning arms and legs. The lights of the patrol were closer. She broke from the edge of the lake and ran for the other side of the compound where they were due to meet Anneke and Khos.

She saw Rhys already ahead of her, dragging Taite with him. Taite had already regained some function, as he was moving his legs, slogging beside Rhys. Nyx tripped, banging back onto the bank. She tasted blood. She'd bitten her tongue.

The patrol was right over the dune. She stayed down, not daring to reveal herself when they were nearly on top of her. She raised her head only as they passed, just in time to see their light illuminate Rhys and Taite getting into the bakkie.

The bakkie juiced up and peeled away from the broken fence just as the patrol arrived; Taite nearly fell out. They hadn't even had time to close the door.

The patrol ran back past her, heading for their vehicles. Nyx pressed her face to the ground, clutching the data net. Her skin was peeling off, and there were swarms of flesh beetles out here, big enough to make giant trees, and this is where she was going to end up, fucking dead beside a data lake for no fucking reason. Why did she die? somebody might ask, if anybody bothered to ask or anybody knew or cared, and they'd say, Who the fuck knows? She needed some rent money.

Nyx rolled over and gazed up at the sky. Clouds had moved back over the moons, cutting off the stars, too, so all she saw was blackness. Like looking inside of herself, a constant loop.

Sound of tires on sand. A heavy bakkie hurtling her way.

A shout, "Nyx! Get the fuck in!"

Nyx scrambled up, snatched the data net, and bolted for the hole in the fence. On the other side, the bakkie was swinging around again. Anneke drove, and Khos was in the front passenger seat, arm outstretched, reaching for her.

She grabbed his hand, and he pulled her in.

They peeled away from the fence a second time and blazed off into the darkness, no headlights on, burning off toward the bumpy road they had mapped out for their escape. Nyx tossed the data net onto the floor at her feet and looked out the back, keeping an eye on their pursuers, whose vehicles still hadn't managed to get around the wreckage near the gate.

She caught Rhys's eye; he sat in the back, wrapped in his burnous. When he saw her looking at him, he closed his eyes and pretended to sleep.

They drove hard for an hour without pursuit before Anneke eased up on the juice.

"You hurt?" Anneke asked. Nyx was in the front, squeezed between her and Khos.

"I'll need a witch."

"Sure thing," Anneke said. She never took her eyes off the road.

The bakkie rolled up outside of a little town called Ikraam, or that's what Rhys said it was called on the map. Anneke found the hedge witch, and got the witch to come to the little abandoned adobe shack at the edge of town where they were squatting.

Khos slept out in the bakkie. He had rolled it away from the road, parked it behind some rock formations, and thrown sand on it for good measure.

Nyx preferred him out there because she found him deeply distracting. The hedge witch sat with her outside the shack in the wee hours before dawn, mumbling over her wounds as she applied a sticky salve crawling with tiny worms that Nyx didn't want to know the name of. The hedge witch was Hedian, and spoke in an accent that Nyx couldn't parse, but her legs were feeling better. What she did understand was the hedge witch setting down a bottle of whisky in front of her and rubbing her thumb and fingers together. Extra, for the whisky. Nyx was happy to pay that, and tucked the bottle up between her feet.

Anneke and Taite were passed out inside the ruin; Nyx heard Anneke's snores. Rhys stood a few paces away, arms folded, staring at the blush blue on the eastern horizon. As the first of the suns crested the horizon, he rolled out his prayer rug. Nyx thought it was a little early for morning prayer, but who was she to judge?

She paid the hedge witch, who totted off down the road, muttering things in Hedian that could be blessings or curses. Nyx figured she deserved a bit of both.

She sat on a petrified log, leftover from some ancient forest long dead here in the desert, and watched Rhys pray.

When he was done, the first blue sun had cleared the horizon, and it turned the whole world eerie and dreamlike. This was her favorite part of the day.

Rhys caught her look and said, "Respite on the crossroads to Jannah? I know you've already chosen your path, but there are days I think I still have a chance to take a new direction."

She snorted. "Paradise is a pretty story, but just a story."

"One nice thing I say, after all that, and you just spout cynical brimstone and fire."

"There's no paradise," Nyx said. "No Jannah. No hell, either, before you get started on that shit, getting all mouthy with me. Just this. This." She tapped the petrified log beside her. "We make of it what we will."

"And this is what you've chosen to make of it," Rhys said, nodding at the ruined adobe. "You chose this tired little place, your ravaged body, your loose morals, your drunkenness. You chose to be alone, adrift, damned. This is the hell you made yourself. I'd ask what you have to punish yourself for, but I've already seen enough in my time with you to justify every bit of this."

"What about you?" Nyx said. She was tired, and not in the mood for his preaching. Maybe he had gotten his second wind; she wished for a first. "You're not living in any paradise. Not one from the fucking Kitab, anyway. Maybe it's different in Chenja, eh?"

"Jannah is for believers," Rhys said. "We make it there by dedicating our lives to the worship of God. This is my hell, yes. It's the trial I must get through to Jannah. I reach many crossroads, and at each one, I must choose the path to Jannah."

"Well," Nyx said, showing her teeth. "That's something we

have in common, then, isn't it? We're both living in our own little hell."

He shook his head. "I'm glad you're not dead, too," he said, and left her alone on the log. He passed into the ruined hut, into darkness.

Nyx turned her face toward the horizon again, because it was the easier view, the beautiful view that she could understand. The air was still blissfully cool. The first sunrise had turned the horizon a fiery blue, and the second was making a violet line there where the desert touched the sky. She closed her eyes and felt the wind-borne sand caress her face. The smell of saffron rode in over the wind, faint, just a breath of it, like the scent of an old lover still lingering on one's clothes. She yanked off the top of the whisky bottle with her teeth and spit out the cork. It skittered across the ground, leaving a wispy trail in the sand. The impression it left there put her in mind of a snake, and that made her hungry, so she drank instead because that was easier right now. She choked on the bitter fire in her throat and squeezed her eyes shut against the brightening sky. Her skin still tingled, sloughing off dead and dying layers. She was alive, alive, alive today; she was never so alive as the morning after cheating death.

She opened her eyes. The sunrise was very beautiful.

PAINT IT RED

"We are they who painted the world scarlet with sins."
—Dante Alighieri, *The Divine Comedy*

NYX ENJOYED DRINKING more than fucking, because when she drank she didn't have to worry about somebody else fucking up her enjoyment with all the gory fetishes and bleeding-heart confessions. She was deep in her latest bottle of whisky—something out of a backyard still on the coast—and whiling away the afternoon listening to some southern beat music, when Rhys pushed into her office waving green papers and using words that had a lot of syllables.

It killed her buzz immediately.

He was good at killing her buzz.

Her com tech, Taite, was off visiting his sister. Khos, her resident shapeshifter, was sorting out some legal paperwork at the local shifter registration office. Anneke, her sniper and weapons tech, was currently thirteen hours into her allotted twenty-six of incarceration for a minor assault charge that involved a joke about someone's mother. That left Nyx and her magician, Rhys, in what should have been relative quiet and comfort. But Rhys could never enjoy a single moment of downtime without inventing some morally compromising catastrophe.

Nyx turned down the radio, if only because—paired with Rhys's nattering—it was starting to give her a headache.

"Slow down," she said. "The fuck you say?"

"Two bounties," he said, thwacking the papers onto her desk with a dramatic flourish.

"What about them?" she said. "We just turned in two. I'm drinking my share of it. Why don't you go eat some gravy or buy a new Kitab or whatever it is you do with your cut?"

"Did it occur to you that if we stopped living bounty to bounty and put something away for the rough times, we wouldn't have to take on more dangerous jobs when we ran low on notes?"

"Not once."

"You're insufferable," Rhys said. "Look these over and then—"

She leaned over her desk and waved her half-empty glass at him. "You phrase that like you're in charge," she said. "You aren't. I decide what we do and when you do it, and I've decided to take today off."

"Fine," he said, "you sit here and drown."

"I intend to."

He huffed out of her study. She heard him knocking around in the keg—the workroom in the back. Nyx polished off her drink and grabbed the bottle. She ducked through the curtain into the keg and went after him. Rhys was in his little nook of a sleeping area, stuffing things into a rucksack.

"What the fuck are you doing?" she said.

"Leaving," he said. "I can't tolerate you another minute."

"Good," she said. "Can't wait to see what kind of a job you get, being a Chenjan man in Nasheen. They'll eat you alive out there, and not in a good way. You'll call me up all bloody and fucked-up and beg me to come back."

"You'd enjoy that, wouldn't you?" he said. "Because you're monstrous and broken."

"Don't forget ungodly, or whatever."

Rhys stormed past her. They were of a height, but he was leaner. She caught his arm. He tried to wrest it away, but she was stronger.

"You listen here," she said, "if you call me for help, I'm not coming for you. I'm leaving you to your stupid choices. Get that?"

He yanked at his arm again, and she let him go. She expected a parting quip, but he went out the front door and slammed it behind him without another word.

"Thanks!" she yelled at the door. "It's about time I get some peace and quiet!"

She expected he would go sulk at a teahouse or a mosque all afternoon and be back before dark. That's usually what he did when he'd had enough, which had been at least a dozen times in the five years they had worked together.

Nyx slumped into her chair, put her dirty feet up on her desk, and took a slug from the bottle. Fuck him.

She spent the next hour drinking and trying to cook plantains in hot oil, which didn't turn out well. She got specks of hot oil all over her forearms; they made little red dots on her brown skin, a smattering of violent stars. Nyx was so engrossed in the project that she didn't hear anyone come in until they were nearly on top of her.

"Nyxnissa?"

Nyx jerked away from the hot plate and came up with her mostly empty bottle in one hand and the pan of hot oil in the other, ready to dispatch one or both at her visitor.

A lean woman half a hand shorter than Nyx stood a few paces away. She had her hands out, empty palms up; the hands and arms sticking out of her red burnous were crisscrossed in fine, pale scars. Her round face was slightly lopsided; the left eyelid drooped, and a corner of the mouth turned down, as if she had suffered some stroke.

"You remember me?" the woman asked. "It's been a while."

Nyx peered at her. Certainly there was something familiar about the woman's voice and manner, but she could not place it. That drooping face should have been a tell, but she didn't recall it. For a moment she thought the woman was a former bel dame, part of an independent group of government assassins that Nyx had been a part of a long time back. But that wasn't right; often Nyx could get a sense of that in a few seconds, and this woman wasn't holding herself right for that. No, it was likely she'd just been slapped back together or rebuilt a few times since last Nyx had seen her . . . if they had crossed paths at all. It wouldn't be the first time someone pretended to know Nyx to try and get in some sob story about a job she should take on the cheap out of goodwill. Nyx didn't have much of a soft spot when it came to money.

"No idea," Nyx said, "did we fuck once?"

"Close," the woman said, "we killed a man together."

"Shit," Nyx said, "that list is even longer. I can recite the ninety-nine names of God and you can tell me when I get close."

"You owe me a death," the woman said.

Nyx held out the frying pan, still sizzling around the browned plantains. "Hungry?"

"Got cold beer?"

"Just the whisky."

"That'll do."

Nyx set the pan on the workroom table, pushing away weapons parts and bullet casings made of bug secretions. Anneke liked to stamp her own bullets. Gave her better accuracy, she said. More reliable. No worries about them being underfilled or badly clipped, unless you put the things together drunk or stoned, which Anneke had been known to do. The smell of gun metal and lubricant mixed with the scent of hot oil and plantains.

Nyx and the newcomer sat around the work table and fished the hot plantains out of the pan with their bare fingers. Nyx tapped out a dirty tea cup of Taite's and poured two fingers of whisky into the bottom and passed it to the interloper. Nyx used the long silence of the slurping and munching to kick-start her sluggish memory. Nyx had been killing people since she went to the front at sixteen. She did her two years, got reconstituted, and gave up the military to become a bel dame. But she hadn't been good at rules, and it wasn't long before they put her in prison for a year and then kicked her out. Now she was almost thirty, which meant she had fifteen years of killing to wade through, searching for a woman's face. Hard enough as it was, but Nyx had spent a lot of those fifteen years drunk or on regulation military-grade narcotics.

"Mahir," the woman said, lifting her glass. "That's my name. I can see you searching for it. We were in prison together. Five years ago."

"Ah," Nyx said. Her stomach churned, and she vomited a little in her mouth. Nyx reached for the whisky and took a long pull to wash down the taste of the past. As she did, she sized up the woman again, trying to fit her face to the one she remembered from her year in prison. The woman's arms were covered above the elbows, so Nyx couldn't match tattoos. But there was certainly only one woman from her prison days that Nyx owed a death to.

"Who you want me to kill?" Nyx said.

"Straight to the point," Mahir said. "I always did love that about you." She took up her glass and swirled the whisky at the bottom.

"You did me a favor in prison," Nyx said. "I clear my debts."

"I saved your life."

"Sounds like a favor, doesn't it?"

"Missed your sense of humor," Mahir said, and leaned forward on her elbows. She clapped the glass back down on the table. Curled up the one corner of her mouth that could still curl. "Quick job, smash and grab. Can't talk about it here, though."

"Just give me a name and I'll—"

"No," Mahir said. "I need you to work a job with my team, tonight."

"I'm busy."

"Yeah, you look it."

"Can't just run off."

"Who'd miss you?"

Nyx grimaced. "You're just as to the point," she said.

"Quiet as death here, Nissa."

"Fuck, I hate that name. Don't call me that."

Mahir tasted the lip of the glass, ran her tongue over her lower lip. "Bad whisky," she said. "I figured you'd have better taste."

"Clearly not," Nyx said, "I ran with you."

"I see you pushing at me," Mahir said, "I don't buy it. But that's your game, so it's as you like." She stood, leaving most of the liquor in the glass. "My team's around the back. Can you do it, or not?"

"Can't, I—"

"Just lock up," Mahir said. "It's only for the night, and then you're free of the debt. You always said how much you hated owing people. After tonight, you won't owe me anymore."

Nyx clung to her bottle. "One night?"

"I'll have you back before morning prayer," Mahir said. She put out her hand, palm up, like a bel dame. "Swear. I can tell your mother so."

"Fuck it," Nyx said, because in truth, she knew exactly how tonight was going to turn out if she said no or put it off. She'd either spend the rest of the night passed out drunk, or have to deal with Mahir some other time. The first was way too predictable and the second would be insufferable.

"That's what I figured," Mahir said. "Come on, Nissa. Grab my hand. One last time."

Nyx didn't take her hand, but she got up and followed Mahir out the back. She didn't even lock the front door. Whether that was her being drunk, or realistic about the odds she was going to bother coming back, she wasn't sure. She did grab her sword from by the door, and sheathed it at her back, then pulled on her burnous and slipped on her sandals with the razorblades in the soles. When she reached for her scattergun, Mahir laughed and said, "We have better gear for you."

"Happier with my own, thanks," Nyx said, and sheathed the scattergun behind her left hip, and her pistols on either side, and then she was following Mahir out the back door, into the alley behind the keg, and Nyx didn't even care if it was a trap or not because whatever happened next was sure to be more interesting than a night getting drunk alone.

A cat-pulled cart waited at the end of the alley. The two big cats were mangy, yowling things, each about as tall as Nyx's shoulder. One had a puss-filled, half-closed eye, and the other was missing half an ear. That should have been a good indication of the sort of "team" Mahir had at her disposal for whatever flash-bang job she had in mind.

The cart driver was a stocky little runt of woman who had to be at least forty, which was old as shit for a Nasheenian. Her dark hair was going to white, and most of her left arm was sheathed in the telltale green skin of an organic wrap, which meant the arm wasn't her own, and had only recently been pulled off somebody else and stuck on her.

"That's Kasib," Mahir said, and the stocky woman spit a gob of sen in reply. She didn't even nod. "Good fighter, passable com tech. You might have fought on the same fronts together."

"Looks like she was before my time," Nyx said.

Kasib showed her red-stained teeth. "I fought twenty years, you piece of shit," she said. "You have the face of a woman who did her two and shit herself."

"Well," Nyx said, "she's salty. I'll give you that."

Leaning up against the cart was a lean Mhorian, maybe a half-Mhorian, whose gender Nyx couldn't guess with any certainty. Their most striking feature was the preponderance of dreaded brown hair, unbound, and the fact that they seemed a little young, maybe seventeen, if a day. Their hands and face were covered in blue tattoos, which were similar, but of course not identical, to Khos's. The blue tattoos had something to do with familial lineages, though Nyx had never really gotten into that with Khos because the less she knew about her team's past, the better. They wore a bulky burnous, far too bulky for the heat, which told Nyx that there were a good deal of weapons likely stowed beneath it.

"That's Eli," Mahir said. "My sharpshooter and weapons specialist."

The last one was a plump woman with a pleasant face that put Nyx in mind of old radio shows about healthy living on the coast. She might have been twenty-five or so, old enough to have seen some shit, and young enough to still do something about it. She wore her black hair braided back and up, all knotted with purple embroidery thread. Nyx looked for scars or tattoos or piercings, anything to make that milk-fed face more normal, but didn't see anything.

"And my magician," Mahir said, "Ada. You won't find a better one working this side of the city."

Nyx noted that bit of praise was terribly specific. It likely only meant she was passably better than, say, Rhys.

"Nice introduction," Nyx said. "But I'm more interested in details on the job."

"Let's go then," Mahir said, motioning to the cart. "I'll fill you in once we're there."

The cart seemed particularly shabby for a bounty team. Good ones invested in a bakkie, even a shitty one. The state of the cart itself was as bad as the cats. Nyx noticed as she pulled herself into the cart that Kasib was barefoot. The soles of her feet were pitted and cracked, the nails overgrown, toes splayed. This was a hard-up team, and if Nyx weren't so drunk, she supposed she might have misgivings about what desperate thing they were going to do for money. As it was, she slid into the cart, and Mahir got in next to her, and they headed out.

Kasib kept the cart to the alleyways, which would have been harder with a bakkie; a bakkie would have been noisier, too. Nyx started slotting all those details into place even before Mahir handed her a bladder of water.

"It'll help you sober up," Mahir said.

Nyx drank, wincing at the rusty taste of the water, and watched the city slide past. Shadows played across the angles of the buildings, making spidery shapes as the suns moved into late afternoon. The worst of the day's heat was just about over, but all the bugs were still sheltering under awnings and behind trash bins, skittering around in the shadows. People, too, were lazy this time of day. They were nearly the only ones out; most folks hung around on balconies or in doorways. A few sat out under awnings at the tea shops and local taverns, but work, such as it was, had lulled for a few hours while the heat passed.

Mahir didn't talk during the ride out. She kept a pistol in her lap and her gaze on the alleys and side streets. Behind them, Eli and Ada were similarly wary. Eli had pulled a big shotgun from the back and kept it on their lap in plain view to anyone who gazed after the cart, which would certainly deter ordinary criminals and petty thieves, but Nyx suspected they were alert to more than that. Who had Mahir gotten herself into trouble with, then? Somebody pretty bad, to risk looking Nyx up after all this time.

Nyx didn't start to get concerned until they left the city and headed north. Bakkies passed, honking and spitting dead beetles at them. They crept up on little broken settlements, a few scattered houses here, some there, many just burned-out wrecks from the last time the Chenjans invaded and briefly occupied this part of Nasheen. Contaminated desert rolled out in all directions. The others placed kerchiefs, scarves, or burnouses over their noses and mouths, and Nyx wrapped her burnous up over hers, wishing she had brought her goggles. The sand and chemicals irritated her eyes, which started to water badly. She turned her tear-streaked face out to the rolling, ragged desert, noting the broken stands of contagion sensors, and the one lonely anti-burst station that still looked like it had a little pluck left in it.

For all the apparent desolation, there was life out here. Giant, many-legged centipedes as long as her arm burrowed in the sand, scuttling across the road ahead as they approached. There were children, too, watching them from atop nearby dunes. The kids were dirty, wearing ragged clothes and cracked goggles. As the cart got close, they ran back down the dune toward a little bristling farm. A patch of green lit up the desert there, surrounded by a fuzzy filter that protected the whole homestead, which had what appeared to be the only working contagion sensor for miles jutting up from behind the low house, still winking green. The dwelling itself was half-covered in sand, purposely, Nyx guessed, with the windows facing south. Nyx wondered how long they had been out here. A few years, no more. Since the last Chenjan incursion. They wouldn't last when another one came. Dumb, hopeful little family. Hope could kill, out here. Nyx had seen it.

"We usually work out of Mushtallah," Mahir said suddenly. The voice, after so many kilometers of silence, startled Nyx. "Lot more work down there."

Nyx was sobering up. The call to afternoon prayer had sounded just as they left the city, and it was getting up toward dusk. She drank more water and spit some of it out along the road. Little burrowing beetles and centipedes emerged from the sand and eagerly sucked up the precious moisture.

"Where the hell we going out here?" Nyx said. "There's not shit here."

"Parrot Temple," Mahir said. "This is where we start. Hopefully where we end, too."

"There ain't nothing out here," Nyx said. "What kind of a job folks do in the wasteland?"

"Eli's sister is one of the temple zealots," Mahir said, as if Nyx hadn't spoken. "She was hard to turn back to sense, but we had some help. We're coming up on it now."

Sure enough, as they came around a massive sand dune crawling with fingernail-sized sand mites, a craggy red spire came into view. Nyx had a moment of dissonance as her mind tried to make sense of the structure. Certainly it was some type of mud-brick, but that didn't seem right. Then she noted the pillars of red stone jutting up from the sand all across the desert here; the sands broke around them, like buoys at sea. While none were more than a few hands high— at least what was peeking out of the ground—the temple had certainly begun as a very massive red stone pillar like these, and the mud-brick compound had been built all around it. The spires were oddly delicate, twining around one another like clasped fingers. While the bulk of the compound still bore the red of the stones, the spires and the tops of the walls were chalky white. Nyx didn't have to ask why. The colorful forms of thousands of parrots clustered on the spires or took wing in great flocks. The flocks engaged in the eerie swarming behavior that herded and trapped insects, making them easier prey.

Nyx expected them to drive right up to the front gates if Eli knew somebody inside, but no. As dusk bled over the desert and the air cooled down, they trotted out around the back side of the Parrot Temple to a tiny, bullet-riddled door.

Mahir jumped out, and Nyx followed. Eli sauntered up to the door and gave a little knock, like maybe they were expected, which sort of made sense if they had recruited a zealot. Nyx was liking this whole thing less and less, but then, she hadn't liked it in the first place. Ada, the magician, kept watch at their backs, scanning the skies for bugs or . . . what? Who knew.

After a few minutes, the door creaked open. The hinges, Nyx saw, were real metal. Expensive stuff, but corroded as much of the metal was in Nasheen. A little wizened woman peered at them from behind the door. If this was Eli's "sister," then Nyx was a fucking mullah.

Eli slapped a hand on the woman's shoulder, though, and leaned in and murmured something to her. The woman stepped out and limped past them. Nyx saw that she had been hobbled in some way. The woman climbed up alone into the cat-pulled cart. As she did, her skirt rode up, and Nyx saw that her left knee was a twisted wreck. Around her right ankle was a twisted bit of studded wire that her skin was already growing over. Nyx hoped she clipped that shit off on the outside before it took off her whole foot. What the fuck was going on inside this place?

Eli entered the temple first as the woman headed out on their cart. Nyx thought to ask what the fuck they were going to do for a getaway, but hell, this whole thing was so weird she was beyond caring. Kasib and Ada followed Eli. Mahir waited outside for Nyx.

"Come on," Mahir said. "We don't have much time."

"Who the fuck was that woman?"

"I told you."

"What the hell job is this?"

"Inside," Mahir said. "Pistols out. Shoot anyone who resists."

"Are you serious? These people are religious zealots. What are they going to do, have their birds shit on us?"

"They're here to protect something we're contracted to pick up," Mahir said.

"Fucking great," Nyx muttered, and pulled her scattergun.

They made their way down the flickering corridor. The halls were close and dark as a fucking tunnel. Mahir and Kasib led, Nyx and Eli were squeezed into the middle, and Ada took up the rear. Nyx would have put the magician in the middle, to make it easier for her to see and counter any bugs, but she knew nothing about this place or its problems. Maybe bugs here only bit you from behind. She sure as fuck didn't know. Her skin crawled with all she didn't know, but there was a thrill in it, too. On her worst days, dying seemed like a great adventure. The last one.

Glow worms shifted in the lanterns along the hallways, emitting soft orange light that played across the gritty stones. The team's feet scuffed against the floor; and the wind keened through the pits and cracks and seams in the walls. But those sounds were muted by the caw of parrots, the flutter of wings. The stench of bird shit was strong. Nyx caught sight of several colorful birds flitting down intersecting hallways. The team passed one room crawling with the goddamn things. Nyx glanced in and up; the door opened into a little courtyard open to the sky, and parrots wound all the way up the walls, bickering in nest boxes carved into the walls.

"Why do they stay in form?" Nyx said.

Eli tugged at her sleeve, encouraging her to get away from the courtyard. "Many prefer it," Eli said. "Stay a parrot, you get endless food and drink, and nobody asks you to fight in the war."

"They can't keep all these people from fighting," Nyx said. "There's a draft on everyone, especially shifters."

"Can't force them back into form," Eli said. "They're deserters, sure, but lots of Ras Tiegans and Mhorians, too. Easier life, being fed and cared for here, safe from the war, worshipped by some cult."

"Sounds like its own kind of prison," Nyx said. "What the fuck is here that's worth anything?"

Mahir hushed them, and Eli shut their mouth and moved away, gesturing with their shotgun for Nyx to follow.

A figure moved ahead of them, coming around a bend in the corridor. Mahir fired; her gun made a sharp, muffled pop that Nyx recognized as a bug-laced bullet. The bullets were quieter than many alternatives, and once they struck flesh, burst apart and flooded bodies with toxic chemicals.

Mahir hurried toward the figure as it went down. Nyx caught up and saw it was a young woman wearing a shimmering purple burnous and wide, skirted dress that covered her from neck to ankle and up both wrists. Blood leaked from the wound in her gut. She clawed at her stomach, moaning; little bubbles of blood formed around her nose, and a seam of red dribbled from her mouth.

"Stash her, Eli," Mahir said. "Rest of you, keep going." Mahir waved Nyx ahead with Kasib, and Ada picked up her pace and joined them.

Nyx cast one look back at the young woman bleeding out on the floor, and remembered when it was her lying on the ground, bound and beaten bloody by a gang of twelve women in prison. None were bel dames, but they were all war vets—everyone in Nasheen was, barring some First Family cowards—and they hated bel dames. Bel dames hunted down deserters, which sounded fine on paper, but in practice meant hunting down women's brothers, friends, and colleagues on the field. Folks tired of the war were tired of people like her enforcing it. They had broken her face, dislocated one of her vertebrae, cracked another one, and broken six of her ribs.

The pain had been among the worst she'd experienced in her life, and as a woman who'd set herself on fire and been reconstituted and totally rebuilt, that was saying something.

What Mahir saw then in her bloodied, broken body, Nyx was unsure. Maybe she saw this: a chance to own a tool, a weapon. Because though Nyx had done a lot of dumb shit in her time, her biggest weakness was always in her word. When Mahir and her gang rolled up out of the showers and encountered the ones beating up Nyx, Mahir had saved her life. Nyx had taken her hand and said, "I don't take charity," and Mahir said, "I don't give it."

Nyx joined Mahir's gang, and they beat the shit out of a lot of people together, and even killed a man one dark night in a scheme she was sure would catch up to her someday. But this part, the debt—Nyx would clear the debt tonight, or die trying. She fucking hated owing anyone a favor. Debts of personal obligation were far worse than money debts. They cost you more, and resulted in a lot more problems.

At the end of the hall was a door lined in jittering green beetles. Ada ran up to coax the bugs away from the door they were guarding. Someone had raised an alarm, though, because above the flapping and squawking of the parrots and keening of the wind, Nyx heard more zealots moving in on them from the hall behind and the corridor to their left. There was no corridor to the right, which meant they had to fight them here or get the door open, because there was no other way through.

Eli got into a crouch, leveled their shotgun, and waited. Kasib pressed her bulky body flat against the corridor behind them and took aim in that direction. Nyx sighed and aimed her scattergun as well. She was too sober for this shit.

Whirling figures appeared from both corridors. A hail of sharp projectiles snapped ahead of them. One landed in Nyx's forearm. She swore and yanked it out. It was a serrated spine from some insect. If it was poisonous, she was fucked. The others didn't bother yanking. They fired into a collection of women coming at them as the women danced and flung their spiny weapons.

Nyx waited until they were in range, then fired her scattergun. It was the most appropriate firearm for fighting this close, and it hammered the nearest woman hard, taking her off her feet. That made the others hesitate. Nyx fired again and again as the little spines burrowed into her cheeks and chest. Most of the women were down now, a good nine or ten of them, all soaking in blood and loose spines. It wasn't until Nyx gazed at their sprawled forms and saw the spiny ridges on their arms that she realized they had been pulling the projectiles out of their own bodies and using them as weapons. She made a face at that.

"They'll send another wave," Mahir said.

"Got it open!" Ada said.

"Move, move," Mahir said.

The bugs that had guarded the door lay dead on their backs, little legs curled skyward. Nyx crunched across them and into the blackness. Cold, damp air wafted out of the dark. She nearly tripped on a step, and grabbed Mahir's shoulder.

"Watch it," Mahir said. "Going down. Ada, lock that behind us!"

The others crowded behind Nyx. She holstered her scattergun and put out her arms until she touched either side of the cool stone walls. Ada muttered something behind her, but

Nyx didn't pay attention; she had heard nagging magicians before, and she knew the tone well enough to get the gist of it.

Mahir took a glow globe from under her burnous and shook it until the worms began to shift, spilling sickly orange light. They were older worms, which meant the light was bad; like light coming through deep water.

"You going to tell me what this is about?" Nyx said.

"Almost ready for your part," Mahir said. "You'll see it up here."

At the bottom of the stairs, the corridor spilled out into a massive half-circle of a room lined in glow globes as weak as the one Mahir held aloft. Sand had piled up over and around dozens of small red and black pebbles scattered across the floor. On the other side of the half-circle was another door, this one bristling with a more diverse web of bugs: spiders, mostly, big as Nyx's fist, as well as cicadas, roaches, and thorn bugs. She grimaced.

Mahir stopped at the bottom of the stairs. Nyx started to go ahead of her, but Mahir pulled her back. "Ah, no," Mahir said. "It's mined."

"Where?" Nyx said.

"The whole room," Mahir said. "We need you to clear a path to the door there on the other side."

"The fuck? You said this was a simple smash and grab."

"It is," Mahir said. "What we're contracted for is behind that door. We smash it open, we grab it. We go."

"You could have fucking said. I'd have brought tools."

"Eli has tools."

"Not my fucking tools," Nyx said. "Shit, what a burst-fuck. You realize clearing a whole path could take hours?"

"We have all night," Mahir said.

Nyx swore; her rant echoed around the room.

"Stop being so dramatic," Ada said. "I can use bacteria to detect the actual mines. You just need to disarm them." Ada pulled a jar out of her robe and emptied what appeared to be regular dirt onto the floor. But as she raised her arms, the little bits whirled across the floor. They began to coalesce in round patches, covering large spots on the floor, where they began to glow. Nyx had seen magicians deploy those bomb-glowing bacteria in the field, and it was always both exhilarating and depressing. She had spent way too much of her time on the front in danger, detecting mines with trained hornets and dogs, when some magician could just walk in and basically take a shit and get it done.

Seeing the extent of the job, Nyx understood why they had brought her. The circles on the floor were massive, at least as big around as Nyx could spread her arms, and they were so close together that none of them would even be able to get a foot in between them. Nyx's only bit of luck was that the size of the mines meant there were only about ten that she needed to disarm, between her and the other side of the room, to get them across. Only ten ways to die! Luxury.

Nyx held out her hand to Eli. Eli put a demining probe in her hand, an expensive piece of titanium with a pointed head that looked fairly new. It had a protective round hilt meant to shield the hand from a blast, but Nyx had seen a lot of friends lose hands despite them. She figured they were just there to make people feel better.

"That it?" Nyx said. "Really?"

Eli grinned. "Kidding." They reached under their bulky

burnous and pulled free a full demining tool kit, all rolled up like a set of painting brushes. Demining kits were expensive stuff because a lot of it was metal fused with bug secretions. Somebody had given them that kit, or they'd stolen it.

Nyx resigned herself to her life for the next few hours—if she made it that long—and waved them all back. "Have a shit and a snack," she said. "This will take a while."

She lay flat on her belly at the bottom of the steps and began working at the first mine, using the probe to determine the actual edges, then brushing away loose soil with one of the brushes from the tool kit. People died a lot using the trowels and even the probes: they tended to get the tools up under the lip of a mine and yank open the casing by accident. Always bad.

Sweat formed on her brow as she worked the dirt and rocks clear of the mine. Little droplets wet the dirt. When the sand was clear, she could make out the type of mine; it was desperately old shit, something she had seen briefly in some lecture back in her early military training. It had to date back at least a century. Old didn't mean easy, though. She hadn't encountered one of these, and though she knew the basics of demining, most of what she learned on was new stuff.

"What's taking so long?" Mahir said. "Can you do it?"

"Shut the fuck up," Nyx said. "You talk again, I'll shoot you myself."

That made the others quiet, too. Nyx heard nothing from the floor above them, but she bet the temple keepers were working on Ada's bugged door. Crushed between religious zealots and century-old mines because she couldn't stand another boring night inside. Fuck my life, Nyx thought.

She explored the edge of the mine with the brush, which

was the least likely tool to trigger the fucking thing, and figured this model was going to be easier to demine from underneath. Getting a couple fingers down from the top was usually a good bet.

While she sweated, a persistent buzzing began at the door on the other side of the room. She didn't look at it, but the noise was aggravating. No doubt Ada was already working on whatever protection was on the door.

Nyx managed to get four fingers down around the mine and finally found what she was looking for—the grooved chamber where the mine's bugged pin had been. She fished around in the demining toolkit, looking for something that closely matched the oblong hole. The closest she got was a round one; they were meant to configure themselves to fit a variety of shapes and bacterial environments once placed inside, but with something this old, there were no guarantees.

She thought to warn the others to get back, but hey, fuck it. Her death could serve as a warning. Nyx pressed the bugged pin into the chamber, letting out her breath as she did it. The soft pin reacted to the shit inside the mechanism, and Nyx held her breath then, because if they were a poor fit and the mine rejected it, they were fucked beyond belief.

Nothing happened.

That was the shitty part about demining. You didn't know if it worked until you picked the fucker up. But these ones were too big to pick up, so Nyx was going to have to test it. Nyx sat back on her heels and grabbed the probe again. She squeezed one eye shut and pressed the probe directly onto the pressure trigger at the center of the mine. If you were going to test something, go all out.

Nothing.

Nyx huffed in a breath.

"You do it?" Mahir said.

"One down," Nyx said, and she gazed all along the row of glowing mine stamps between her and the door. "Nine to go."

She wasn't sure how long it took to get to the last one. Nyx had to crawl across all the mines she had deactivated as she went, highly aware that the pins could fall out or have a bad reaction at any time and blow off her legs. She kept moving, not thinking, just doing, listening to that annoying fucking buzzing from the door.

Nyx pressed another pin into the last mine, and breathed deep as she raised her head. There, on the other side of the deactivated mine, was the door she had spent all this time clawing her way toward. Now that she was close, she saw lettering winding around the door itself in the language of the Kitab; they were likely phrases from that book, but they were hard to read because of the bugs still crawling over and around the doorway. A couple of the biggest spiders were dead, but there was another fat one above the door that seemed to stare down at her balefully. Nyx sneered back at it.

"We're coming over!" Mahir called.

Nyx got to her feet and stepped from the path of deactivated mines to the clear stone floor in front of the door. Her arms ached, and she was still sweating heavily, even though the room was cool. The spider, her new nemesis, slid down a thread of silk and bounced to a halt just in front of her. It opened its jaws.

Nyx pulled out her scattergun and shot it.

The spider burst, and bits of it splattered in all directions.

A big hunk of it landed somewhere to her left. An explosion rocked the room, throwing rocks and dirt across the room. Nyx's ears rang.

"Goddammit!" Mahir said, and her voice was muted. She took Nyx by the shoulder and yelled something at her. Mahir was shorter, and Nyx just stared down at her and nodded at whatever she was saying. "No shooting!" Mahir said. "You want those bugs to careen around and set off more of those things?"

Ada stepped up beside them, wiping bug guts from her pleasant face. Nyx shrugged. Ada shook her head, expression disapproving, like a much-put-upon mother of a batch of twelve. She knelt in front of the door and pulled a few more jars from hidden sleeves in her burnous. Various bugs emerged, including a buzzing cloud of hornets. Ada spoke a few soft words and directed the swarms at the bugs on the door.

This took another big chunk of time, enough time that Nyx's ears stopped ringing and she could hear some banging upstairs, the zealots above them, but Ada finally grinned triumphantly, and the whole wall of bugs around the door dropped off, dead.

Mahir rushed to the door and pushed it open. Nyx waited behind, not particularly interested in what all the fuss was about at this point. She was hungry and tired and her head fucking hurt. Eli waited outside with her while Ada and Kasib went in.

"Got any sen?" Nyx asked Eli.

Eli palmed over some.

Nyx thumbed a square of it into her mouth between her

teeth and her cheek, and felt slightly better. "What kind of a smash and grab is it?" Nyx said.

Eli shrugged. They had their hands on the shotgun still. "Same as it always is," they said. "Grab something somebody will pay for. Might as well go in. Only way out is through here."

Nyx grinned. "Ah," she said. "You were waiting for me."

Eli nodded. "Sorry," they said. "Orders to keep you moving."

"I bet," Nyx said.

She stepped through the door onto a spongy floor. The light here was much better, nearly bright as day. At the center of the room a young man sat at a desk. He stared at Mahir, open mouthed, as Mahir brought up a machete. He couldn't have been more than twelve or thirteen, not quite old enough for the draft. All around the room were paintings and pictures; Nyx didn't know much about art, but she could tell what they all were, mostly landscapes. Very green. Purple skies. Bugs. The whole place smelled of lilac and saffron, which put her in mind of the bursts at the front, and for a minute she reeled at the memory of it.

Mahir drove her machete directly into the boy's chest. He grabbed at the blade as he went over and made a little mewling sound.

"The fuck?" Nyx said. She made her way over just as Mahir was gutting open the still gasping boy.

Mahir was up to her elbows in blood, digging around in the hot, wet torso while the boy kicked his legs. His eyes rolled, and his mouth made little gaping motions, like a gasping fish, then stopped. Mahir yanked something from his body. It took a moment for Nyx to realize it was his heart, because there was something wrapped around it.

"Got it!" Mahir said. "Out, now. Out the back."

Nyx got a look at the thing as Mahir ripped away the muscle of the heart it surrounded. It was something shiny and metal, dotted with tiny blue and red nodes. It almost looked like an expensive piece of jewelry, only it glowed faintly. But before she could see any more, Mahir stuffed it into a pouch and into her breast binding, and ran after Kasib.

Kasib took out her gun and blew a hole in the back wall. Eli and Ada helped her tear away a large chunk of the spongy covering, revealing another door, this one unguarded. Nyx wondered who had helped them plan this heist, because the knowledge it would have taken to get in and out of here sure as fuck wasn't anything this band of misfits could have figured out on their own.

Nyx followed after them, glancing back just once into the boy's cell where his body lay cooling on the floor.

Fuck of a night.

They crawled up through a slimy, ill-used corridor and up again via a creaky ladder dripping with mucus. Eli slipped and twisted their wrist, but it wasn't bad enough to slow them down. Together, they sloshed through what must have been an old sewer system from back when there was a real city here, no doubt all buried under sand now, and came up at least half a kilometer from the back end of the Parrot Temple. Nyx was exhausted and covered in filth, and the others didn't look much better. She had seen enough not to be surprised when Kasib and Mahir pulled a sheet covered in sand from over the top of a bakkie that had been stowed here for them, camouflaged by the dune. Had they done it, or had their contact, the one who really planned this whole shit?

Nyx piled into the back with Eli and Ada. Mahir rode shotgun, and Kasib drove. Kasib hit the juice, but didn't turn on the lights. It wasn't until they bumped out of sand and onto the road that Mahir started to laugh.

"Holy fuck!" Mahir said. She reached back and slapped Nyx's knee. "Did you see that shit? Did you see what we just did?"

Nyx didn't say anything.

Mahir laughed some more and turned back around. "Baths all around! Booze! And fuck, yeah, food, I'm fucking starving! You hungry, Nyx? I never could eat on a job."

"I could eat," Nyx said.

"Fantastic," Mahir said.

They hit a tavern an hour later, some busted-out halfway house that had likely survived by having no qualms about going dry and serving Chenjans their gravy-soaked yams whenever they took over the area. Nyx heard the call to midnight prayer as they piled out of the bakkie, and couldn't believe it had only been five hours since they descended into the goddamn temple.

"Sure you don't want to keep going?" Nyx said. "Put some distance between—"

"This is where we meet our contact," Mahir said. "At dawn. Hey, your shit is done! Debt paid. But stay for a drink on me, all right?"

Nyx knew she sure as hell wasn't going to get a ride out of this place before their dawn meet-up with their contact, so grudgingly agreed to stay. It was better than trying to hitch back.

Ada grinned as Nyx came in after her. "Wasn't so bad, was it?" Ada said. "We're all going to be rich!"

"Good for you," Nyx said.

"I have sisters," Ada said. "Eli's got debts. Kasib—" she lowered her voice—"Kasib's got some shit to take care of with magicians. We got no problems now, though, hey?"

"You'll spend your money like every team," Nyx said. "You'll be back doing this shit in a few months, half a year at best."

"*Awwww,* sad sack!" Ada said, playfully poking at her.

Nyx grabbed her hand.

Ada cocked her head and grinned. "I don't mind it rough."

Nyx released her. For fuck's sake, these people.

Ada flounced into the tavern, and Nyx followed her, looking for food and a bath, in that order. Mahir put down some notes on the bar—far more notes than Nyx would have advised anyone to carry—and bought a round for them and the six or seven local patrons.

Nyx rubbed her head. Mahir was going to get them killed, celebrating this close to the temple. Nyx walked over and pulled her aside as the bartender handed Mahir a drink.

"Hey, you understand low key?" Nyx asked. "Those women are going to look for you."

"Not tonight," Mahir said. "Not ever."

"The fuck you talking about?"

Mahir handed Nyx the drink, and thumped her hand on her shoulder, pulled her close. "They won't bother us. It's taken care of."

"By who, Mahir? You are fucking with some powerful people."

"Not fucking them," Mahir said, "working for them. And it's great. You saw how slick that was? We ain't never pulled off a job that slick."

"And you never will again," Nyx said.

"Get that bug out of your ass," Mahir said. She pressed herself closer. "I remember when you were fun."

Nyx snorted. She pulled away and went in search of a hot meal. The bartender said it would be a while; most people didn't order food this late outside the holy month. Nyx opted for a bath while she waited, and went in the back to find a tepid pan of water and a wash cloth. She was clearly still in the desert. Nyx wiped herself down and beat the dust out of her clothes, then got dressed again. When she came back into the common room, the food was ready, and she sat down with the crew to eat.

Eli was telling a joke about their family, something involving fishing, and Kasib laughed uproariously while patting her belly with her slick green hand. Ada got herself a seat right by Nyx, and Nyx found she couldn't help glancing at Ada's roundly pleasant face throughout the meal. Mahir sat across from Nyx, urging her to try the red wine.

"It's made with grapes," Mahir said, "from Heidia. It's good. They can put some iced bugs in it."

"Makes me shit regular," Kasib said, and guffawed.

The tavern keeper kept the food coming: twisted rye bread, rice and hunks of fried dog, salted grasshoppers, sweet mealworms, and other stuff that Nyx didn't recognize. Ada pressed her leg against Nyx's, and Nyx let it sit there. Nyx saw danger here because she didn't have all the cards. Clearly Mahir did, and she was carefree as a fucking bird.

When Nyx stumbled upstairs, Mahir followed her up to her room. Nyx opened her mouth to protest, but Mahir kicked the door closed and pushed her onto the bed; she was tough for a little fuck. Mahir put her mouth on Nyx's, and it was just like the old days. Mahir tasted of wine. Nyx pushed off Mahir's burnous, and for a moment they tangled with it until they were both laughing in a heap on the floor.

While they untangled themselves, Ada came in. She made no pretense, just started shedding her clothes. Nyx wasn't going to complain. She pulled Ada down with them, and they spent an awful long time fucking on the floor until the tavern keeper came in and told them to quiet the fuck down.

Ada snickered at that, and the three of them moved to the bed. It was a cool night, but they were covered in sweat and breathless in the end. Nyx hung off the edge of the bed, suddenly bone tired. Mahir laid her head between Nyx's shoulder blades. Ada was out almost immediately; she snored softly at the other end of the bed.

"You should join the gang, Nissa," Mahir said, running her fingers along her arm. "We could spend every day like this, you know?"

Nyx stared across the room. Ada had opened a window at some point to let in cool air. The stars peppered the sky like the flinty eyes of the dead.

"Can't have every day the same," Nyx said.

"This is a good crew," Mahir said. "We get along, don't we?"

"I don't know who you're working for," Nyx said. "That shit bothers me."

"It's just a job," Mahir said. "We weren't all bel dames. You have to start where you start."

"Somebody got you into that place. Got you a map. Had a way out all set up. That's not your planning, Mahir. You plan worse than I do."

"So what? You never get help?"

Nyx thought about her team back at the keg: sulky Rhys and drug-addled Anneke and morose Khos and needy little Taite. It all felt exhausting. Truth was, some days she didn't feel like they helped her as much as she took care of them, like they were some big family of kids still shitting their pants and yelling at each other. Maybe she was, too.

"I could use a change," Nyx said.

"See?" Mahir said. "It'll be fun." She kissed the back of Nyx's neck, the way she had done in prison, and Nyx's skin prickled.

"You could have gotten another sapper," Nyx said.

"I wanted you," Mahir said.

Something moved in the window. Nyx lifted her head and peered at it. It was a parrot.

Nyx got up.

"What is it?" Mahir said.

"Get dressed," Nyx said. She went to the window. The parrot stood on the sill, head cocked. "Out," Nyx said. "I have pistols, you little shit."

The parrot cawed. An answering caw came from outside. Nyx peered out and saw a massive black shape moving across the freckled stars.

"*Fuuuuuuck,*" Nyx said. She slammed the window closed. "Up!" she said. "Ada! Get dressed! Move, move!"

Mahir scrambled for her clothes.

Nyx shook Ada awake. "We've got a swarm of those fucking parrots," Nyx said. "We need to get to . . . fuck . . . somewhere. They'll come through. These windows aren't filtered."

Ada muttered something and rolled over, then: "Wait, what?" and then she was up and moving. Nyx had to give them all points on taking direction.

Nyx dressed quickly and then checked to make sure she had all of her weapons. She was an old hand at fast changes, but the flock was faster. Parrots thumped against the windows.

"We can't go outside!" Ada said. She was mostly dressed.

Mahir opened the door. "Can we make the bakkie?"

"Let me think," Nyx said. "We need a filter. Parrots can't get through most filters that are tailored to keep out bugs. City filters, like Mushtallah."

"We won't make it halfway across the country," Mahir said.

"I said something *like* it," Nyx said, "doesn't have to be . . ." and then she remembered the settlement they had seen on the way to the Parrot Temple, the farmstead with the patch of green and the grubby kids and that lonely, winking contagion center.

"I know where to go," Nyx said.

They pounded down the stairs and through the common room, startling the last of the patrons and making the tavern keeper yell. "You should all be in bed anyway!" Nyx yelled at them, and wondered where the fuck that came from. In bed or not here, for sure. This was a shitty place to be.

Nyx went out with her scattergun first, firing before she

even saw anything. Preventative measures tended to be useful in these types of situations. The bakkie wasn't far—the lights from the tavern shone on the front end—and the parrots hadn't circled around the front yet.

"Go, go!" Nyx said to the others.

Kasib tried to get in the driver's seat, but Nyx pushed her out of the way. "I drive," Nyx said. "You shoot."

Nyx slammed the door, and put her scattergun on the seat next to her. The flock of parrots reeled around; there must have been thousands of them. Nyx said, "Everybody in?" but didn't check to see that they were before she hit the juice and blasted out of there.

The parrots flocked the bakkie, obscuring her view. Nyx snapped on the lights and turned on the wipers. Kasib hung out the passenger side, firing. Eli and Mahir lolled out the back two windows with their own guns blazing. A swarm of hornets swept across the hood of the bakkie, which meant Ada was in play now, too. At least Nyx didn't have to give them directions once the shit hit.

Nyx drove until she hit the crossroads with the main southern artery they had come up on, and just kept feeding juice to the bugs for all the fucking bakkie was worth. It wasn't her bakkie. If the bug cistern overpopulated and burst, that wasn't her problem until a lot later, if she lived to see later at all. What she needed now was speed.

She could make out the road if she concentrated on the thin stretches of it she could see through over the flapping wings and soaring bodies of the parrots. Then one of the parrots started morphing right there on the hood, throwing off streamers of mucus as its wings elongated and its beak shortened and it began to take on its human form. The thing grabbed at the edge of the window with its wing-fingers. Kasib shot it in its half-shifted face, and the thing rolled off the hood and onto the road.

Nyx yelled at them to keep an eye out for a farm compound, but they all seemed too busy to pay much mind to anything but the shooting. She peered out both sides as best she could as half-shifted parrots kept peeling away from the bakkie. The ride up in the cat-pulled cart had taken a lot longer, and she knew she was making good time in the bakkie. They would be on it any—

The green eye of the top of the contagion sensor careened past.

Nyx jammed on the brakes, taking the bakkie into a full spin. Eli screeched and nearly fell out of the bakkie. Ada grabbed their burnous and pulled them back in.

Nyx blasted forward again, turning sharply left off the paved road and onto the sandy drive of the homestead. The happy, twinkling lights of the farm grew closer. If she squinted, Nyx could just make out the sheen of the filter around the place, protecting the grounds from all the toxic shit that came in from the front.

"Hold on," Nyx said.

"Fuck!" Mahir yelled. "How do you know it's not tailored for people? It could fucking kill us!"

"You got a better option, Mahir?" Nyx said.

They hit the filter.

The bakkie shot through and ground to a halt. The hood reared up, and the cistern blew bug juice and the heated, popping carcasses of dead red beetles across the lawn.

Nyx grabbed her scattergun and pushed open the door. Bug juice bled across the ground; the red beetles protected by the cistern hadn't been completely fried to ash, but they were sure as fuck dead, and they floated down the rivers of bug juice like sad little soldiers.

Nyx raised her scattergun, pointing behind her at the filter. A heap of colorful feathers lay on the other side of it. A few partially burned parrots limped around on the other side, missing a wing, a beak, a foot. There were more parrots in the swarm, but they had circled off and regrouped. Nyx saw them resting at the top of a nearby sand dune.

She lowered her gun. Behind her, Mahir was talking to Ada, asking her to send a message.

"The fuck?" Nyx said.

"I want my money," Mahir said. "She'll send a beetle swarm to our contact and let them know to meet us here."

"There any alive in here?" Nyx said.

"Out there," Ada said. "I can manipulate them from here. She'll get the message. We can hide out here."

The porch light came on at the homestead.

Nyx wondered how to play it—put the gun away or hold it up?—but Mahir was already moving, waving Eli and Kasib ahead of her.

"Hands up!" Mahir said. "We'll be out of your hair in a minute."

"Leave it," Nyx said, but Mahir was already on the porch, talking down a beefy woman who bore a long scar on one side of her face.

A gunshot came from inside.

"Goddammit," Nyx said.

Mahir and Kasib bolted into the house. The beefy woman tried to stop them, and got the butt of a gun to the face in response.

Nyx stood outside with the injured woman while the others cleared the house. The woman clutched at her face and leaned hard against the door jamb. She snuffled and snorted snot and blood. The woman wore a breast binding and trousers, and she was barefoot. A battered old shotgun lay nearby, no doubt tossed when Mahir came down on her like a fucking sandstorm.

Mahir yelled from inside and told Nyx to escort the home-steader back in. Nyx helped the woman up and half-dragged her inside, where Nyx found herself staring down the sorriest bunch of folks she'd seen in a while.

There were six kids total, four of them clearly from the same batch. The other two didn't seem to be related to the batch or to each other, and they were older, maybe ten and twelve. The beefy woman Nyx pushed toward the others was maybe thirty, and there was a legless woman in her twenties and a battered war vet who must have been over forty babbling to himself in one corner. He smelled like urine. The house was neat enough, but poor as shit. Everything was simple, well-worn; the kids wore patched-up clothes with cracked goggles around their necks. One of them had some kind of rash spreading all up his face and along his left shoulder. Another kept wiping her nose and sniffing.

"We ain't staying long," Mahir said. "You all sit tight here, don't try any shit. We're meeting someone, then we leave."

The beefy woman spit. "You take what you want," she said.

"Don't mind us. Need water, food, you take it. We got some weapons in the back. That's all we got."

"Shut up," Mahir said. "Just . . . fucking sit tight. Shit."

"I have to pee," one of the kids said, and that's when Nyx had to go sit outside.

Nyx slumped into one of the chairs on the porch and gazed out at the fence. The beefy woman had bled all over the porch, spraying blood from her burst nose. Smears of it ran across the stones. Nyx was dying for a drink, for some sen, for sex, for anything to take her mind off this fucking night.

Nobody came out for a long time. Nyx didn't hear any gunshots, which seemed like a good sign.

Finally, as the first hints of the blue sunrise tickled the horizon, Nyx heard a bakkie buzz up to the edge of the filter. It parked on the other side, and someone got out.

Mahir opened the door behind Nyx. She said nothing to Nyx but walked down onto the path to meet the newcomer.

Nyx pegged the newcomer as First Family, one of the rich old families whose kids never seemed to serve much at the front and who spent most of their lives behind filters that protected them from the sun. She heard some of those pampered pieces of shit lived to be sixty or more. Interesting, though, for a First Family to send one of their own out here to pay off Mahir, instead of just a lackey.

Nyx shifted in her seat, making it a little easier to grab the butt of her scattergun if she needed to. She also tugged up the hood of her burnous, just in case. This wasn't a job she wanted to be remembered for.

The woman reached Mahir, and stepped into the light

from the porch. Nyx realized the First Family woman was someone she knew. It was Yah Reza, a magician who ran one of the major boxing gyms and magician training operations in Faleen.

"You got my piece, baby doll?" Yah Reza said. Her speech was a little slurred, and her teeth were red with sen use. She was a regal older woman, all wrapped up in a red burnous.

Mahir produced the complicated bit of metal, or whatever it was. "Just where you said it would be," Mahir said.

A grin split Yah Reza's face. "That's just fine, baby, just fine."

"We've got . . ." Mahir said, "the parrots. You saw the parrots outside?"

"No problem," Yah Reza said. "I can take care of those. Now." She closed her hand over the piece.

"You have what we agreed?" Mahir asked.

"It's all been transferred," Yah Reza said. "Ask Ada."

"Great, great," Mahir said, and she smiled wide. "Great doing business with you."

Yah Reza glanced at Nyx now for the first time. "Come on down here, Nyxnissa."

"Shit," Nyx said.

"Go on in Mahir," Yah Reza said. "I want to talk to Nyx."

Mahir raised her brows, but did as she was told.

Nyx didn't go down to Yah Reza. She just pushed back her hood and put her feet up on the railing.

Yah Reza, bemused, made her way up the steps. "Been a long time, baby doll."

"Why you have that shit team do this?" Nyx said. "Mine could do it."

"Yours wasn't as desperate," Yah Reza said. "And lest you forget—you, child, tend to make a terrible mess of things."

"I saved them from the parrot problem."

Yah Reza pursed her mouth. "As I said."

"Ah," Nyx said. "They weren't supposed to survive that. How would you get your trinket?"

"Trinket?" Yah Reza held it up and laughed. She tossed it onto the porch and ground it under her foot. It was surprisingly fragile, clearly not metal at all, and it turned to jagged bits of dust easily under the magician's foot in a way it certainly hadn't while traveling in Mahir's breast binding. "It wasn't the trinket, it was the boy. It's done now."

"You all work on some other level up there," Nyx said. "Someday I'll figure it out."

"No, no, child," Yah Reza said. "You don't want that. If you do that, we couldn't abide having you around anymore." She patted Nyx's cheek. "We prefer your ignorance."

"Thanks?" Nyx said.

"You're welcome," Yah Reza said. Yah Reza put her hood back on and started down the steps.

"You really calling away the parrots?" Nyx asked. "Cause if I'm—"

"Already done," Yah Reza said. She gestured to the ground-up trinket. "They've been released."

Nyx stood, walked down into the yard and watched Yah Reza go. Shifters bound to a temple, but why? Pulled there and kept in a prison? For who? To do what? And where would they go now? Fuck, she was glad getting paid didn't involve understanding First Family catshit.

She caught a whiff of smoke, and wondered if somebody

was cooking breakfast already. The bluish haze of the first sunrise was still dim. Not even Rhys would be cooking that early.

As she turned, Nyx saw the team coming out—Mahir first, squat Kasib, little Eli, and Ada with her sunny face. They looked happy, cheery, two words she would never use for her own team.

Behind them, flames whorled from the open door of the house.

"The fuck?" Nyx yelled.

"Huh?" Mahir glanced back at the house. "Just tying up loose ends," she said. "Come on, they have a bakkie. We can cut the filter and get out."

"You just . . . those people are still in there," Nyx said. "Did you just fucking torch a house full of kids?"

Mahir raised her brows. "We've murdered any number of people today," Mahir said. "Children, women, men. What's it matter? It's the job, Nyx."

"They weren't part of the job!" Nyx said, and her own ferocity surprised her. It seemed to surprise Mahir, too, because she took a step back. "Shit, Mahir, yeah, you do what you need to do for the job, but it's over. There was no need for that. They don't have to die for you to get paid. That's just fucking . . . it's not . . ."

"Are you all right?" Mahir said.

Behind her, the flames leapt higher. Her face was a fiery silhouette.

Nyx had to look away. Her mind worked furiously, exhausted and dehydrated and sore as fuck and here she was with this blazing house of kids and Mahir was right, who cared? She had done worse things, hadn't she? But those were on a job. A job. This was different, it *was*.

She had brought these people here, yeah. But the homesteaders shouldn't have been out here. Something was bound to happen to these people way out here at the edge of nothing, sooner or later.

But Nyx knew the difference, now, as she gazed at their happy faces. The difference was, this killing wasn't for the job. It was for their own pleasure.

Mahir was patting her shoulder. "Come on," she said. "Let's head out. They would have been taken out by the next Chenjan raid. I was doing them a favor."

They piled into the bakkie, and Nyx followed, because what was she going to do, run into the house? Hitch a ride? Walk home? Ada took down the filter. Kasib drove until they got back to town, and the blue sun was up over the horizon. Kasib stopped outside a hotel, and as they all got out, Mahir pulled out some notes and stuffed them into Nyx's hands.

"Here," Mahir said, "you deserve it," but all Nyx saw were the smears of blood on the porch. "You all right?"

"Think I'll walk from here," Nyx said.

"Wait, what?" Mahir said. "Don't you want to be part of the team?"

Ada gazed at her from outside the bakkie, pleasant face all scrunched up. Kasib was sitting on the hood of the bakkie, eating a roti. Eli had their shotgun over their shoulders, standing watch outside the ratty hotel.

"No," Nyx said. "I've got a team. We're square, though, huh?"

"Sure," Mahir said, "we're even."

Nyx turned her back on them and walked and walked as

the sky began to brighten. She stopped at a mosque where the muezzin was stepping out onto the sidewalk to head up into the minaret to call prayer. Behind her was a mullah.

Nyx held out her hand to the mullah. "My tax," Nyx said. "For the waq. My mother was on the waq, the dole. Giving it back, maybe, for somebody else."

The mullah raised her brows.

"I'm a pretty bad person," Nyx said.

"I'm sure you like to think that," the mullah said, and took the money.

Nyx came within a couple blocks of her storefront just as, at her back, the big orange demon of the second sun crested the horizon. She waited, not sure if she could go back there, to either team. Sunrise warmed the city and the call to prayer sounded. The heat bathing her back soothed the muscles there. Her ass and thighs still hurt from all the fucking, and she looked forward to lying on the roof and soaking up more heat before it got too hot to bear.

It was the promise of the warm roof that decided her.

As she came up under the awning of the storefront, she saw that the front door was open. She froze and pulled her pistol. Nyx crept to the doorway. She went in pistol first.

Anneke was in the foyer, passed out on the divan. Nyx knew she was passed out, not dead, because she was snoring like a fat old dog. A bottle of whisky sat at the head of the divan, and smears of sen shown on Anneke's fingernails.

Nyx lowered her pistol, but kept it out. Someone was banging around the keg, and whistling. She walked to the curtain over the partition between foyer and keg and gently pulled the curtain aside with the barrel of her gun.

Khos cleaning up the remains of Nyx's dinner with Mahir; she'd completely forgotten about it. Grease smeared Taite's workbench, and some of the whisky in the bottle had leaked all over one stool and onto the floor. Behind him, Taite was at the com, already plugging in the scents to call and direct another day of hacking communications associated with their bounties.

She didn't get much further into the keg before she saw Rhys bent over in the little nook he called a bedroom rolling up his prayer mat after morning prayer.

"What the fuck you been up to?" Khos said, wiping at the table. "Looked like you had company."

"Not too much," Nyx said, holstering her pistol. "Just the usual, you know? Painting the town bloody red as a wound."

"I'd expect nothing less," Khos said, tossing her the rag. "Could you help me paint this one a little less greasy?"

"No problem," Nyx said, and she saw the surprise on his face at her quick acceptance. She'd like to tell him she'd be a better person, clean up more, look after herself, give a shit about them publicly, but that would be a lie. And she didn't like lying to them, or to herself. Not unless money was involved. Not unless it was part of the job.

"You're back," Rhys said, moving past her toward the foyer. "I really did not miss your face."

"Didn't miss yours either," Nyx said, and kicked out of her sandals. She began to disarm, pulling the scattergun, the pistols, the sword, and laying them all out on the workbench. Khos watched her do it. He didn't say a word. He simply reached out, and wiped away a bit of blood from the back of her hand.

It was good to be home.

ABOUT THE AUTHOR

KAMERON HURLEY is an award-winning author and advertising copywriter. Hurley grew up in Washington State and has lived in Fairbanks, Alaska; Durban, South Africa; and Chicago. She has a bachelor's degree in historical studies from the University of Alaska and a master's in history from the University of KwaZulu-Natal, specializing in the history of South African resistance movements.

Hurley is the author of the space opera *The Stars Are Legion* and the Worldbreaker Saga, which is comprised of the novels *The Mirror Empire, Empire Ascendant*, and *The Broken Heavens* (forthcoming). Her first series, the God's War Trilogy—which includes the books *God's War, Infidel*, and *Rapture*—earned her the Sydney J. Bounds Award for Best Newcomer and the Golden Tentacle Kitschy Award for Best Debut Novel. Hurley is also the author of the essay collection *The Geek Feminist Revolution*, which contains her essay on the history of women in conflict "We Have Always Fought," which was the first article to ever win a Hugo Award. Her nonfiction has appeared in numerous venues, including the *Atlantic*, *Bitch* magazine, the *Huffington Post*, the *Village Voice*, *LA Weekly*, *Writers Digest*, and *Entertainment Weekly*, and she writes a regular column for *Locus* magazine.

Hurley has won two Hugo Awards, a British Science Fiction Award, and a Locus Award, and has been a finalist for the Arthur C. Clarke and the Nebula awards. Her work has also been included on the Tiptree Award Honor List and been nominated for the Gemmell Morningstar Award. Her short fiction has appeared in magazines such as *Popular Science*, *Lightspeed*, *Vice Magazine's Terraform*, *Escape Pod*, *Strange Horizons*, and *Amazing Stories* as well as anthologies such as *The Lowest Heaven*, *The Mammoth Book of SF Stories by Women*, *Year's Best SF*, and *Year's Best Science Fiction and Fantasy*. Her work has been translated into Romanian, Swedish, German, Hebrew, Chinese, Turkish, Spanish, and Russian.

In addition to her writing, Hurley has been a Stollee Guest Lecturer at Buena Vista University, a LITA President's Program speaker, and taught copywriting at the School of Advertising Art. She is also a graduate of Clarion West Writers Workshop.

Hurley currently lives in Ohio, where she's cultivating an urban homestead.